I0674906

The Extricated Soul

M. Suzanne

The Extricated Soul

By M. Suzanne

© 2019 M. Suzanne

Cover Designed by Acepub

Graphics provided by Acepub

Published by Blue Spruce Publishing Company
2175 Golf Isle Drive, Suite 1024
Melbourne, FL 32935
610-647-8863
info@BlueSprucePublishing.com

ISBN: 978-1-943581-13-9

Forbidden Fruit

Succulent fruit hanging on the vine.

Humans and animals living in

harmony with the Divine.

Beauty of the creating Lord

flourishes in blooms and grasses

across the garden floor.

Adam and Eve stroll among the grasses and leaves,

Living a life of grace and easy.

Man and women created to celebrate

the harmony and joy of this garden so great,

can pet the lions and play with the hounds,

and live in a world without barriers or bounds.

A garden of love for animals, insects, plants and trees.

A love of one another and the Divine Creative Source.

Through their choices and thought's, they made,

God gave them the ability to co-create.

Universal Law a gift from God,

says it is your thoughts that create the life

and feelings you procreate.

In contemplation of wanting more

Adam and Eve ventured to the forbidden tree

protected by a serpent of truth.

Eve asked, "What is it you protect in this tree?"

Slithering in silence the snake left his perch,

to look the couple in the eye,

to see what questions

the souls were hiding inside.

As he looked he saw the souls trying to re-align,

"One choice can send your world in a spin,"

is what this serpent said to them.

"It is our right to know…what it is this tree does grow?"

Responded Eve.

The serpent moved closer to see what Adam didn't show,

"Why are you so silent and not asking to know?"

Asked the snake then hissed and moved slow.

"It is my partner's plight to see the truth in a different light,

and there is no one else for me to love so joyously."

"Ahhh," said the serpent,

"A couple so free, in a garden of bliss,

so eager to separate

from the Divine that created all of this.

Yes, it is your choice to taste the fruit.

And, I will tell you it is your choice that

grows the Garden of Eden

or creates a world of fears and hate.

Use your thoughts and choices wisely…

For they will quickly procreate."

The serpent slide from the tree

to reveal the lush fruit.

In last words he said,

"You have received the message from your Creator,

Who has given you this freedom to choose.

And always, God will sit and wait for you,

Receiving you back regardless of what you think and do.

In re-alignment you will find the Garden of Eden is still divine."

Further from the tree he slid,

and one last time looked back to see

the forms of Adam and Eve lose their radiant light

as they bite the fruit from the forbidden tree.

It did not take long for the ego to take hold

and the life of contrast ignite

into a world of illusions and fright.

Thank You!

As a first-time novelist, I am very grateful for the coaching and editing from my editor Richard Dalglish. He has worked with me over this past year and a half as I wrote this story. He has exercised patience and always coached me kindly. He would share writing tips and critiqued my writing with honesty and professionalism. Sometimes it felt hard to go back and make the alterations and corrections he encouraged, but I stuck to it. It was his writing expertise and coaching that kept me focused on finishing the story in my words while strengthening my writing skills.

I thank my friends who made up my beta reading group, George Austino, Abigail Barrett, Catherine Frank, Trish and Allen Ruane. They read sections from first drafts through to the final fully edited story. I am grateful for all their love, support, and honest feedback.

And most importantly, I am grateful for the Divine Creative Source who delivered this story through me. For decades I felt an inner desire to write, yet I allowed the voice of ego to say, "Who, you? You can't do it."

I am blessed, the Spirit of the Living God kept pushing and prodding me until I sat down and allowed this story to flow.

Chapter 1

China moved quickly through the darkness. As she pivoted around she could see the outline of the small garden. Looking beyond the stone pond, she felt her heart pounding. Her eyes swept across the tight landscape searching for him.

The courtyard garden was a collage of darkness and shadows formed by the dim garden lights, with empty pots of various sizes and small, sleeping garden beds. She felt his presence just seconds before he grabbed her by the neck. She turned to face him, and Soul to Soul they gazed into each other's eyes. Sadiki's darkness was deep, and she felt the violence of his thoughts. The power of his egotic mind blocked her gaze from seeing his Soul. She could detect not a glimmer of light, not a speck of light to grasp. Lifetime after lifetime, Sadiki's Soul, denied and starved of the Divine light, needed to be saved.

His strong hands held a steady pressure on her throat as he let out a laugh. "Tell your God, not today. I will kill you before you can save my Soul. You think your White Soul is stronger than me?"

He tightened his hold on her neck, and she started to feel weak. "The darkness within me is growing every moment, and when the time is right I will come back for my son," Sadiki shouted with a hateful tone that ripped through her. "He will serve me, I will have the great strength of 'All Darkness' and will soon overpower God and the minion angels."

China tried to pry his hands from her neck. *I must hold on, Spirit flow through me with strength*, she thought. With full force, she jerked her knee into his crotch. He spiraled back in pain, releasing his grip. Doubled over, he fell to his knees, his hands clutching his groin. She moved quickly to him and kicked his face, aiming for his nose. A crack sounded, and blood spurted from his nose, landing on her clothes. He fell onto his side. With a fierce desire to survive, she pushed him onto his back and dropped her full weight onto his neck, leading with her right knee.

She heard the crackling of his trachea and the snap of his neck. Stunned at first, she just looked at him under her knee and then slowly moved away. Still kneeling beside him, she watched his body convulse with seizure-like movement until his last breath left him. His Spirit released and hovered over her.

She sprang to her feet like a wildcat and reached to grab his Soul from the dark cloud of hate. Her strong grasp went right through the withered Soul as she watched it crumble around her hands. He quickly engulfed his Soul within the dark mist. Laughter emerged from the darkness. "Not today, not today." His energy dissipated, and he was gone.

She screamed after him, "I am more powerful than you. The light will always win." She stood there watching his body start to decay.

"Mom, Mom, are you all right?"

Bernard stood next to his mother, a startled look on his face. She was wrapped tight in an old sleeping bag she used in the garden on cold days. He put his hand on her shoulder and tried to shake her out of her groggy state. In a trembling voice he asked, "Are you with me?"

China's eyes were glazed over and devoid of energy.

"Are you okay?" Bernard asked again. "Mom, you're scaring me. I heard you screaming at someone. Was someone here? Are you okay? Did someone try to hurt you?" His voice quivered with fear.

China began to focus on her surroundings. Her mind and energy slowly shifted as she returned to the present moment. She felt a soreness around her neck, and as she breathed in deeply, she noticed the return of the ground beneath her feet, the chair under her body, which was wrapped in her father's old green sleeping bag. She looked up at Bernard, saw that his big brown eyes were moist, saw his look of fear. She cleared her throat. "I'm fine," she said, her voice weak and raspy. "I must have fallen asleep. It was just a dream." She cleared her throat again and put her hand to her neck, wondering if she had any marks.

"What's wrong with your neck?" Bernard asked. "Did someone hurt you?" Large tears rolled over his lower eyelid and down his face.

"Bernard, I'm sorry, don't be scared." She glanced at the pond where Sadiki fell. There was nothing there. She pushed the sleeping bag down off her shoulders and looked at her shirt where the blood had spattered. The shirt bore no evidence of the struggle.

Bernard dropped to his knees next to her and reached for her hand. "Mom, were you fighting with someone? What happened?" A shiver went through him as he knelt on the cold stone and the chill February air stung his wet cheeks. "Why are you holding your neck like that, let me see?" He tried to sound brave, but his trembling voice betrayed him, and he could not control the tears as they ran down his face.

China put her hands on his soft chubby cheeks. "No honey, nothing to worry about here. I'm fine and will come in shortly." She leaned over and kissed him gently on the forehead. "Go on in, finish your homework and I'll be there shortly." She watched her eight-year-old go into the house. As she sat alone in the garden she asked, "Spirit, what happened?"

From within her mind she heard the words echo.

You did not protect your Aura.

In her mind's eye she saw a cloud form and the vision of the attack play like a movie. She recognized the cloud was a "thought form." She relaxed into the knowledge and heard a voice within.

He sent his negative thoughts out to you, and your ego grabbed them and completed the scene. It occurred as you were traveling in Consciousness while meditating.

Still with some confusion, she asked, "Did I actually kill him?"

She sat silently waiting for the words to bubble up in her thoughts.

No, he still lives in your dimension of time and matter.

There was a pause and she felt her energy stir within her heart space.

As your Soul continues to expand, your ego will become more still. Today it showed its protective instinct.

China breathed again and felt a response bubble up.

Continue with your spiritual work of prayer and meditation.

She allowed herself a feeling of comfort knowing she had not hurt Sadiki. She took several deep breaths to allow the thoughts to surface. "Will Bernard be safe?" she asked.

This time the impression came quickly.

He has no use for a boy so young. He will wait until he is a man.

"Mom, it's dark, please come in." China heard fear in Bernard's plea from the back door. "I'll feel better if you come in."

"I will finish my prayer and be right in. Stop worrying," she said in her best maternal voice.

"•. .•*"*•. ☆•*"*•. .•*"*•☆

Bernard, overwhelmed with fear, turned from the back door and stomped through the house to the living room. He turned on the TV and sat on the sofa to see the large red words "Breaking News" as the picture went to a reporter on the streets of New York.

"What we know is there was an explosion in the garage of the World Trade Center earlier today," the reporter said. "The explosion took place approximately at 12:15 p.m. It is being reported that over tens of thousands of people were evacuated after the explosion. So far, the death toll is at six, and hundreds to thousands are believed to be injured."

Sirens sounded, and an ambulance passed behind the reporter, who turned to watch it pass. He turned back to the camera and said, "The explosion was more than six hours ago, and people are still being triaged and taken to hospitals throughout the city. The first responders are still trying to clear the crowds to make sense of what happened."

Bernard felt a paralyzing fear as he thought of the time that he, his grandparents, and his mom went to New York for a Fourth of July weekend when he was five years old. "They could kill me. I was in the towers. Now they want to kill my mom." He pulled his legs up onto the sofa and curled into the corner, leaning against the arm. He wrapped his arms around his knees, put his head down, and started to sob. "What if she gets killed? I will have no one. My father's dead, pops and grandmom are dead, I will have no one. Why didn't she come in? If she loved me she would come in." He let the tears fall as he hugged his knees tightly.

China sat quietly on the patio chair watching the darkness before speaking. "Spirit, am I strong enough to serve you?" She felt a cracking in her voice and tightening in her throat. There was silence and a feeling of stillness within her. Finally, she heard herself say out loud, "Do not doubt the Divine within, for you are Spirit in manifest." She sat in silence for several minutes and then said, "Ashey," before getting up to go in.

Chapter 2

China rushed in through the front door of the old Victorian home in West Philadelphia. In the vestibule she hung her University of Penn tote bag on a coat hook. She sat down on the old church pew to take off her nursing clogs and slipped her feet into her fuzzy slippers. Her feet, tired from her shift in the neuro ICU at Penn, felt relief from the warm, cushiony slippers. The vestibule, with a floor of large black and white tiles, was the entryway to the only home she had ever lived in. Since her parents' deaths she had redecorated almost every room to maintain the old charm while also creating a more modern flow and family feel.

She closed the vestibule's double doors behind her to keep the draft out of the large living room. A large wedding photograph of her parents hung over the old brick fireplace. China had whitewashed the old red brick to give it a warm and more elegant look better suited to the large wood mantel. Smaller photos of both sets of grandparents flanked the one of her parents. She always loved the contrast of her African American paternal grandparents to the left and her Filipino grandparents on the right. Sometimes she liked switching her grandparent's photo, so her father's parents sat next to her mother and her mother's parents next to her father.

Looking at the pictures, she could still feel the love between her strong ancestral lines. She always knew she had grown up blessed and always felt loved.

Whenever she entered the living room she followed the same ritual—she looked at the photographs, smiled, and said, "Thank you, I love you all."

She wanted Bernard to feel that same love. China had told him stories of how much his father loved holding him as a baby. Her parents supported the lie and always spoke of how proud his father was to have a son. Deep inside, she worried that someday his father would show up and Bernard would learn he was not dead. *When he is older I will tell him myself,* she thought.

She shuddered at the thought that Bernard might feel betrayed. Looking back at her parents, she felt a sadness that they were killed in the same way she told Bernard his father had been killed, on the Schuylkill Expressway in a car crash with an 18-wheeler truck. A feeling of guilt overtook her. "It's like the lies I told to spare Bernard pain became your story, your tragedy," she murmured. She shivered at the thought. "Karma in full circle." Her throat tight, she released her gaze from her parents' portrait and whispered, "I am so sorry."

The six-bedroom home, built in 1869, had remained in her family for 56 years. Three generations of the Hope family had lived there. Once considered a home for the wealthy, it fell into disrepair during the Depression and sat boarded up until it was purchased from the city at a cheap price by her grandparents in 1943. It was restored by the Hope men, her grandfather, his father, and his uncles. At that time the young couple had two boys, her father, just four years of age, and one in first grade.

After Bernard's birth, her parents sacrificed one large bedroom to make a master suite with a walk-in closet and an elegant spa-like bath. They gave the new suite to China several years before their death. It was the only home her father remembered, and the only home she and Bernard ever lived in.

Raising her son as a single mom in the old house was bittersweet. She was grateful for the inheritance of the home and disappointed her parents would never see Bernard's adulthood. Instead, they died when he was six years old.

She stopped at the bottom of the steep stairway, closed her eyes, and took a deep breath. "Spirit forgive me for my lies," she whispered. She opened her eyes and called up, "Come on, Bernard, you're going to be late for your soccer game." She waited for a response, but none came. She listened for movement. "Please don't make me come up there!" she called. "We don't have time." Still she heard nothing. "Okay, I'm coming up," she yelled in frustration.

As she came to the landing, she turned toward Bernard's room and saw the door was open. His school clothing lay in a pile on the floor, and his cleats sat on the bed. She walked to the bathroom and knocked on the door. "Bernard, are you okay? We need to go."

Her call was met by silence. She opened the door, saw a towel on the floor and puddled water on the countertop. Surprised, she started down the hallway and passed the guest room, which was empty and seemed undisturbed. The door to the third-floor stairway was closed, the eye hook lock still in place. She kept going and entered her bedroom. She did not see him. Her room was as she had left it, her prayer books in a pile next to her old Queen Ann arm chair. Her meditation altar, with candles, crystals, and a piece of old wood from an oak tree that once stood in the garden, was undisturbed.

When China turned to leave, she heard a sound in her walk-in closet. She walked around the bed and saw light peeking out at the bottom of the door. She opened the closet's French doors and went in. She walked to the back of the closet and turned to the left. Bernard was there, sitting on an old bench that sat at the foot of her grandparent's bed when she was a little girl. Her old journals were scattered around him on the floor. He was looking at an old photo, tears streaming from his eyes.

"Is this him? Is this my dad?" he asked through his sobs. "He didn't want me, he hated me."

China, unsure what to say, sat next to him on the bench and put her arm around him. As she pulled him to her, he turned toward her and screamed, "You lied to me. Why? Do you hate me, too?"

"Oh no, it was not like that," she said, trying to make her voice soothing.

"No one loves me!" Bernard screamed. "My father deserted me, grandmom and pops died on me, and you lied to me." His face turned red with anger and his plump fists banged on his legs. "I have no one who loves me. Kids at school don't like me. I hate them all!"

China swallowed hard. "I love you very much. I lied because I wanted you to feel that love and never feel rejection. I am so sorry." She pulled him closer, but he wriggled free and jumped off the bench.

"I hate you, I hate you, I hate you!" he screamed and ran out of the closet. She heard him running down the hall, and then he slammed his bedroom door. She sat quietly on the bench until the room was flooded with darkness. She got up and turned on a dim light. She picked up the old journals and placed them back on the corner shelf.

She sat on the bed and thought, *Teenage years. I hope this is not a sign of what is to come.* She got up to leave and stopped at the mirror. "How do I fix this now?" she asked herself.

China wandered down to the kitchen where she put the TV on and saw students running across a campus, their arms in the air and police pointing rifles at them. Startled, she turned up the volume.

"Two teenage students from Columbine High School killed 13 and injured at least 21," a reporter announced. "The carnage started during the first lunch period outside the cafeteria and moved into the library. It is believed the two gunmen committed suicide in a main hallway sometime after noon. Parents of the high school students sat for several hours at a local elementary school not knowing if their child was dead, injured, or alive. Police are still going through the high school looking for more victims and bombs placed by the perpetrators. Just ten minutes ago reporters were told that several teachers and students who were hidden in a secluded room behind the library were safely evacuated from the building."

China felt a sick feeling run through her. She closed her eyes and silently prayed for a healing for all involved. She sat down at the kitchen island and wondered what had become of a world where children were no longer safe in school.

Chapter 3

There was a stillness in the early September morning in the Upper Paro Valley in Bhutan. High in the mountains, the Paro Taktsang Monastery sat quietly. The heavy wooden doors at the side entrance of the stone building opened, and two monks holding blazing torches emerged into the cold early morning air. Dressed In heavy wool robes, they proceeded cautiously under a cloud-covered sky. The fiery light of their torches illuminated their forms as they made their way down a steep stairway carved into the rocks. Each monk stepped carefully. The older man leaned into the rock wall to steady himself. A step too far to the left could send him tumbling over the low wall along the cliff's edge.

As they moved through the cool morning, they caught glimpses of the once-white buildings with golden roofs. They stopped to stabilize themselves and slow their momentum on the steep stairway.

The monks began to move again. They descended the stairs for several minutes, eventually turning right, away from the cliff's edge. They moved off the steps and walked toward a large wrought-iron gate, which depicted the tree of life. Only a small scrap of the old gate's pealing gold leaf remained. The young monk pushed open the heavy gate as the elder held the torches. They entered the courtyard and placed their torches in torch stands inside the gate. The torchlight illuminated the small stone courtyard, and they bowed and chanted in Sanskrit as they walked to the prayer wheel. The men stood on opposite sides of the wheel and rotated it to mark the new day. In the still night, their chant could be heard throughout the monastery grounds and down the mountainside.

The two monks remained at the prayer wheel while they finished their chant of gratitude for the new day. They retrieved their torches and left the courtyard. Moving along walls built into the hills, they climbed the steep steps, still chanting. As they approached the monastery, they saw a figure up ahead. An unfamiliar voice joined in their chant. At the top of the hill, the third man fell in behind them as they made their way to the monastery doors. They bowed to each other and entered the monastery's main building.

The newcomer followed them inside. He was a frail man in worn and dirty robes. His sandals were torn and flopped off his feet with each step. His hair was grey, his beard long and straggly. The symbols on his robe revealed his status as a high priest from a Tibetan church. The older monk nodded at him, signaling that he should follow them.

Their shadows fell on the monastery's stone walls, fluttering like a bat's wings as the torch flames wavered and flickered. The men entered a room with floor-to-ceiling shelves along every wall, each shelf organized with books placed in a perfect array. Spiritual bookends and Buddha statues were strategically placed on the shelves. The room had a single window, opposite the door. A small wooden desk with an inkwell sat below the window. A stone fireplace was set in the middle of one wall, and in the center of the room was a table of old twisted driftwood. A smooth, flat stone sat gracefully on the driftwood. A thick piece of blown glass was balanced on top of the stone. The glass had been made more than a century before in the village below.

The men placed their lit torches in stands just inside the door. The younger man went to the fireplace and started a fire. The other two sat down on oversized worn red pillows that were on the floor around the table. The younger man soon joined them. In the fireplace, logs hissed and crackled, as bright flames licked up and warmed the room.

"Blessings, my friend," the older monk said to the newcomer. "I am Angyo, and this is Banko. What brings you to us today?"

"I am called Eleazar. I have been tasked by the Spirit of the Living God to seek your support and the support of all monasteries, mosques, churches, and temples throughout the world for a spiritual healing for the entire planet."

"Go on," Angyo said.

"The earth is inhabited by many Souls who have not expanded in three lifetimes," Eleazar said. "With each life without expansion they are losing the use of free will as their Ego drives them into darkness, hence they become known as Dark Souls after the end of the third life without expansion. If these Souls enter their next incarnation and add their numbers to those already on their fourth life or more, the result will be devastating to our planet's ability to live in peace. Many humans will die because of hate, greed, and the desire for power. The Dark Souls will reincarnate quickly without returning to our Source. They will multiply the hate, anger, greed, and violence. Many of these low-vibrating humans have been gaining power through extremist groups, religions, and politics, and they have linked with others like themselves. They have become violent terrorists, and some have infiltrated their own governments. These fanatics have become powerful and want to use their power to suppress those they don't like and those they lead. They are devastating the world's environment and destroying God's creations. They are killing   God's   divine   human   creations   with discrimination and hatred."

"Is there a particular country we need to be praying for?" Angyo asked.

"Hate has ramped up around the world and reached a tipping point in the East, in countries with Muslim extremists. In East Asia the threat of nuclear warfare is growing. And now the United States has passed the threshold and entered a state of imbalance, with hate and divisive power gaining on liberty and the common good. The political establishment will eventually fall into a divisive disarray. Without divine intervention, America will no longer be able to use its power for good and will turn against its own people for financial and political greed. Over the next few decades we will see many countries around the world spiral into a darker time."

Eleazar closed his eyes and nodded as if he were listening to someone. The room was silent, Angyo and Banko barely breathing. Eleazar opened his eyes and started again. "Our Divine Creator has called upon White Souls, or those known as Wise Old Souls, to intervene in ways never seen before. The Creator intends to intensify the power of the White Soul for a Spiritual healing."

He paused and sat quietly for a moment before continuing. "When the world's tipping point is reached, the earth's excess of unexpanded Souls will start to spiral out of control if divine order is not restored. God's granted free will is being used destructively, but there is still time for nuclear devastation to be averted. Let it be known that once a Soul hits the fourth incarnation, it is living fully in the dark shadows of ego and cannot be converted during the incarnation. Intervention must occur right before the Soul extricates. A Dark Soul needs divine intervention at death, and the window of time for the intervention lasts only a few seconds. When intervention is successful there is no choice to reincarnate as a Dark Soul. The Soul will be folded into the Consciousness of the Spirit of the Living God."

Eleazar paused again, closed his eyes, and nodded in agreement as he relaxed into a small smile. "Spirit will call upon many advanced Souls to intervene. The White Souls will come in many guises—advocates, caregivers, healers, even politicians. God wants to save all Souls from the egotic mind of self-destruction, and this divine intervention is the means. This is the only planet with free will."

Eleazar closed his eyes again and took a breath before continuing. "If the world goes to the Dark Souls, the reincarnation schematic will end. If the problem is not corrected within one hundred years, human life will cease to exist. If the White Souls, Archangels, and others called to this mission can make an impact, then it may be slowed and eventually reversed."

"What is our role?" Angyo asked.

"Spirit asks you to write and sing new chants that focus on the expansion of these Souls. Some Souls, especially the ones on their second life without expansion, will feel the spiritual strength and awaken their human form to the truth of who they are and reject the spell of hate and separation they live under. Once the spell is broken, they will join other Souls in building a peaceful and harmonious universe. Many others will require interventions before they transition and reincarnate. The younger ones in their third life will have on-the-ground interventions with Angels and White Souls. Ordinary people, White Souls, living ordinary lives around the world, are answering God's call to help. Some are saving Dark Souls at the end of life. While I refer to these Souls as dark, in truth they have become so disenfranchised from the Divine, the power of the egotic mind produces dark thoughts that put the Soul in the shadows of their negativity, hate, and deceit. These Souls need to gain the energy required for expansion prior to the body's death to break the illusions of the egotic mind. Once that occurs, they will be reabsorbed for the remaining reincarnation schemata. Their energy will not return here but will be folded into the loving embrace of the Divine."

The high priest paused, his face showing an expression of despair before he took a long breath and continued. "These interventions will be more dramatic and drastic than any prior to this time. Raising the earth's vibration is required to counterbalance the hatred, discrimination, greed, and misogyny that has been suppressed for decades. It is best if it surfaces sooner rather than later, for the later it rises the more hatred will grow, and more Dark Souls will unite. God has every intention of saving all beloved Souls whether Dark or White."

"Will this lead to Armageddon?" Angyo asked.

"The earth is on a path to a downward spiral, and we must slow the momentum and work to reverse the trajectory. Without these interventions, there may be a nuclear holocaust that will end life on this planet. Every attempt is being made to allow expansion before death. God has intervened to help the spirits that live within these low-vibrating beings, but the free will used unwisely has stalled the progress. So now this help must be increased one-million-fold."

"How can we help?" Angyo asked.

"I am traveling to monasteries, temples, churches, synagogues, and mosques and asking each to contribute to the Spiritual Web, our Spiritual Oneness, through prayer, chanting, and meditation for the expansion of these Souls. An increase in the world vibrations will aid these misguided humans. You are being called upon by the Spirit of the living God. I am only the conduit for the Divine's words."

"We will answer God's call," Angyo said. "We will start today. You will need food and rest before you leave us. You may rest here until you are ready to go. Stay as long as you need."

Eleazar nodded. "In meditation, ask for the words, and God will speak them to you. Each chant is unique and intended for the Souls of many different levels of expansion. Your chant has been selected specifically for you and those that chant here."

The two monks stood up, and with their hands in the prayer mudra position, they bowed to their guest. "We will fix you a good meal," Angyo said. Banko went to the fireplace and added wood to the fire. He turned and said, "I will bring more wood." Then the two monks left.

The sacred Buddhist temple Paro Taktsang clings to a hillside, 3120 meters above sea level. The buildings are interconnected by stairs carved into rocks. It was built in the 1600s.

Angyo means peacemaker.
Banko means everlasting.
Eleazar is a biblical name.

Chapter 4

"Bernard, what do you mean you got in a fight again? You can't solve your problems with your fists." China's voice was raised and vibrating with stress as she spoke to Bernard. "Do you understand that what you do in high school sets you up for the rest of your life?" She turned from him and felt her jaw tighten. "I didn't raise you to fight." She turned back toward him and watched as he paced the kitchen floor.

"No, you raised me to pray and be a doormat to others," Bernard replied. "You are so righteous, yet you lied to me. You live in your fantasy world of prayer and meditation. You have no idea how I feel, and you never cared." His face contorted with anger as he spoke, and his eyes were dark and piercing.

"That's not true. I love you very much and would do anything to help you, I just don't know what to do anymore." China sat on a kitchen island stool and dropped her head into her hand as she let her frustration out in a loud sigh. "I've said I was sorry over and over. What else do you want from me to help you feel loved? Truly, all I wanted to do is to love you, yet it is never good enough."

"I want you to have the same pain I had when I lost gram-mom and pops. I want you to experience the pain I felt when I sat inside the house alone waiting for you to die in the garden when you refused to come in after you were in a fight. I want you to have the same pain I felt when I read your diary and learned you were lying to me about my dad." He turned from her and started pacing again. Finally, he said in a strained quiet voice, "I want you to have all my pain so I can live without it."

"Bernard, it doesn't work that way. You can't find freedom from pain by inflicting your pain on others."

"It doesn't matter," he responded before walking into the dining room and through the living room and exiting through the front door.

"Ms. Hope, this is the third fistfight Bernard has gotten into since starting high school," said Leo Barrett, the vice principal at West Philadelphia High School, as he rolled a pen between his fingers. China faced him across a desk in a small cluttered office.

"I know," she replied. "He's been struggling since his grandparents died when he was in first grade. We see a counselor, but he doesn't open up."

"Well, for him to finish his junior year here, he needs to improve. Three suspensions for fighting and two for cutting class. His saving grace has been his ability to get good grades. The next suspension he will be kicked out." Mr. Barrett looked up from his pen and asked, "Is his father in his life?"

"No, he left when Bernard was a baby." China hesitated before adding, "Unfortunately, I lied and said his father died in a car crash on the Expressway when Bernard was four months old. When Bernard found out his father was not dead, things went awry. It was the beginning of his anger. He's expressed his anger through physical action, and now he breaks things and gets into fistfights."

"I see," Mr. Barrett said, nodding his head.

China gulped and took a deep breath. "I felt so loved when I grew up, I just wanted the same for him. I never wanted him to know that his father did not want a baby and deserted me when I was pregnant. I never saw his father after he graduated from Wharton." She dabbed her eyes with a tissue as she felt her own sadness emerge. "He was such a good baby and a sweet little boy. It made it easy to carry on the lie. I thought I was giving him a loving image of his father, thought I was helping him grow up feeling good about himself."

"I see," Mr. Barrett said again, as if he could think of nothing else to say.

"The psychologist said that I protected him so much he never learned to navigate negative emotions. So, as it flares in him, he releases it through his physical action." She looked away and took a deep breath, but Mr. Barrett made no response.

"I keep praying he lets go of his father's desertion and my lie." A tear rolled down China's cheek, and she dabbed her eyes. "I will talk with him and we will see what we can do to turn this around."

"I'll start checking in with him more frequently to see if I can help direct him a little better," Mr. Barrett said, finally dropping his pen on his desk. "He's a smart boy and I'm sure inside he's a good kid."

"He is," China whispered.

China left the school and started to walk home. The day was clear and warm, a fine September day. She had walked several blocks when she heard someone scream to another, "We are under attack. They destroyed the World Trade Center."

Startled, she looked around to see the man on the corner in front of a diner yelling to others at an adjacent bus stop. She crossed the street and entered the crowded diner. She navigated the crowd until she came up to the counter and saw the overhead TV. In horror she stood and watched as the video feed played the crumbling of the World Trade Center over and over.

China looked at the clock on the wall. It was 10:11 a.m. She stood silently and listened to the morning show host report in an excited voice the events as they were known. In the background she watched the first plane hit the north tower and then less than twenty minutes later another plane crashed into the south tower. Feeling weak in her knees as she watched, she felt herself falter when a large black man behind her grabbed her arm. "It's pretty sickening," he said. "Are you okay?"

"Yeah, but I can't watch anymore. I need air, I need to get home." She forced a smile and nodded before leaving the crowded diner.

As she entered the sunlight she quickened her pace. "Spirit, I just don't understand what is happening. Help me understand how I can help Bernard, and what I can do to make a difference in this world." After several minutes of silence as she walked she added, "I trust you to lead me."

Chapter 5

Early the next morning, the two monks entered the monastery and found the high priest waiting in the entryway.

"I must leave now, and I thank you for your hospitality," Eleazar said. "I appreciate the clean robes and new shoes." He looked down at his high-top sneakers and smiled.

"How long have you been traveling on this mission?" Banko asked.

"Nearly one year," Eleazar replied. "I have six or more years to travel. Then I will be given a new task. Until then, I will continue to walk from place to place and travel by boat when I need to."

Angyo nodded and said, "Wait here." He went to the library, took a wooden box from a shelf, and opened it. He pulled out a satchel that was filled with paper money and coins. As he returned to the entryway he handed the satchel to the priest. "Please take this to support your travels."

"Thank you," Eleazar replied. "Spirit has provided for me all along the road, so I accept this with great gratitude as a gift from Spirit through you. Many blessings. I will join you in chant and the welcoming of the new day. I hope to be at the bottom of the mountain as the day is breaking."

The two monks looked at each other, and Angyo nodded to Banko. The young man went to a backpack that was leaning against a wall and picked it up.

"We want you to take this backpack for your journey," Angyo said. "We have filled it with clean robes, another pair of sneakers, food, and a tablet. Our young apostles arrive with laptops and tablets, and we have no purpose for them. Sometimes we go down to the village to use the Wi-Fi in the local cafes."

Eleazar smiled and took the backpack. "Thank you."

"We have had the computer reset for you," Angyo said. "I wrote your password and directions on a paper and put it in the backpack. You can use it for directions, reading world news, communicating with temples and monasteries that have such technology, and many other things. In many coffee shops and libraries around the world, you can connect to the World Wide Web. The Universe asked us to give this to you. Last night, we and our apostles recorded our chant in the prayer garden. You will find it on the computer."

"Again, I thank you," Eleazar said as a tear slipped from his eye. He bowed his head. After a moment, he looked up and said, "Soon the rooms of this monastery will fill with life and a new purpose."

The three men picked up torches and left the monastery, heading toward the steep steps that ran along the stone wall. They began to descend, chanting as they went, their torches flickering in the darkness. The cold early morning air made them shiver, and their exhalations sent out little streams of fog.

In the prayer garden, the two monks took their places across from each other at the prayer wheel and started the rotation. They continued their chant of gratitude for the new day, and after several chants, they stopped and looked at Eleazar, who was standing at the garden wall. The monks bowed to their visitor before turning back to the prayer wheel and starting a new chant. The chant became louder as they raised their voices in unison.

Eleazar bowed as the monks continued the prayer chant, and a tear of gratitude fell from his eye. He left the garden knowing the words would resonate through the spiritual web, the universal consciousness, or, as scientists call it, the unified field. He proceeded down the steps as the sounds of chanting filled the early morning air.

Eleazar reached the valley after sunrise and felt the instant warming of the early sun's rays. He walked into the town and stopped outside a coffee and tea shop as he watched a young man set up outside tables and turn the closed sign to open. The young man held the door and encouraged Eleazar to enter. "What can I get for you? The coffee should be ready in a few minutes." He spoke in his native language.

"Do you have a Tibetan chai tea?" Eleazar asked. After a pause Eleazar added, in Dzongkha, "With goat's milk?"

The young man nodded and started to make the old man his tea. "You can sit down. I will bring it to you."

"Very nice," responded Eleazar. He sat at a corner table and faced the big window to enjoy the coming of the day. He placed the backpack on his lap and slowly started to empty it, looking at everything that was packed for him. In the middle of the new robes was the tablet that Banko told him about. He pulled it out and repacked the other items into the backpack prior to placing it on the empty chair next to him. He looked at the tablet, turned it from side to side and even shook it, not sure what to do with it.

The young man approached with Eleazar's tea and set it down on the table. "Wow, you have the newest tablet," he said. "That's pretty cool."

Eleazar looked up. "It does not seem to be working."

"May I see, please?"

Eleazar shrugged and handed him the tablet.

The young man took the tablet and sat down across from Eleazar. He was smiling. "I want one of these." After several movements of his hand, the computer started to boot up. "See, you push this button here." He had his finger on the button on the side of the tablet and showed it to Eleazar. "Watch the screen, it's booting up. Is this your first computer?"

"Yes, it was just given to me at the monastery. I thought I would sit for a little bit and learn how to use it." He felt his cheeks flush from the idea of having a computer. "Are they hard to use?"

"Nope, I love using them," the young man replied. "In fact, I am learning how to repair and program computers."

"Oh, very good, God brought me to the right place for my lessons." He was about to say something else, but he hesitated and a sheepish expression crossed his face.

The young man laughed and said, "Yeah, I'll help you."

"Thank you," Eleazar said, and he told the young man his name.

"My name is Ram," his new friend said.

Another customer came in, and Ram went to serve him. When he returned to Eleazar, he picked up the tablet, tapped it a few times, and then handed it back. "There you are, ready to start your internet surfing. What would you like to know or find on the internet?"

Eleazar thought for a moment and said, "What is happening in the world?"

"That's pretty broad, so we will set you up with a website for world news." Ram set up the computer to open to the BBC site. "Okay, just tap on this to open the news page." He pointed to an icon on the screen.

Eleazar did as instructed and tapped the icon. He was surprised to see the headline "America Under Attack" pop up. He looked at Ram. "What happened? Are they at war?"

"It was a terrorist attack yesterday, a very bad one."

Eleazar proceed to read the article as the young man got up from his seat.

"Thank you, Ram," responded Eleazar.

Ram nodded and returned to his work.

March 11, 2004

Chapter 6

China and Bernard sat in the living room watching ZNN.

"One hundred and ninety-two people were killed in the Madrid train bombing and approximately two thousand were injured in yesterday's attack," the reporter said. "The authorities are reporting that an Al Qaeda terrorist cell has taken responsibility for the bombing."

China turned to Bernard. "I thought the roughest thing we would encounter was your adolescence. Now I worry every time you walk out the door. You're an honor student at Penn, and I can't protect you from the world, from hate and destruction. My heart is heavy that so many people are cut off from the Divine and creating such destruction and senseless killing."

"Mom, I know my teen years were tough on you," Bernard replied. "I know I still struggle with my anger and wanting to blame you for things that may not be fair. Even I don't always understand my feelings. But now I just want to be successful and on my own."

"On your own without me?"

"No, just on my own. If I can see myself as successful, then I'll be happy, and that will help our relationship. I won't have anything to blame you for." Bernard looked at his mother, his face pensive and remorseful. "Nine-eleven scared me to death. I prayed that day, and I told God I wanted to forgive you but wasn't there yet. I told God, when I am successful and feel real love, I will be ready."

China felt her heart swell with the love of a mother. "What I offer you is real love, the real love of a mother. It's okay, honey, you no longer need to answer to me. You are an adult and I respect that. Regardless of how you feel, I will never stop loving you, I will never stop seeing the good in you, and I will always honor the divine that lives within you regardless of where you are on your spiritual journey." She gave him a sad smile and swallowed hard before saying, "As long as you put conditions on forgiveness, happiness, or love, you will most likely stay stuck where you are." She stood up and turned from him and headed up the steps to her room.

Chapter 7

Sam Benoff looked up the steps of the Paro Taktsang Monastery. He started his climb with a backpack and an overstuffed gym bag. At 32 years of age he had felt driven by an internal urge to leave his position at M.I.T. He had a good reputation for his work in quantum physics. He spoke at conferences around the world, collaborated with universities and physics labs on most continents. Many scientific leaders referred to Sam as the next Einstein. Yet an inner unrest about where he was in life sparked a new curiosity to explore the dimension of Universal Consciousness.

Looking up the steps that climbed the wall of the mountain, Sam could not see where they ended. "This must be the stairway to heaven," he said with a laugh as he continued his journey. After an hour he turned to look down and realized he could no longer see the village below. The stairs had turned in an upward spiral. Above him it looked like the steps vanished in the clouds. The old stone wall on the right stood less than 10 inches high and did not provide protection from falling off. The steps were uneven in size and depth. Sam resumed his climb, looking to his left for rocks that jutted out that he could grasp to keep him steady on the harrowing incline.

Two and a half hours into his climb, Sam thought he could see a gate at the top of the rocks. With a feeling of relief, he hoped it was the end of his climb. He'd first heard of the monastery when he read an article on the Bengal tigers that live harmoniously on its grounds. When the monks meditated in the woods, the tigers often joined them and walked alongside.

The journalist who visited the monastery spent three weeks there. He learned to meditate and felt the peace and love transmitted by beasts, humans, and plant life. It was the perfect depiction of the garden of Eden. The tigers were not known to hunt within the grounds of the monastery. The monks believed the tigers traveled several miles around the back side of the mountain to hunt the mountain goats and deer. Sam had added the monastery to his bucket list of places to visit. Since the article's publication he felt a growing need to visit. He wanted to feel the harmonic energy alignment of beast and human.

Sam was not a very religious man. Raised in the Jewish faith, he found himself less connected to the practices of his family's religious belief the more he delved into quantum physics. His studies of vibrations and the "God Particle" had drawn him into believing in oneness and the unifying vibrations of the Spiritual Web. His decision to leave his position was to gain a better understanding of how the spiritual connectiveness worked. Studying this harmonious microcosm could help him develop a greater understanding of the Universe and this thing call God.

Sam saw a big black gate looming over the steep steps. He thought he saw eyes peering down at him, between the opening of the wrought iron gate. He blinked to help him focus and saw nothing more than pine tree branches swaying in the wind, but the wrought iron pattern revealed itself more clearly with every step. The pattern of a large leaf sat in the center of the gate.

Sam stopped to rest, his left shoulder leaning into the mountainside. He took a few deep breaths then counted the steps ahead of him. The last eight steps appeared to be the steepest he had to climb over the past few hours. His legs felt like lead as he took each step, but he reached the top and walked onto a flat landing lined with big stones. The steps continued up in another spiral ahead of him.

On his left was the gate that had drawn his focus. He held on to the old metal to steady himself for a few moments while he scanned the area around him. He pushed the gate open and entered the courtyard. He thought the stone courtyard was a meditation garden. Large flat rocks lined the side walls. Sam dropped his bags at the end of the big stone and sat down. He saw torch holders in all corners and by the gate. He stared at the large stone wheel. From his seat, he bent over to see how the massive wheel was supported off the ground. Under the large stone there appeared to be a large wooden turntable. Looking up at the top of the stone, he saw something etched into it.

He was too tired to get back up and figured there was plenty of time to see the prayer wheel. He set his legs onto the stone and lay back onto his backpack to rest. Rest came easily as he felt himself drifting into the distance. The sounds of the mountain were around him as he drifted into a warm, loving space. He let himself go deeper and he saw himself morph into the tree of life. In the silence of his mind he asked, "Teach me about the oneness of the Universe."

Sam continued to float for what felt like several more minutes. He heard himself say within his journey, "Yes, I choose to serve." As the words tapered off he felt an awakening to the winds and sounds around him. He sat up quickly and realized he was no longer alone. A young bald monk sat across from him in meditation. As Sam started to pick up his bags he heard the man speak.

"I will take you to the monastery, you can eat and rest there." Sam followed him through the gate and they started to climb higher up the mountain.

Chapter 8

China moved around the monitors and machines as she gazed down at her patient. "Sally, I'm changing your IV lines," she said in a soft voice as her long, slender gloved hand worked on the lines. "Don't worry, it won't hurt."

"Hello," Sally murmured, her first communication in twenty-four hours.

"Hello, Sally," China said, and then she went about her tasks.

"He who dwells within."

China looked at Sally again and leaned close to her ear while speaking in a soft voice. "Yes, Sally, you need to turn to 'He who dwells within' to discuss if you stay or go. You had another stroke this morning, the third in three days. Your heart has been very irregular, and we're doing everything we can to stabilize you." She turned back to the IV pumps and lines.

"Hello." The voice had a digital quality.

China stopped what she was doing and looked at Sally. Their eyes locked for several seconds. China knew that Sally was at a point of decision. She wondered if she would decide with her Spirit to remain in a debilitated form, put up a good fight and try to recover, or if her Spirit would detach and leave. As she turned away to change the IV bags and lines, she thought to herself, *I will honor your Spirit's wishes.*

"He who dwells within," the digital voice uttered.

"I can't tell you what to do, Sally, it is the Spirit that dwells within that can guide you. Maybe you think of it as your Spirit, your Soul, or your higher self. It doesn't matter what you call it, it's your inner power. You must turn within to find your direction and make your decision. It isn't mine to make, but I will honor and support your decision." China looked up at the monitor and watched Sally's heart rate slow and the irregularity change to a steady beat.

"Good, Sally, you're responding nicely to the new medicine. I'm here with you and won't leave you if you need me." She reached over to the pump and changed the rate of flow.

China removed her gloves and rubbed her brown fingers on Sally's pale white skin. As she looked up, she felt a presence enter the room. She looked around, saw that no one had entered. "So, you're here," she said in a quiet voice. "Is this a checking in, or are you here for a transition?"

She felt a sensation of checking in—there would be no transition today.

China bowed her head. "I will serve Spirit however I'm needed," she whispered. "Tell me what to do so I can honor Sally's Spirit, He who dwells within."

The air thickened in front of China and elongated into a formless image, with energy waves moving out from the center. "Thank you," she whispered. "I welcome your presence."

Sally slipped into a quiet sleep, her breathing rhythmic and easy. China stroked Sally's head and said,

"You are so loved. Spirit loves you and so do so many people. So do I love you."

China took a deep breath before reviewing all the monitors and IV pumps. She charted the information and left Sally's bedside.

China, feeling tired, moved to a corner of the large work station that filled the center of the Neuro ICU. She sat in front of a large monitor so she could watch Sally and her vital signs. She liked the corner of the busy station where she could sit away from the frenetic activity that occurred right in the center of the station. The phones rang continuously, the staff spoke loudly to each other, and alarms rang through the monitor system. Yet in her corner she felt calm and clear in her thoughts. Staring at Sally's monitors she felt her Spirit move within her.

China's peace was shattered by the harsh screaming from the third year fellow Dr. Jill Buggy. "God damn it, I didn't ask your opinion. I am telling you what I want, and I expect you to do as I say and don't think you know better than me." Jill's face twisted in a fit of anger as she stood shaking her finger at a nurse who looked flustered and shaken.

An attending who was sitting behind the desk got up and walked to the young nurse. "I'm interested in what you think," he told her. Then he turned his back to Jill and escorted the nurse back to a patient's cubical.

Jill let out a loud "Ugggh" and pushed a medicine cart into the wall. Several bottles of IV medications fell off the cart and crashed to the floor. Jill turned on her heels and stomped out of the unit.

China was in and out of Sally's room over the next thirty minutes and then sat down to finish her charting. Finding her corner of the station empty, she settled in.

"How is she doing?" Dr. Jill Buggy broke through China's peaceful moment and sat down next to her. "Are you, all right?" she asked. "You look tired."

China looked at Jill and frowned. "You know, you were way out of line over there. And if you're still in a mood, I'm not interested in talking with you."

"I took a break and feel better now," Jill said, sounding like a child who was caught in the act of doing something wrong.

China looked at Jill like a mother who could not stay angry and gave her a nod. "As for me looking tired, three twelves in a row feels different in my fifties than it did in my twenties and thirties. But I'm grateful I'm not one of the three on maternity leave. Too old for that, and poor Jennifer still fighting cancer."

"Hopefully, you'll have some time off soon," Jill responded.

China shrugged. "I'm off tomorrow, back on Friday."

"Sally's so unstable you may want another assignment if she's still here."

Jill's concern felt genuine to China and she allowed herself a smile. "Just one more hour, and then

I'm off for a glass of wine and dinner with my son. He's cooking."

Dr. Buggy grinned. "That's awesome. He's a good son. Of course, he has a good mom. Have you found him a young nurse yet?"

"I'm keeping myself out of it. Now that he's finished law school and passed his bar exams, he needs to get a little more settled. He's only been working for three months, but he's talking about getting his own place. I suggested he stay another year and save some money, maybe enough for a down payment."

"Sounds like a good plan," Dr. Jill said, standing up. "I'm off on my rounds." She looked at the monitors one more time and then walked away.

China watched Jill leave, remembering how difficult it had been for her to adjust to the many personalities of the ICU. Jill's rigidity and quick temper had been difficult for many on the staff, including the physicians. "I send you love and blessings, Jill," China whispered. As she refocused on the monitors, she heard raised voices on the other side of the unit. China turned to see Jill demeaning the same new nurse over her documentation. Her preceptor came rushing out of a cubical to intervene.

"It's still bumpy for her Spirit," China whispered.

China entered Sally's room and felt the warmth of the Divine energy filling it. She stopped, smiled and said, "I honor and love the Spirit that lives within." She proceeded to make her assessments. When she was finished, she said to Sally, "I'm almost done my shift, but your next nurse will be here soon and will take good care of you. I'm back on Friday, so if you're still in the ICU, I will see you then. If you get transferred to another room, I'll stop in and visit." China bowed her head and put her hand on Sally's arm. She said a brief silent prayer. China looked around the room and smiled as she felt the warm loving presence that lingered in the room.

Sally's digital voice said, "I'll be here."

"Okay," said China. She smiled at the frail woman as she looked deep into her eyes. She knew she was looking at Sally's soul, which was looking back at her. Sally's eyes were unusually large, like those of a frightened deer. Yet her eyes radiated a sense of divine knowing and inner peace. This was something China had seen many times. She had learned early in her career that many disabled and autistic children and adults do this Soul gaze. She always felt her own Spirit move within her, and her own eyes felt fixed and focused on the eyes within. They are the spiritual eyes that look through the filters of the human ego's lies and misbeliefs.

After report, China gathered her pocketbook and tote bag from the locker room. The walk through the large medical center of the University of Pennsylvania went quickly. She boarded her bus, sat down, and closed her eyes. As the bus traveled down Spruce Street, she was lost in thoughts about Sally. The sweet old lady with a confused family made China laugh when she first came in. At first, she had a sweet gentle voice, until she yelled at her grown son. Then her pitch was high and her tone sharp. Each day since her arrival Sally had deteriorated. The Divine Energy that so often accompanies the dying was with Sally when China left the room. In her heart, she knew that Sally would soon transition back to spiritual form.

"•.,,.•*"*•☆•*"*•.,,.•*"*•☆

As she closed the vestibule door behind her, China was embraced by the smell of a roasting chicken coming from the kitchen. "Smells delicious!" she called out as she walked through the living room. "Do I have time to get cleaned up?"

"Yes," her son, Bernard, called back as she walked around the dining room table approaching the kitchen. "And there's a bottle of chardonnay in the refrigerator. I'll pour you a glass. You can take it with you while you get a hot bath."

He retrieved the wine, uncorked it, and poured a glass. He handed it to his mother when she entered the kitchen.

"Thanks," China said. She took a sip and nodded.

"Dinner should be ready by the time you're done," Bernard said.

China took her glass into the bathroom and started to run the water. She linked into the Agape radio station out of L.A. The spiritual music lifted her Spirit after an exhausting twelve-hour shift.

She sat by the old clawfoot tub on a Japanese-style wood cedar bench. As she watched the hot water pour in from the faucet, she unconsciously tapped her big toe on the black and white tiles. The walls around the old tub were surrounded by a white subway tile. The floors were custom made to match the original black and white basket-weave tiles that her grandparents had in the hallway bath. She now had a stand-alone spa shower and a crystal chandelier that was on a dimmer. Her grandparent's old dresser was used as a converted vanity and sink. The renovation of her master suite was worth sacrificing the sixth bedroom for the bath and walk-in closet.

She raised her glass and toasted the moment. "To a moment of luxury with you, Spirit! Thank you for this blessing." She sipped her wine as she watched the tub fill.

Working as a nurse, China had grown more spiritual over the years. Unlike the newer and younger nurses, she no longer thrived on the adrenaline rush of saving lives. Pushing drugs and performing CPR were not stimulating. She found herself drawn into the warmth and comfort she felt around the dying. She always felt honored to share in the transition of energy from one dimension to another. Some of her peers did not like being involved with death. They saw it as a failure of medicine and were quick to assign China the patients they thought were hopeless.

China shut off the faucet before sliding into the deep tub. Hot water covered her, and her mind drifted into a relaxed state without thoughts. She heard herself say, "Yes, I will help Sally. I serve you, Spirit, with love and devotion." As she said the words she refocused on the room and her long thin body in the tub. She lathered up and washed away the smell and feeling of the hospital. "Thank you, Spirit, for asking me to help. Just let me know how and when."

After dinner, China fell into a deep sleep while watching TV. At 11:30 she awoke and looked around. There was no sign of Bernard, and she assumed he had gone to bed. She got up and went to her bedroom and got ready for bed. She drifted into an easy sleep.

"China."

China was startled awake by the voice. She glanced at her alarm clock. It was 1:30 a.m. She looked around the room and saw no one, but she knew the voice was Sally's.

"I'm awake, Sally," she said in a low voice. "I can hear you."

Sally told China about her fear of leaving and said she had failed her children, who were still suffering as adults.

"Sally, they are grown middle-age adults, and they need to fix themselves now," China said. "You did the best you could with what you had. Every parent makes mistakes."

China heard Sally's words inside her head, in the same sweet voice she had when she first came into the ICU. Sally told her she had lived her life for the love of money and sold her children out for money. She said she had done terrible things.

"Sally, forgive yourself and ask your children to forgive you for your actions. Often that's what a person needs to hear from a parent for them to move forward and heal. You can still give them that gift."

China was sitting up in bed, her pillows propped behind her. The dark room had a fading flameless candle dimly glowing on the dresser across from the bed. China focused on the light as they talked. By three o'clock Sally had gone silent. China slid back down and cuddled her pillow. "Spirit, how can I help?" she whispered, and then she slipped back into a peaceful sleep.

By 5:30 a.m., China was sitting up in bed, a burning feeling in the center of her forehead, her throat tight, and her stomach churning. Spirit's words moved through her. She heard them clearly within her. The words flowed in an even, monotone voice.

This is the third lifetime that Sally's Spirit has not expanded. She needs the expansion to occur before her transition, to break the cycle she is stuck in.

China spoke quietly, "Yes, I will help." As she spoke she felt the room get warmer as another energy was present. China's Spirit within was expanding in her heart as the words flowed through her mind.

Sally is here now with us. Sally, are you willing to accept this help?

Sally agreed. This time her voice sounded like the digital voice China had heard in the ICU. A feeling of gratitude filled China. She understood that this was Sally's gratitude. Sally's energy shifted, and China felt her presence leave. "What will we do?"

China took several deep breaths, and with closed eyes she focused on her heart space. Finally, she whispered, "I am open to hear your words." She could feel her heart space expand as the message flowed.

Sally needs an energy infusion to allow her Spirit to expand. If she transitions without it, she will return quickly to a more difficult life. If she enters her fourth life cycle without expansion, her next life will be even harder, with greater pain for herself and others. Her egotic mind will take away her right to free will. Sally is asking your help today with her last chance to use her free will.

"I've never done an energy infusion before," China replied. She felt the confirmation of Spirit's words.

I will guide you. You will be the conduit to provide the infusion and the healing energy work required.

"How should I prepare?" Quickly she knew she needed to pray and meditate to build her energy source and receptivity to receive Spirit's directions. "Good, we will do it Friday." She said it aloud to verbally confirm what she intuitively heard and felt within.

China felt a blissful feeling of gratitude move through her. "Thank you for choosing me," she murmured.

"•.₃₃.•*"*•☆•*"*•.₃₃.•*"*•☆

China began early with morning prayer, speaking her words aloud. "There is one God, that God is the Source of all, that is all. This Divine Energy is the creator of all I know, think, and do. This energy is manifesting through me and through Sally. This is the energy of love, light, peace, harmony, beauty, and abundance. I am so grateful for this knowing and the oneness in which I live with Spirit and Sally. Today I choose to serve Spirit in all that is requested. I serve with love, with an open mind and heart. I accept the gifts of this day, and Spirit to lead me. For I know only good can come to me and to Sally. I release these words and it is done. Amen."

She spent time in her living room praying and meditating. After lunch, she moved to her fenced-in courtyard garden and sat by her small fish pond. She prayed and meditated.

Later that day, after dinner, she continued with her third session of prayer and meditation. By night she was filled with peace and calm and a feeling of great alignment with Spirit. She slept soundly and awoke early Friday morning refreshed and ready for her day of work and service to God.

Chapter 9

Bernard walked slowly along Rittenhouse Park. He approached the restaurant under the dark cloud-covered sky. The night was damp and cold with a forecast of sleet and rain as the temperature dropped to freezing. Fallen leaves crackled under his feet. The light showering down from the street lights lit the restaurant's entrance. He stood directly across the street from the big front window and saw the restaurant's busy activity, servers rushing from table to bar, patrons eating and laughing.

He felt an annoyance flare up within him that they had the perfect life and laughed so easily. The thought of their happiness was like a knife in his heart. He took a deep breath of the cool damp autumn air and sighed, a queasy feeling of apprehension turned in his gut.

"I have nothing to fear," Bernard murmured to himself. "We're only meeting. He must be ready to have a son." But he wondered if he was ready to have Sadiki as his father. Sadiki had called him. Bernard had not been looking for Sadiki.

Bernard stood still for a few seconds as he let that thought settle into his being. Feeling more confident, he looked across the street and saw a tall broad black man enter the restaurant. He looked like the man he imagined his father to be. The man in his old faded picture appeared to be broad-shouldered and tall. Back then he appeared thinner. His face was blurred in the picture, and it was hard to see the tribal mark on his right cheek. He reminded himself to check for the markings.

Bernard darted across the street between cars and stopped at the large glass window to see where the man was sitting. He saw him at the bar speaking to the bartender. The restaurant was full, no empty tables and only one empty bar stool, next to Sadiki. Bernard opened the door and was greeted with a mixture of scents, from Italian seasonings to a sultry Moroccan seasoning on his favorite fish dish. He walked to the hostess desk. "Bernard Hope, I have a 6:30 reservation for two."

"Mr. Hope, the other party is waiting at the bar. Your table will be ready around 6:30. Help yourself to a drink and we will call you shortly." She smiled and turned to answer the phone.

As Bernard walked toward Sadiki he saw him stand up. He felt his eyes watching him as he weaved through the tables. His chest felt tight and his mouth dry as he reached his father. "Sadiki?"

The tall, broad man smiled. "Yes, Bernard, it is me, your father." His voice was deep and he had an African accent. The first thing Bernard noticed about Sadiki was the sweet and musky scent of his cologne. Bernard recognized the cardamom, cedarwood, and mandarin fragrance as a Clive Christian cologne, the same cologne worn by one of the firm's partners, a scent still too expensive for Bernard to buy. Sadiki's pigmentation was much darker than Bernard's, and his smile appeared too bright a white for his black skin. He was ruggedly handsome and exuded a confidence that bordered on arrogance.

"Yes, the blood test shows you are my biological father. My grandfather was my father. Pops died when I was six years old." Bernard's jaw tensed up as he spoke. He felt his mouth go dry. He turned to the bartender to order a beer. "A Dock Street, please."

"When did your grandmother die?"

"At the same time. They were killed in a car accident, right before my sixth birthday." Bernard did not look directly at Sadiki. His gaze went past him as he scanned the pictures on the bar wall.

"That must have been hard on your mother. She was very attached to them." Sadiki finished his whiskey and dropped his glass on the bar. The bang of the glass on the wood startled Bernard from his daze. Sadiki called to the bartender, "Another double."

"She did better than I did." He picked up his beer and took several gulps. The cool drink felt good in his mouth and warmed him quickly as he swallowed. He sighed a deep breath as he felt his composure slowly return.

"What's wrong with you, boy? I thought you would be happy to meet me after all these years."

His deep African voice left Bernard devoid of warmth. He hesitantly looked at Sadiki's forehead. He couldn't look him in the eye.

Bernard finished his beer and ordered another, quickly downing half the pint. "I'm trying, just help me right now. So where have you been traveling to recently?" He heard the strain in his own voice as he spoke.

Sadiki had a skeptical look as he peered at his son. "In May, I was in San Diego, June in Paris, July I was in Knoxville, and September I did not travel. I sell my diamonds all around the world."

Bernard felt his interest pique. "Were you in San Diego when the courthouse was bombed? And there was a shooting in a church in July in Knoxville. Were you there when they happened?"

"No, I was in San Diego prior to the bombing and did not arrive in Knoxville until after the shooting. Very sad events." Sadiki picked up his drink and looked away from Bernard before he slugged it down in one gulp.

"I have a lot of mixed feeling about us," responded Bernard. "I can't do this," he sputtered. "Not this way, like we should be best friends. You deserted me and my mother. It took me years to get over it when I found out the truth. And now you want to be friends, just walk back into my life like nothing ever happened." His voice was elevated as he spoke. He jumped off the bar seat and balled his hand into a fist.

Sadiki quickly reached out and took Bernard's fist into his big, powerful hand and said, "That would not be wise, boy." He turned to the bartender and ordered another round for both before releasing Bernard's hand.

"I sometimes do that when I'm upset," Bernard said. His voice was even now, almost apologetic. "It's like a reflex."

"You ever hit anyone with that fist?" asked Sadiki as the drinks arrived.

"Yeah, a few times. Got suspended from high school several times for fighting. They threatened to kick me out and press charges." Bernard let out a chuckle. "Now I'm on the right side of the law."

"I had a temper as a young man. We have that in common. Must be in the genes. Now what truth are you talking about? What did your mother tell you about me?" Sadiki looked directly at Bernard with a deep penetrating gaze.

Bernard felt uncomfortable by the intensity, and he instinctively knew not to lie to this man. "I grew up being told you loved me very much and were so proud when you held me after my birth. You supposedly died when I was four months of age in a fatal car crash on the Schuylkill Expressway. That was the lie she told me. I found the truth by reading her journals after my grandparents died. I was desperate to connect with you in some way. At first, I loved reading about your dates, I felt so close to you. Then she told you she was pregnant with me." He felt his voice crack and could not look at Sadiki. "You told her to abort me, she refused, and you just cut her out of your life." This time he looked at his face to see Sadiki's reaction. "You never held me—not once!"

"Now, that is the lie. The first part was true. I was so excited when she was pregnant. I wanted to marry her. Your grandparents refused to let her marry me. They were ashamed of my heritage. My family was from a tribe in the African bush and did not match the social status they saw for themselves."

"Why would my mother write a lie in her journal?" asked Bernard in disbelief.

"Because she wanted to ensure if we met you would hate me. She wanted to protect her parents and their rejection of your father. Your mother could never go against her parents." Sadiki looked at Bernard before standing and removing his leather bomber jacket. "Looks like the hostess wants us for our table."

Bernard caught sight of what was once a deep scar cut into Sadiki's right cheek. Bernard's mother told him it was the tribal marking given to the first son of the tribal leader.

They moved to a table by the front window. As Bernard sat down he felt an overwhelming guilt move through him as he thought he was betraying his mother. *Why do I care? She betrayed me with her lies,* he thought. He felt a deep stirring turning his stomach and an ache in his chest.

"Tell me about yourself and your career," Sadiki said.

"I've been working for this firm for the past three months. Right now, I do a lot of the research and write briefings for the partners. I like the work and I'm continuing to learn. The partners seem to like me, so it feels good."

"Do you plan to specialize in any area of law?"

"Yeah, I want to specialize in discrimination law. Our firm takes on discrimination cases and they have been discussing launching a specialized discrimination department. It's just talk right now, so we will see where it goes. I hope by the time they launch it, I'll be ready to take the lead with cases and go to trial."

"Good boy, shoot high and it will be yours," responded Sadiki.

They shared some mindless chatter as they sat waiting for their dinner to arrive. When their meals arrived, Bernard had a hard time eating his favorite fish dinner. He watched his father devour his steak as if he was starved. "You downed that fast," said Bernard as he watched his father clean his plate.

"Yes, I was very hungry, meals on the plane never satisfy me," responded Sadiki as he looked to capture the attention of the waitress. He raised his empty glass and pointed to Bernard's beer glass. Without a word he communicated his expectation to receive another round of drinks.

Bernard felt the tension in his face and jaw. Not sure how he was feeling, he was reluctant to continue drinking. "I don't need any more beer, thanks."

"Humor me, we are celebrating our reunion," responded Sadiki. "I am very happy to be with you and proud of you and your success."

Looking at Sadiki, Bernard hesitated before saying, "I'm not there. I'm really struggling right now to even like you, to trust you, let alone to celebrate with you our reunion. If you didn't screw things up when Mom was pregnant, we wouldn't need a reunion."

Bernard's voice was filled with bitterness and a sharp tone of anger.

"Let's change the subject," said Sadiki. "Are you going to vote for a black president next November?"

Bernard felt anger flare within him. "I'm voting for the best candidate for president who happens to be black. And just like me, he has a mixed heritage. Ironically, he had an African father. But what matters most is he is sincere, intelligent, empathetic, a good husband and father. He will make America proud of who we are." Bernard laughed before adding, "That is more than I can say about my own father."

Leaning over the table towards Bernard, Sadiki said, "Americans are too prejudiced to vote for their first black president. In the heart of many Americans is fear of those who are different from them. It is a country heading toward white nationalism, and the hate will soon bubble over. Even if your black president is elected, in time the hidden fears of Americans will destroy the illusion of freedom many think they have. Your country will soon be led with greed, prejudice, lies, and destruction." Sadiki's eyes darkened as he talked, and his face became cold and flat, as if devoid of emotions.

Bernard felt a chill go through him. "Who the hell do you think you are, depicting Americans that way? You don't know anything about us."

"I sell diamonds to the elite, the politicians in the highest of positions, and they pay greatly for my services. Every diamond purchase to your Washington politicians reveals their fears. They fear all that you and many young people represent. They fear inclusion, diversity, acceptance of those who are different. They pay me to give them a flawless gem and a flawless society." Sadiki's response was direct, clearly stated, and filled with a knowing that scared Bernard.

Bernard stood up. "I can't do this, I can't listen to you anymore." He pulled out his wallet to pay for the meal.

Sadiki shook his flattened hand over Bernard's wallet. "No, my treat." He leaned back in his seat. He knew he had hit Bernard's deepest fear, not being accepted.

"Yeah, it was a real treat," Bernard said. He felt the angry feelings of his youth surge through him. "Fucking asshole," he muttered under his breath as he stomped out of the restaurant.

Bernard stepped into the street and felt the cold October rain strike his face. He was grateful to have his tears washed away, and he allowed his pain to flood out.

Chapter 10

China's trip to work, on an early October morning before dawn, felt magical. She was full of inner peace, and everywhere she looked she saw the light within everyone and everything. She felt their spiritual radiance. Rain from the day prior had left an early gray sky. Her bus trip was quick, and she felt her oneness with the trees and plants along the way. At times she could see the energy waves around the trees and those connecting with the energy of the people passing by. She saw the radiance of the Spirit even within the dogs that walked their owners.

The bus stopped on Spruce Street by the hospital, and she got off. There sat a large mutt who looked at her and bowed its head. She felt the energy of gratitude within her heart from the big beast. China smiled and nodded back and said, "Thank you." He lifted his head and turned it side to side to show his smile and big canine teeth. China laughed at the endearing action.

China was assigned Sally as her only patient. During the night Sally's heart had become very irregular, which lasted several hours into the morning. She was weak and did not respond to questions. But her eyes followed China and watched what she did.

China felt Sally's gaze, so she bent over the bed rail and said, "Spirit will guide us to the right time and what will be done." Sally's eyes gave China the Soul gaze. "I trust all will go well for you."

After Sally's heart went back into rhythm, she fell into a deep sleep. By one o'clock, China had completed all of Sally's care. She went to the unit's station, which was lined with monitors and work stations. China gave an update to Dr. Jill Buggy and the charge nurse. She felt the tension between them and knew Jill was in one of her moods. Younger and less experienced nurses continued to struggle with Jill's demeaning personality and demanding expectations.

When China returned to Sally's room she pulled the curtain closed, blocking visibility into the glass ICU cubical. She grabbed a chair and sat by Sally's side. Placing her hands on Sally's arm, she began to pray.

"I call upon my Angels, Sally's Angels, Archangel Michael, and all the Archangels and ascended masters to join me in this healing."

She bowed her head and felt the warmth of the energies who came to assist. The room filled quickly with the Divine Energies. A web of oneness was created. China looked around and saw the densities in the room as vibrating air, some thick, some thinner. China knew which energies were in each position. Archangel Michael was over Sally's heart, and the other Archangels were positioned at her chakras. The ascended masters were at her head and feet. Jesus laid his hands on Sally's head. Sally's and China's angels created a circle of energy around everyone who worked on Sally. Sally remained in a deep sleep. China started a meditation with three deep breaths. She was fixed and frozen as she meditated on the healing. Quickly she heard words of prayer flow through her.

As China prayed, she felt herself drift to a place of peace and stillness. A flow of energy started to fill her and move through her aura at her crown chakra, the top of her head, past her third eye, throat chakra and down into her chest, heart chakra, and out through her arms and hands and into Sally. Energy flowed up through the floor into her feet, up her legs, and through her lower chakras into her heart space and out her arms and hands. The continuous flow moved through her easily. China watched the energy move through Sally and pour into her heart space. Occasionally, China heard the words she prayed and would be drawn back into her sacred space of stillness and peace where the energy flowed easily. The energy was visible to China in pure white waves of liquid that glistened and sparkled brightly. Watching the waves flow mesmerized China into an even deeper state of peace.

After some time, China felt her focus return to the room. Her eyes opened, and she felt her hands release, like a spring rod that snapped open. Her hands still on Sally's arm, she re-rested them gently on Sally's skin. China felt the infusion slowing down and energy settling into her own human form.

Sitting in stillness, China heard the words within.

We need to create a gentle webbing around her heart space to hold the energy in place while her Soul absorbs the infused energy.

Accepting the direction, China continued in her trance without hesitation. Without effort, China's eyes started to move in a circular motion as she saw threads of light building the webbing around the heart space. Glittering gold and silver threads were spun around and around the heart space.

Ever so gentle. Ever so gentle, Spirit whispered to China. She heard the word in this sacred space, Spirit right there within her, giving her clear directions in a loving tone.

When the procedure was finished, China was refocused on the room and the inner presence as it communicated, *The last thing we need to do is build an aura for the expansion.* Spirit's voice reminded her of the sound of whispering winds.

China continued with her prayer and again was pulled into the oneness grid that filled the room. Her eyes started circling Sally's body, and she watched as the flickering light strands were laid down like straw in a stable, one strand settling on the previous strand as the aura took shape. The layers of strands were the colors of the chakras, one layer at a time. Her eyes moved mechanically without hesitation, without her control.

Ever so lightly. Ever so lightly.

The words vibrated within her heart and mind. She felt a warmth and she smiled in acknowledgement of the Divine coach.

China watched the aura thicken in beautiful sparkling threads and was directed to lay a webbing of light fibers on top in a lightly woven pattern. The light fibers were continuous in a steady stream of energy in a brilliant white. In a few more minutes, the webbing was complete. As the light fibers glowed from the completed pattern, China felt her eyes refocus. Her mind returned to the present dimension, back into the room and her surroundings. Her eyes were open, and her hands were still resting gently on Sally's arms. She looked at the clock. An hour had passed.

"All this time, and no one walked in on us," China murmured. She felt a gleeful response bubble up from within.

I took care of that.

Just as the words were said, the curtain around the glass cubical flew back. Dr. Jill Buggy entered and said, "How you doing?" Jill appeared hurried and her tone came across as aggressive. Her movements seemed unsteady.

"We're good," China replied as she forced a smile.

"She looks more peaceful than she did earlier," Dr. Jill said. She glanced at the heart monitor. "Rhythm looks regular and strong. Good work, China." Her voice was unusually animated, and she seemed to force her words.

"Thanks," China said. She felt awkward but knew Jill had no idea she was standing in a room full of Angels and Spiritual energies.

"The patient in four just gave us a challenge," Dr. Jill said. "He was trying to check out, and we brought him back. Guess it wasn't his time. He kept everyone

busy for the past hour, which surprised me. I thought he
was our most stable patient. I was planning to transfer
him out of here around five o'clock. It ain't happening
now." Her laugh was awkward and felt inappropriate to
China.

"I'm glad you brought him back," China said.

"Yeah, me too. Hey, isn't it kind of warm in here?
You may want to drop the temperature in case her
stroke damaged her temperature regulation." Jill turned
to the wall and walked to the thermometer. "Yikes,
China, it's 76 degrees in here. You know better than
that." Her tone was sharp, her words slurred, and her
eyes narrow as she looked back at China.

"You are right, sorry I missed it," said China. She
continued to chart Sally's numbers and check her IVs
without looking at Jill. "Thanks for checking in, I
appreciate it."

"Anything to add to your last report?"

"No."

"Okay, I'm off on rounds, then."

China smiled and went back to work on Sally.
She wondered about Room 4 being stable. She felt a
wave of communication go through her.

*I asked the Spirit in 4 to aid in Sally's healing.
He made a free will decision to accept the request. He
will recover perfectly.*

Chapter 11

Sam started on a walk around the monastery grounds. The fall day was crisp and cool. The temperatures on the mountain seemed to be cooling more each day since his arrival. After several days of good food, rest, and meditation, he was feeling an inner stillness emerge. Everywhere he looked he saw the beauty of the Divine Creative Energy, the perfection in nature's intricate plan and harmony.

He took a meandering path from the back of the monastery into the woods. The woods looked deceptively small and narrow. Sam had learned on his first walk that the woods wrapped around the mountain and widened in some areas as it climbed up the peaks and spread down the back. He liked to follow the footpaths that were loosely stamped between bushes, trees, and rock formations. At times he had to climb over downed trees and through thick weeds to continue.

Soon Sam realized he was heading far down the mountain. He decided to turn around and head back. He was already two hours into his walk and had gone much farther then he intended. He passed many footpaths cutting off on each side. On his way back, he took a path to his right, thinking it would cut short the long meandering path he had hiked on the way down.

Sam breathed in the clear crisp air as he entered the forest. He counted each path off to his left as he moved deeper into the woods. After a half hour he turned to his left on a very narrow path. He wondered if this was an animal path. Along his walk he saw a few mountain goats grazing on the green grass, and as he saw more rock clusters he saw a ram standing on some rocks. As the landscape became rocky, the forest began to thin. He zigged his way through until he came to a strong rushing river. The sound of the fierce water burst through the quiet of the forest as he emerged into the opening. His senses were overtaken by the roar as he walked closer to the river's edge. Looking up, he saw what looked like a steep fall of water that propelled the fierceness of the river. He looked down but could not see an end, just the rapids moving down the mountain.

Sam sat down on a rock to listen to the forging waters. After several minutes of watching the mesmerizing river, Sam leaned back against a rock. He took a deep breath and felt something stirring inside. He took another breath and closed his eyes. "I am open to connecting to your great strength, your infinite intelligence, your eternal peace and joy," he whispered. "I am here to experience oneness."

Sam felt himself drift into a warm comforting state of being. A effervescent sensation filled his mind, as if little bubbles were percolating up through water and popping on the surface. Staying relaxed, he allowed the percolating to continue. The sound gradually dissolved while the sensation grew stronger. Quickly a thought percolated up.

Water is divine energy.

Sam acknowledge the thought as true. Another thought arose in his consciousness.

Everything is energy, the energy of our source.

Again, he felt his acknowledgement of the thought. In his mind he saw the water rupture as it splashed on a rock, sending little gushes of energy flying up before they reentered the water. He thought, *How*?

Little triangles formed around the water. As the droplets burst, they were contained within a triangular field of energy. The shattered molecules returned to the water and reemerged as one molecule. His vision morphed as he watched the individual molecules reenter the flowing mass of water. Each molecule now merged with the massive body of water, each contributing to the massive force of the white rapids. Waves of energy drifted up from the rushing water, and the energetic aura emerged over it.

His vision expanded, and he saw the energy waves of trees, plants, and animals as the image continued to grow. He saw all the energy waves merge together, waves intertwined into one large energetic scene. Sam acknowledged the vision and knew this was the confirmation of oneness. As he spoke the words, "Thank you," he quickly returned to see the river flowing past him. Sam sat up straight as he saw what lay across the river. "Hello," was all that came out as he watched the big tigers lying peacefully watching him. "I heard you only hunt outside the monastery property. Hopefully, I am still within the borders of harmony."

Sam stood up slowly, turned toward the path, and began the hike back to the monastery.

Chapter 12

A few minutes after seven o'clock Sunday morning, China entered Sally's room and approached the bed. "Good morning, Sally, I heard yesterday was a good day for you and your family." She touched Sally's arm and caressed it with two fingers. "Last night was tough and you had another stroke."

Sally's eyes flew open as she looked directly at China.

"I am here to serve your Spirit," China said. "What have you decided? Is today the day you transition?"

Sally made no reply, but China felt the acknowledgement that Sally would transition today.

"I will support and honor your Spirit," China said. She began her care and worked with the certified nursing assistant to ensure that Sally was clean for her family.

Sally's family arrived around eleven that morning. China encouraged them to talk with Sally and hold her hand. Her youngest son struggled through the morning, tearful and angry. He had the hardest time touching her and showing love for her. China offered a prayer to Spirit for this man to come to a place of peace with his mother.

Shortly after one o'clock, Sally's heart became irregular. China adjusted the medications and tried to stimulate her heart with a sternal rub before the medical team rushed in with the code cart. As Sally deteriorated, the team gave her medicines.

Outside the room, Dr. Jill turned to Sally's son. "We don't have a Do Not Resuscitate order. What do you want us to do?"

In shock and feeling overwhelmed he said, "Just keep her alive." He began pacing outside the room.

China left Sally's side and approached her son. "She's made her decision and you can't stop that."

He shook his head. "No. I'm not ready for this."

China looked at him and acknowledged his pain and sadness. Then, in a soft voice, she said, "I'm sorry, but this is not about you. It's between Sally and her God. She loves you and that will never change. No parent ever does it perfectly. She told me all she did, and she wants you to know she is deeply sorry. It was too hard for her to say it herself."

Tears welled in his eyes and flowed down his cheeks, and a shudder ran through his body. He took a long breath, turned from China, and walked away.

China returned to Sally as the medical team was setting up the ventilator. She took Sally's hand in hers and said, "Sally, regardless of what happens here, you are free to go. No one can stop you once you've made the decision to leave. It's your decision with Spirit and no one else's. You are loved by Spirit and will be taken care of by Spirit. Ignore all that is happening and release yourself from this physical form. There is no fear with Spirit. Fear is only earthbound."

Their eyes locked into the Soul gaze as the team continued to resuscitate her body, without success.

China held her hand, and as the gaze broke, she felt Sally's energy leave her body.

Just as Sally's Spirit released, her son entered the room and said, "Stop, let her go. It's okay to let her go."

The medical team stopped the resuscitation. They quickly shut off the monitors and removed the wires and tubes from Sally.

China encouraged Sally's two children to touch her body. "Your mother is still here in the room."

"I feel her," Sally's daughter said. "She's right here at my shoulder."

China smiled. "Yes, that's your mother's spirit."

China watched as Sally embraced her daughter, and then her energy moved toward her son. As his mother's energy form went to embrace him, he turned away and said, "No, I do not forgive you," and then he walked out of the room. China watched as Sally's energy followed him.

"You can stay with your mother's body for a few more minutes," China said to Sally's daughter. "I'll let you know when it's time to leave." She turned to the thermostat and dropped the temperature in the room 10 degrees before turning back to Sally's daughter. "I changed the temperature, so you can have more time with your mother."

When China left the room, she looked down the hall but didn't see Sally's son. She went to the desk monitors and switched screens until she found him by the front double doors to the unit. He stood in the corner facing his mother's energy. China quickly prayed,

"Spirit, I ask of you to flow through him to allow his mother to reach him and ease his pain. He is deserving of self-forgiveness and to forgive his mother."

As she watched, Sally's energy moved closer. Her son slumped to the floor, sobbing, as her energy engulfed him with divine love. China felt a tightening in her throat and chest as she watched the flow of love energy move through them both.

"What are you watching?" inquired Dr. Jill as she sat down next to China. She looked up at the monitor. "He's a pretty angry dude."

"I think he's accepted the first steps to healing."

Jill looked at China as she pulled her legs up against the desk. "Sometimes I wish we could do our jobs without all the drama."

China looked at her and laughed. "Our world is full of drama. Health care is the biggest drama of all, maybe even bigger than politics."

"Ugh." Jill jumped up and walked away. "At least ours is science and facts."

China smiled as she silently thanked Spirit for the opportunity to serve and to know the truth.

Chapter 13

"Hey, Mom, how was your day?" Bernard yelled to China as the vestibule door opened.

Closing the door behind her, she wondered what type of mood Bernard was in. She called back, "Good, honey, I just had a lovely walk home. I love these warm winter days." She walked through the living room and dining room and into the kitchen, where Bernard was tending dinner. "I saw a few crocuses blooming next to a melting snow pile. How was your day?"

"Mine was good, too," Bernard replied. He opened the oven door and basted the pork, then closed the oven and turned around to look at China. "Mom, I've hesitated to say anything to you, but I'm worried."

"About what?"

"You. Also, the presidential election later this year."

China sank into the stool at the kitchen island. "I think I'd like a glass of wine. Do you want one?"

Bernard nodded. "Sure, but don't get up, I'll pour it." He opened the refrigerator, pulled out a bottle of white wine, and poured two glasses. He handed one to China, and they clinked glasses and took sips.

"I have my concerns about the election, too, but I do my best to pray them away," China said.

"Mom, I'm scared of what will happen if Americans aren't ready for a black president."

"A lot of people feel that way, but we still have more than a year and a half to the election. Good things can happen to show we're moving forward with more acceptance." She sipped her wine.

"At work, the partners are gearing up to take on more discrimination suits. In our weekly briefings, we're discussing the increase in violent crimes against blacks, Muslims, and gays. The statistics are showing these events are occurring even though the media is not reporting them. We discuss the possibilities of what happens based on which side wins and if a black man is voted in as president. The partners have been meeting about this for some time. They're worried about the impact on civil rights. And when I was talking to Darren, the mail room supervisor, he told me there was a meeting in his neighborhood yesterday. Many are preparing to fight. They think the KKK and the neonationalists will rise and start another civil war."

"Trust in God and let it go," China said. "The more friction you put out there, the more attention you give your fears, the more power you give the negative situation. I raised you to know and honor the Spirit that lives within. You're a spiritual being who inhabits a human form. We don't engage in the low-vibrating negative thinking of humans led by their egos." She ended on a sharp tone.

"That's the problem," Bernard replied as he leaned in closer to her. "You live in a fantasy spiritual world. I'm out there working for the common man and woman. For the blacks, the Hispanics, for the gays. What happens to them? Will they all be thrown to the wolves while you pray to some pretend God?"

As China looked at him she saw not only the anger on his face but also the slow, dense energy that formed his aura. His thoughts were taking on more of the negative vibrations of the cultural and political consciousness. "I've chosen to live the truth of who I am," she said, feeling her own anger rising. She took a breath and calmed herself. "I respect the path you've taken. I'm proud of you for your service to others, but there's more than one way to look at things. When we lock ourselves into one way—tunnel vision—we lose sight of the truth." Raising her voice again, she said, "You have lost sight of who you are. A Divine Spirit in manifest, who can do so much good if you hold on to that knowing. Yet I can see you are living in the pain of ego's lies."

"Pain, you called me living in lies?" he shouted back. "All my pain is caused by you. You are my pain. You're locked into one way of looking at things, and it's not reality."

China felt his anger and fear rip through her, but he wasn't finished.

"You go to work in that picture-perfect ICU with the newest and greatest technology. You scurry around as super nurse and then come home and pray. You've stopped living."

"I'm sorry my praying concerns you. I'm going up to take a bath and won't be back down for dinner. When you're calm, I'm glad to talk." She stood up and poured more wine into her glass. She started to leave the kitchen but stopped and turned back to him. "On second thought, let me take the bottle with me." She picked it up and left the kitchen.

"Remember you're the one who told all the lies," he shouted after her, his voice still angry. "You lied to me and you pretend to be so saintly!"

The words sent a sharp chill through her. She felt her heart ache as she climbed the stairs.

"'•ᵎᵎᵎ•'*"'*•☆•*"'*•ᵎᵎᵎ•'*"'*•☆

Reclining in the tub, China felt the heat of the water embrace her. The Divine presence moved within her, loving her and filling her with joy. "Oh, Spirit, I so love you and love to serve for you. What can I do now?" She felt her energy start to move, and the sounds of spiritual music playing on her tablet began to fade into the background.

China heard a response inside her mind.

Would you be willing to do this work full time?

"Of course, I would, but I'm not sure how, with my job, my home, the bills that need to be paid. Tell me what I would do." As she sank deeper into the tub she felt a response emerging from within.

There are already tens of thousands around the world serving in this capacity. Only White Souls can do this service.

China looked up and said, "Should I sell my house and leave my job?" She waited as she relaxed her head on her bath pillow. Then the words flowed inside her mind.

You will need to go into a coma. When your time of service is done, you will return to your normal state of being. Everyone will call it a miracle. Or you can choose to transition back to your eternal form. We can do much more in a short amount of time if your Spirit extricates itself from the human form. Some of your energy will remain to keep the cells of the body alive.

China's eyes widened, and she sat straight up in the tub. "I don't want to be on a ventilator or in that type of coma. I'm a nurse, and I know the risks—skin breakdown, clots, infections—I don't want any of that. I don't want to be looked at like a slab of meat or empty carcass. Spirit, I love you and love to serve you. But I'm not sure that a coma is the way I want to do it."

She took a sip of wine, then another, and before settling back on the bath pillow she slugged down the contents of her glass. Her mind was spinning as she felt the warm water engulf her body. She was excited but nervous. Finally, she said, "I want you to find a way I can do this without being in a coma in the hospital or a nursing home. You're the creator of the universe, the infinite intelligence, so create a way to support my body with energy so my Divine presence can do your work without risking my human life. I still feel committed to living in human form, and I'm not ready to vacate my body or leave my son. You have always said it is my right to choose the time and place for human death. To accept this service as you describe changes that." China felt her energy shifting, felt the calm and peace settle within. She let herself drift into a more focused meditative state.

After some time, she felt drawn back by the chill in the water. The music of the Agape Choir playing on her tablet again became audible and filled the room.

Chapter 14

Eleazar was feeling tired and drained from his many years of travel. Somewhere along the way he lost count of the days and years. He visited mosques, temples, monasteries, and many churches of various denominations. While most spiritual leaders were open to the words of God, there were those leery of participating for fear of losing their followers. Always following the lead of Spirit, he felt the Divine leading him back through Europe. "Spirit, I will always follow your direction, but we have passed the seven years of service you asked me to commit to."

Eleazar closed his eyes and heard the response within his heart.

In my dimension there is no time.

He then heard a chuckle within.

As he passed an old library in Rome, he felt an impulse to enter. "I hear you, I'm coming," he said in response to the call from within. The old stone building with round turrets and arched windows was from a different time. A time of reverence, formalities, and growing prosperity. More than a hundred and fifty years old, the building was a symbol of knowledge. The stained glass windows told the story of Isaac Newton and gravity. Other windows showed the stars and planets.

As he approached the front of the building, Eleazar smiled and said again, "I hear your call." As he took his next step he said, "I am here." He entered the foyer to pass through the metal detector and X-ray for his backpack. This type of security practice had become familiar to him as he traveled. As the guard looked at him and his tattered clothing, Eleazar asked, "Why the security?"

"Many of the buildings within Rome have security like this. We no longer live in peaceful time."

"Hmm," Eleazar murmured as he picked up his backpack and headed to a table of computer screens. He sat down in front of a large screen and pushed the mouse. The screen lit up and Eleazar proceeded to answer "yes" to the terms of agreement. The library home page lit up. He read the tabs before clicking on World News. After several minutes of scanning headlines, he clicked on Health. He was intrigued by the headline, "WHO reports escalating numbers of people in comas." He opened the link and started to read about growing concern regarding an unknown illness that was causing people to go into a coma with decreased brain waves. Some required life support, and when the life support was stopped they continued to live in a vegetative state.

He looked at the chart that showed a steady jump in comas of unknown origin. The numbers had escalated more than 10,000 times over the past decade. It was expected to continue to climb. The World Health Organization reported that until a cause and treatment could be found, this situation was rapidly becoming a health threat around the world. The illness did not discriminate, it impacted people across the lifespan and from every ethnic, religious, and racial background. In some countries, the authorities had to build facilities to house the people in comas, who continued to survive for years without life support.

Eleazar, sat quietly after reading the article. He took a deep breath and closed his eyes. Within seconds he felt an internal stirring that confirmed this was the work of the Divine to aid in the healing of the Dark Souls. He nodded in understanding and whispered, "I am here to serve and soon to end my travels." He took another deep breath and looked for the tab on Religion. The first article he saw after opening the link read, "Seeing the Divine in Everyone." The article was a teaching written by the Pontiff himself. As Eleazar read the beautifully written words, he recognized that the Pontiff was sharing the teachings of oneness disguised as Catholic doctrine. The focus was mainly on the immigration aspect of acceptance. "Yes, your way of sharing the ancient teachings."

Eleazar remembered the Pontiff and his previous discussion on the cloak of doctrine and how it clouded the true Spiritual teachings. All religions had the ability to highlight the parts of the true teachings that supported their doctrine and leave other information in a locked vault. "So, when will you share the teachings that have been hidden for so long?" He relaxed into the thought before he answered his own question. "Nothing can be hidden forever, God always shines the light on the truth." He bowed his head in reverence and said, "Thank you, Pontiff, you will know the right time."

Eleazar spent the afternoon in the comfortable library, and at one point a young couple caught his attention. They were mere teenagers hiding behind the bookshelves and giggling. He looked between the books and saw them kiss sweetly. He smiled and sent them a blessing for a life of love and goodness. The afternoon filled him with an inner peace and a belief that the world was moving in the right direction. He felt a swelling within his heart that he had aided in the healing and love he witnessed that day.

He left the library and set off for Vatican City. As he approached an old church, he heard the bells ring, and then a faint chant started to rise through the old building. He walked to an old marble fountain that sat in the center of the piazza and sat down. The chant stirred within him, and the sounds continued to rise as if it was moving closer to where he sat. He closed his eyes and felt the love and harmony of the chant resonate through him. It was a beautiful collection of sounds and words in Italian, which stirred his spirit. When he opened his eyes, he saw two long rows of nuns entering the square from the church. They formed a half circle as they continued to sing and chant.

Off to the side he noticed a young couple standing before the blessed mother. The young man knelt on one knee and showed the woman a small box. Eleazar felt elated as he watched the young couple. *I'm here to witness love*, he thought. As the couple hugged and kissed, Eleazar saw a middle-aged woman emerge from behind a pillar with a bouquet of red roses. She handed them to the young woman and started to hug the young man. The excitement and joy mesmerized Eleazar. "Oh, Spirit that is a love I have never known. Can an old man die or go into a coma without knowledge of love between a man and a woman?" He looked pensive, then thought, *I kissed my mother goodbye for the last time when I was 17 years of age and I never saw her again. The only woman I ever loved.*

Eleazar sat listening to the chants as he watched the activity on the square. He saw the beauty of the energy vibrations growing around the crowds. It was a light, airy vibration that flowed easily and freely, connecting all that participated in that moment. Many travelers and locals were bathed in the vibrations of love. As he felt an inner acknowledgement of the moment, he also knew the Pontiff was on board with the God Project. "Thank you, Pontiff," he acknowledged again. Eleazar was lost in the sounds of the chants and had no concept of time. It was dusk when the singing stopped. He smiled, knowing each Soul was touched by the sounds and more open to love, just as it had impacted him.

He started to rise when a nun approached him. "We can give you food and a room before you continue on your journey."

He smiled in surprise. "Thank you, I accept your kindness as a gift from the Divine." She offered him her arm, and he slowly rose on his stiff legs.

January 2009

Chapter 15

China turned down the volume on the blaring TV while she spoke to her patient. "Your wife said you like to watch the news and want us to leave it on. Today is the inauguration of our new President." She continued to talk as she gathered her clipboards and supplies. "This was the first election I remember in a long time that was filled with a sense of hope and promise for a more unified country and hopefully a more peaceful world. I wish my son felt the same." As she turned back to him she said, "In the job I do, as a nurse, your politics, religion, nationality, or race have no impact on your care. You can be the poorest of men or the richest, I will give you the same care. I will honor the Divine Spirit that lives within you. That Spirit is the true you, the outward body is just a garment to house the Soul that lives within." She turned back to the curtain and pulled it closed around the glass cubicle.

She looked at him and he showed no response as he lay sedated on the ventilator before she continued. "I guess I'm most worried about my son," she said. "He's been a lawyer for the past few years, and he's getting lost in the weeds of politics and all this divisiveness." She sighed, and her face showed an expression of remorse. She glanced up and saw the crawl at the bottom of the television screen: "Spirituality on the rise."

She turned the volume up and listened to the reporter doing a stand-up report. "There has been an unusual influx of highly trained scientists and technology geniuses heeding a calling to enter monasteries, temples, mosques, and churches," the reporter declared. "According to the Silicon Valley giants, many of their best and brightest are leaving for what they call a life-altering experience away from the science and tech culture. MIT reported that three of its top physicists left tenured positions. One moved to a monastery in Bhutan. NYU's acclaimed physicist Dr. Jeff Fei will be on the World News this evening to discuss this rising phenomenon." When the report ended she turned the volume back down.

China's patient, James, a man in his mid-forties, had fallen from a ladder at home while painting. He was conscious when he arrived at a small community hospital. A CAT scan of his head revealed an 8-cm mass close to his brain stem. When his breathing stopped unexpectedly, he was transferred to University of Pennsylvania, where he had remained in a sedated state on a ventilator. A few days earlier he was a father, husband, and businessman. Now his life was uncertain.

"This morning, you'll get your bone scan," China said to James. "It's the last of the testing. The doctors will meet with your wife this afternoon to discuss the results and formulate a plan."

James showed no signs of responsiveness as she spoke to him. She checked his monitors frequently. His heart rate and breathing were in normal rate and rhythm.

She heaved a deep sigh and placed both hands over his chest. "Turn within to find the answers you will require. It is always your choice with the Divine Creator, God, Spirit, that wonderful energy that manifests through you."

James's eyes flew open and became wide and intense as their eyes locked. "I honor your Spirit and will do as the Divine within requests," she whispered. China felt a deep stirring within her body and her heart space. "Soul to Soul we gaze. I hear your call for help for your Spirit to engage—my answer is yes."

As quickly as their eyes locked China felt the sucking power of his gaze. Breathless and weak, she felt her legs start to buckle, and the lock on her eyes was painful, as if he was sucking out her Soul. "Spirit, we must disengage." Her legs went limp and she staggered several steps to the bedside chair. She understood his Soul's thirst for energy. It was a painful feeling, and she knew in that moment he was her next assignment. Too weak to stand, she pulled the bedside table towards her. She recognized her mistake. She had ignored her first impression of darkness within him. When she met his wife, she was so sweet and loving, it was easy for China to push the impression of darkness away. "Oh, Spirit, I allowed myself to get caught in my human impression."

"Are you all right China?" asked Dr. Jill as she saw China sitting limply on the chair.

China let out a chuckle. "You never let me have a moment, do you?" Still too weak to stand, she grabbed the clipboard from the table.

"His rhythm went a little crazy, so I had to check in. It looked like a pause, with a rhythm I would expect post-shock. Did you stick his fingers in the socket? Better check your alarms. They didn't go off at the desk despite the changes." Dr. Jill's voice was sharp.

China stood up despite her feeling of weakness. Holding on to the bedside rail, she moved to the monitor. Reaching up to turn on the control panel she felt her muscles shake from fatigue, "Nope, everything is on. They were on when I started my shift, and they're still on."

"Perhaps it was a malfunction," Jill said as she moved closer to China and the patient.

"We can have our biomedical guy check it for any problems," China said. She hesitated to look directly at Jill. "Do you think it was someone else's rhythm and you confused the room numbers?"

Jill shook her head and responded angrily, "No, I'm sure it was his." Within that second China noted a faint smell of alcohol on Jill's breath. Jill glared at China. "I'm not a novice like most people in this place." She moved to the patient and placed her stethoscope over his heart. "Sounds strong and steady." Jill stood right next to China as she spoke and leaned against the bed rail as if she was steadying herself before moving back toward the doorway. China had an uneasy feeling that Jill had been drinking.

With a weak laugh China said, "You know I'm an energy healer, so maybe when I put my hands on him for his bath, I just zapped him." Seeing a demeaning look on Jill's face, she frowned and said in a meek voice, "I didn't see anything on this monitor while I was bathing him. I was talking to him and he was peaceful. My alarms never rang."

Jill looked perplexed and disappointed. "Okay. Is he almost ready for the scan?"

"We go down in ten minutes," China said. "Respiratory will be here to help with transport."

"I'm going to send one of our second-year critical-care fellows with you, just in case, something is going on. His tumor is close to his brain stem, so he's at risk." Jill's words started to slur as she spoke. "We can't wait any longer to finish the staging." Again, Jill seemed to stutter, and this time to lose track of her thoughts. "Oh … Oh, we're losing precious time." Jill turned on her heels and rocked unsteadily for a moment before she headed out of the room, pulling the curtain closed behind her.

China stood watching the doorway after Jill left. "Spirit, I pray this is not what it seems." She moved to James's bedside. "Don't do that again," she whispered in his ear. "You'll get what you need when the time is right. Your ego's patterns here on earth will be broken, and you will be free to expand. Your Soul has lived under the shadows of ego, while mine is in pure white light. I am far stronger than you, and you just took me by surprise."

His eyes flew open and he made a hissing sound around the intubation tube.

"I will serve Spirit to bring in light," she said and turned away from him. She was careful not to look at his eyes as she continued to prepare him for transport.

By four o'clock, the doctors had all the results and were ready to meet with James's wife, Linda. China and Jill met with her in a small conference room. The small room had six plastic chairs around a round table and bare walls. It was a tight squeeze but worked for family meetings.

"This has been a grueling five days for James, you, and your children," Jill said without a look or sound of empathy. "It must feel like a shock, to go from a fall to a brain tumor." Jill looked at her papers as she talked. "We completed the testing today, and we have some good news and some not so good news. First, James's tumor appears to be encapsulated and has not spread to other areas of his body that we can see." She forced a smile as she glanced toward Linda. "He has no bleeding, but it's close to his brain stem, which is the area of the brain that controls the heart and lungs. This morning he had what appears to be an isolated event, with an irregular heart rhythm." China rolled her eyes as Jill continued, "We see no evidence the tumor has penetrated his brain stem, so we will continue to monitor his lungs and heart. At this point, we see no evidence the tumor has spread to his bones or organs, so that's a big plus for his long-term survival. And for a tumor this size not to spread means it's more likely to be benign."

"Doctor, why is he still unconscious?" Linda asked.

"Right now, we're giving him medicine to keep him unconscious. We're still not clear what type of event occurred before he was transferred here. It might have been from the fall. A concussion does not normally stop someone's respirations unless there's a bleed, but his brain doesn't have any bleeding that we can see on the scan, and the pressure in his brain continues to be in the high normal range. I'd like to share the conversations I've had with our neurosurgeon. He's in the O.R. now and will stop in later today to introduce himself. As I said before, your husband's tumor is very close to the brain stem, so as it grows it can cause fatal dysrhythmias and suppress his respirations. There's only one good option, which is to remove the tumor. Once we do that, we can do biopsies to let us know what other treatment he'll need, if needed at all." Jill continued to look around the room and past Linda when she was speaking. She never looked directly at China. It seemed as if she wanted to hide something. "My guess is that this is a benign tumor, but I can't say for sure without the biopsies. "

"When will he go to surgery?"

"I've booked the O.R. for first thing Monday morning. The next few days he'll stay on the ventilator, and we'll wean him from the sedation and start the ventilator wean after surgery. It may take up to a day or two to get off both the sedation and ventilator. I expect he'll start to wake up as we decrease the medications.

For now, we'll monitor him and give him some nutrition through his vein so that he's strong when we go in. Think about everything you've heard and write down your questions. I'm on service from now through Monday. The neurosurgeon will see you later today or tomorrow."

"Don't people's personalities change when they have brain surgery?" Linda asked.

"Sometimes, but we won't know until after the surgery and his recovery," Jill said. She stood up quickly and again seemed to balance herself with one hand on the table. "I'll check in with you later." Jill left abruptly. China watched Jill leave with a growing feeling of concern.

China turned back to Linda. "What do you fear the most?"

"He's an angry man already," Linda said. "He screams at the kids and me. Sometimes we don't even know why. Some days I feel so beaten up that I have no energy. I just want to shrivel up, but the thought of my kids keeps me going." She dabbed her eyes with a tissue.

"Has he physically abused you or the children?"

"He's never hit the kids, but he's hit me a few times. When he hits me he says I deserve it. Mostly, it's verbal abuse and the anger. After his fall, when he stopped breathing, I thanked God for taking him." The tears burst from her eyes. "All I could think was that I'd be free of him. Now he may be worse." She dropped her head as her sobbing increased.

China put her hand on Linda's hand and closed her eyes in silent prayer. After a moment she said, "We don't know if he'll be worse. His tumor may have caused some of these behaviors as it was growing. Was he always like this, or did it show itself over time?"

"Our honeymoon ended three weeks after we got married, seventeen years ago, when he first blew up at me. I don't know what set it off. I've been walking on eggshells all these years. I was pregnant when we got married, and I didn't want our son to be without a father." The tears fell intermittently as Linda spoke.

"We have a psychologist who will start working with you," China said as she watched Linda struggle to regain her composure. "Once James recovers he'll have to work with the psychologist as well. It's an important part of follow-up when someone has brain surgery. While he's here you're safe, and we'll work with you to ensure you're safe when he recovers. If he's worse, you'll need to leave him for your and your children's safety." China held Linda's hand in both of hers. "You can stay here longer if needed. Feel free to use the phone to call family. I need to go back to see your husband. I'll have the psychologist contact you."

China returned to the intensive care cubicle. James's heart and breathing were strong and steady. She went through her monitor and IV checks as she documented his condition and care.

Years had passed since China was first asked to help Sally. At first, she thought her role was to aid the dying, but she'd learned that energy infusions could also work for those who would recover. She had done many infusions from her home. She moved her meditation altar from her bedroom to a room on the third floor. China had come to prefer the remote transfer of energy. In the quiet, comfortable meditation room, or in her garden, she could turn inward quickly and easily. The energy flow through China's consciousness to her patient was powerful and healing as it was with her first infusion for Sally. China's infusions were always supported by the angelic beings and God, and her desire to serve never wavered.

China left the hospital after her shift ended. Still feeling drained, she was anxious to get home to meditate and restore her energies. Once she arrived home, she went to her garden and sat by the pond wrapped in her old sleeping bag. She planted her feet firmly on the cold stone to ground her. "Spirit, can I do James's infusion from home?"

A confirmation resonated within her as she felt her Divine self, embrace her.

"Thank you for loving me so much and for protecting me," she said. She was overcome with gratitude, and tears slipped from her eyes.

"Gaia, Mother Father God, Mother Earth, The Spirit of the Living God that flows through all, is all, and is manifesting as me, I place my feet on the living earth. With love and gratitude, I accept the Divine energies from the core of the earth. I open my heart and mind so you can flow freely through me for my healing and for the task at hand."

She took several deep breaths and was pulled into her sacred heart space. She felt the energies flowing from the earth into her feet and up through her being, opening every chakra from the root through to her crown. The energy surge was a welcome feeling, one she had come to know well and love. With her mind free of thoughts, she saw the energy flowing through the earth into her, filling her with loving energy and light, her aura taking on a brighter white as her Spirit absorbed the Divine love and light.

Her Angels joined her and built the energetic web around her. James's Angels built a web around his form in the hospital room. The Archangels and Ascendant Masters stayed with James. After the infusion ended, China felt the release of tensions from the energy flow that ran through her. As she refocused on the garden, she felt the presence of her beloved Archangel Michael. His warmth embraced her as she lay back into the garden chair. His love and protection engulfed her, and she was healed completely, her energies replenished.

Chapter 16

China looked at the daily printout for Wednesday, April 22, 2009. She was the preceptor for a new RN, Melissa Jeiven, a young blond-haired nurse who had recently finished her critical care course. China enjoyed mentoring new nurses and teaching them the old-fashioned skills of physical assessments and the nursing process.

"Melissa, our patient today is Ms. Maxine Jones in 17," China said as the two stood at the unit station. "Here is her daily report sheet and a list of current computer orders. I would like you to make your assessments, review her information, and come back to me within thirty minutes with your plan for the day."

After Melissa left, China flipped through the computer documentation system to ensure she had the most important information. Lost in the medical history and clinical data, she was surprised when Melissa returned.

"I'm ready, I think," Melissa said.

China smiled and stood up from the computer and stood next to Melissa. "Okay, let's review what information you gathered and what you want to share with the MD about our patient."

Melissa nodded and said, "Her heart rate was irregular at 168 beats a minute, blood pressure was 180 over 102. Her respiratory rate was irregular at 30." She spoke quietly, as if she wasn't sure of her information.

"Okay, was this your assessments or was this from the monitors?" asked China.

"Mostly the monitors and past reports," she smiled.

"Okay. Now those are two ways of gathering information. Let's walk to the patient's bedside and talk about other ways to gather the information needed to make a good assessment."

They both got up from the unit station and walked to their patient's bedside.

"First, I want you to count her heart rate with your stethoscope over the apex of the heart for 30 seconds, then check each of his radial pulses for 30 seconds and do not look at the monitors." China pulled out a teaching stethoscope with one heads, one tube, and two sets of ear pieces.

"Yikes, I heard you use that thing a lot. I don't think I'm good at this, what if I get it wrong?"

China chuckled. "That's why we do it together. How else will you learn?"

After forty minutes both nurses left the patient's room and returned to the desk. "Okay, you just did a very thorough assessment using your assessment skills, technology, clinical data, and understanding the history of this patient's hospital course. If the patient was conscious you would include her concerns and information as well." China looked at Melissa, who appeared to be focused but nervous. "You did a good job giving the pertinent information back to me as if you were giving report to the MD. So now you're ready."

China looked around the unit until she saw Jill Buggy in front of a medication station next to the pharmacy technician dropping off the medications. China thought Jill was scheduled to be off every Wednesday in April. She wondered if Dr. Byrom had switched with her.

She watched Jill turn to the computer to chart the delivery of the medications. China watched with an uneasy feeling in her stomach. Turning to Melissa she said, "Dr. Buggy is over at the medication station. Never interrupt her when she is doing something unless it is a critical situation for a patient. She will be done in a moment and we will approach her as she leaves the station." They both moved to the front of the desk and waited for Jill to finish her work.

"I've been warned that she's difficult," Melissa whispered. "I don't even know her, but I'm scared of her." Just then Jill turned and started to walk toward the unit exit.

"Go and say excuse me, Dr. Buggy, I would like to give you an update on Ms. Maxine Jones in 17," said China as she pushed Melissa forward. "I will be right behind you."

Melissa's porcelain complexion turned a bright red as she approached Dr. Buggy and said, "Excuse me, Dr. Buggy, I would like to give you an update on Ms. Maxine Jones in 17."

Dr. Buggy did not stop walking and didn't look at Melissa. She picked up her pace and said in a loud voice, "Not now!"

Melissa turned toward China, a confused look on her face. China took the clipboard from Melissa and followed Jill, who had gone through the double doors. The hallway near the unit was congested as China passed through the double doors into the crowd at the elevators. Looking down the long hall, she saw Jill walking into the Critical Care lounge. Still carrying the clipboard, she navigated through the swarm of visitors and staff thronging the hallway. Just as she passed the crowd, she almost ran into Dr. Byrom. "Misha, so sorry, I thought you were off today."

"No, Jill is off today not me," Dr. Byrom said. "Who's charge today?"

"I'm in a rush, be back in five," China said, and she turned and sprinted toward the lounge, feeling confused.

With a sense of anxiety, China quickly threw open the lounge door, surprising Jill, who was standing in front of her open locker. China's eyes caught sight of a cluster of pill bottles.

Jill jumped, and the brown pill bottle slipped from her hand and dropped to the floor. Small round yellow pills spilled out and scattered. "Oh no, damn you, China, what is your problem?" Jill dropped to her knees and scooped the pills up in her hand.

China watched the bottle roll under the sofa. "I'll help." She knelt in front of the sofa and reached her arm under to find the bottle. Blindly she swiped her hand back and forth until she had the bottle in her hand. She pulled it out and held it up as she turned the bottle to see the label. She blinked twice as she read, "Mabel Graves, 20 mg valium." As she read the label her stomach churned with a sickening feeling. It quickly moved through her body and she heard the inner voice say, "Jill needs your help." She glanced over at Jill crawling on the floor scooping up the pills. "Jill, why does this bottle say Mabel Graves?"

Jill seemed startled by the question. "I dropped my bottle in the water and just grabbed an empty bottle from the med cart. I didn't notice it had someone's name on it."

China narrowed her eyes at Jill. "Did you take this from Mrs. Graves's med drawer? Why do you need Valium?"

Jill dropped the pills in her hand into a small pile on the chair. "My nerves. It's prescribed because of my nerves."

"Jill, you're the prescribing MD on this prescription. I need to check, but Mrs. Graves never had a Valium order."

"You don't need to check," Jill said in a quiet voice.

"Jill, you ordered this prescription. It just got delivered by pharmacy, and I saw you at the medication station."

China was still on her knees and Jill sat across from her on the floor, her legs crossed. Jill looked down, and tears fell from her eyes. "Please don't report me," Jill whispered. "I could lose everything."

China stood up and walked to Jill's locker and saw an array of pill bottles. "Oh my God, I can't ignore this, Jill. You need help. Give me the pills."

Jill dropped the pills back into the bottle, and China sealed it.

"HR has a program," China said. "If you self-report, they'll work with you. You will have to go to rehab and will be enrolled in the state program for tracking medical providers. That's your only option."

Jill shook her head. "No, I can stop using any time I want. You know me, China, I'm strong, I'm not an addict, I just have anxiety." She got up and wiped the tears from her face. "Leave me alone, China. If you're my friend, you'll forget about this." She turned and headed toward the door.

China followed. "I will not forget about this. If I report you, which I will, you will lose your license and possibly serve jail time, Jill. Is that what you want?" China's voice was strained as she spoke.

Jill spun toward China, her eyes flashing both fear and anger. "You would do that to me? I thought you were my friend. Now you're making me into some kind of criminal, a drug addict?" She pushed China away from her, turned and flung open the door, then turned again and glared at China. "I'm a doctor!" she yelled. "You're only a nurse. You think you're better than me? I hate you, China Hope."

Jill stormed into the hallway and came face to face with the chief of Neurology. He looked at Jill then China and said, "Please call security," he spoke to

China. "Jill and I will be in my office. Please join us when you're done."

"No," Jill whispered.

The chief looked at her. "If you run, your life will never be the same."

Chapter 17

More than ten years had passed since Eleazar's first visit to the old monastery high in the mountains of Bhutan. Over that time, the once small and sedate flock of monks grew into a new spiritual awakening as young men and women heard the voice within call them to a new type of service. Behind the old stone building of the monastery, hidden in the woods, a physics lab had been built into the mountainside. Inside, scientists from around the world worked on building etheric incubators. They created new ideas and new ways of supporting the life of the human body so Souls could extricate.

In the old monastery, renovations occurred. Solar panels and water wheels were used to give the old and new buildings electricity. The bedrooms and common areas were refurbished for the most important part of the God Project, the arrival of the White Souls who had answered the call for extrication.

Temples in India and throughout the Asian countries, mosques in Turkey and the Mideast, and churches around the world accepted the new apostles to work in nontraditional roles. Energy labs forged ahead with groundbreaking quantum physics discoveries, and physiologic energy generators, energy resuscitators, and human-form energetic incubators were designed and built. Many spiritual institutions with declining membership and dwindling funds enjoyed a burst of energy and a new spiritual purpose. The transition, slow to start, was in full swing and soon would enter the third phase of the God Project.

At Paro Taktsang Monastery, the monks, apostles, and community members continued with daily meditation and chanting to raise the vibrations of humanity. The numbers of apostles grew as others came to work in these nontraditional roles. The new community members built the extended community as they designed, built, and opened the energy and IT labs. A full community flourished on the grounds of the once sleepy monastery.

Angyo checked the monastery's sleeping quarters, soon to be occupied. The old stone rooms with large wood-burning fireplaces were now equipped with electricity and beautiful handmade furniture and beddings. Each room connected with an updated private bathroom.

Angyo reviewed the plan with the lead scientist, Sam Benoff. In the physics lab, Sam and Angyo walked to a sterile glass cubicle and entered. At first glance it appeared empty, with only a long wood rack and a mat made of stones and crystals laid on top.

"Hold your hand over the mat," Sam said. "What do you feel?"

Angyo held his hands over the sparkling crystal. "I feel energy pulsating up and hitting my hands. Is this what maintains the body after extrication?"

"Not exactly," Sam replied. "We need to add more crystals for a smoother flow of energy. Diamonds, quartz, and amethyst will be delivered later today. The frame of the bed will be made from diamonds. It will insulate the energy flow that the Angelic beings will be transferring to the body. The mat will be a combination of stones to create a fluid flow of energy required to suspend the body in the etheric energy channel. While you cannot see it now, the energy around the body will be in a pyramid, much like the energy pyramid our human form is suspended in here on Earth."

"I see," Angyo said.

Sam pointed at what appeared to be round silver globes embedded in the wall above the level of the bed. "Look at the wall over there. There is one at the head and one on each wall above and past the bed and again below the bed. This will triangulate the energy." Sam pointed out each of the globes as he traced lines in the air with his index finger.

Angyo asked, "How long can they be suspended in this state?"

Sam laughed. "As long as the Angels can handle it. Since they don't live in our time and dimension, one of our years is no different to them than a moment in eternity."

"Our first White Soul is scheduled to show up tomorrow," Angyo said. "Will we be ready?"

"At first, they should just rest and eat well," Sam said. "They'll need a fat layer to handle the energy flow. Increasing nutrients and vitamins will help with the initial transfer of energy as their Spirit releases itself from the human body. Give them wine, it will help with the shift into the unified consciousness where there is no ego interference. The Angelic beings will support and channel energy in that same dimension." He chuckled to himself and his eyes twinkled.

"You find something amusing?"

"If my parents knew I left MIT for this, they would think I'm the one who flew over the cuckoo's nest."

"They would be proud you answered this calling. I must admit I have asked Spirit why go to all this extreme, since Spirit can just call us all back home. Dark, White, and every Soul in between answers that call. No nuclear war, no more destruction of the earth, no more hate or discrimination. The natural habitat could replenish itself for our return when Spirit is ready."

"Did you get an answer?"

Angyo nodded. "I was told it would soon be revealed."

Angyo left the lab and walked a path that led him around the side of the mountain and through a thick wooded area. He emerged into a sunny clearing to see a large A-frame structure using all the natural elements of the mountains and forest. The front of the building had floor-to-ceiling windows on three sides, creating a beautiful garden room. He glanced up and saw solar panels across two-thirds of the building's roof behind the sun room.

He entered the building and stepped into a large, glass A-shaped room with a wood frame and stone floor. All the natural elements were flooded with light from the large glass windows. Tropical plants, herbs, vegetables, and some fruit trees thrived in large planters, plant beds, and baskets hanging from the walls and rafters. Overstuffed chairs, recliners, and bistro tables were scattered among the planters. In one corner, a waterfall trickled down a wall of rocks into a shallow pond.

Angyo placed his index finger on the fingerprint plate next to two large sliding doors and read the message, "Fingerprint undetected." He removed his finger and tried again. Three green lights flickered with the message, "Fingerprint detected." The doors slid open.

Angyo entered a cool room filled with computers and IT specialists moving from station to station. The IT technology lab was a vital part of the monastery's new mission. Some of the young people acknowledged him. The diverse group came from many different cultures and religions. His hands folded in prayer, he smiled and bowed to each area of the room. Many stood up and bowed in return. The old monk felt a swelling in his heart as he thought, *Spirit, these are your children, and I am grateful you sent them here. I honor and love your presence in each of them.*

Angyo walked to a door at the rear of the large computer room and knocked. He placed his index finger on the ID pad, and this time it acknowledged his print.

He entered a large semicircular room set up in half-moon rows of workstations. Each row was set on inclining steps from lowest in front to highest in back. The central workstation featured a computer and two screens and was occupied by a busy IT specialist. Multiple large screens were mounted on the front wall displaying a mass of colorful lights, all interwoven and sparkling. Other screens showed wave forms and graphs. The center screen showed the earth from a satellite view with the energy vibrations beating from the core of the earth and resonating out. On each end of the combined large-screen units were three smaller screens. Each IT specialist had a job that supported what was happening on the large screens. Others watched the screens as information was diverted from the workstations into a global picture of energy tracking and the world energy matrix. Angyo walked down the stairs to the front row and bowed as the team leader looked up from her work station.

"Can you give me an update?" Angyo asked. "Where are we today?"

The team leader, a young woman with fire-engine-red hair pulled back in a ponytail, stood up. She was slightly rounded at the waist and hips, had full freckled cheeks, and wore dark horn-rimmed glasses that contrasted with her bright hair. The old monk remembered she was the first woman to arrive at the monastery. Angyo was pulled back to the memory of their first interaction.

"God sent me here?" she asked in a soft voice.

Angyo nodded and said, "Welcome. We are a monastery and our apostolates are usually male, but this is an unusual time, with unusual things happening. The Divine Source, our Universe, works that way."

"Thank you," she said as she looked Angyo over.

Angyo heard words inside his head. *"The old way of being must break down for the new ways to emerge."* The monk smiled slightly and bowed to the voice in agreement.

"I hope I can be of some service," she said.

"Do you know your mission here?"

She nodded and quickly said, "I'm supposed to set up an IT lab to track vibrational frequencies here at the monastery and around the world. I'm excited about it. It sounds like fun."

His eyes widened and then he frowned. "Fun, when the world is in a downward trajectory? I suppose I must learn this type of fun." He bowed his head to her as he invited her into the monastery.

The young woman extended her hand. "My name is Tammy Grant. God said this would be fun and satisfying."

"Perhaps it will be," Angyo said.

"I was unhappy in my last job, and one day I said, 'God, if you are real, find me something fun, exciting, and challenging.' Three months later I was packing my bags to come here." She gave a little laugh. "Who could have guessed I would come to a monastery for fun, excitement, and a challenge?"

He shook her hand and said, "Yes, who would guess?" He shrugged his shoulders before bowing to her presence. As she entered the monastery he closed the door behind her.

"On the plane, I thought maybe the men would be the challenge and the fun. I had never met a monk before." She smiled sheepishly with her eyebrows raised.

Her unrestrained banter alarmed him, but he also felt amused by her honesty and lively personality. "Please remember, the monks and apostolates are not here for your amusement," he responded in a stern voice.

"Of course," she replied, her rosy cheeks flushing even more.

"We've been able to connect with the vibrational frequencies of each of the Spiritual command sites," Tammy said, bringing Angyo back to the moment and his task at hand.

When Angyo looked at Tammy working in the IT lab, he understood that her mind and skills were tapped into the Infinite Intelligence of the Universe, which was working through her. "How are the world web frequencies doing?" he asked.

"We're doing better this month since seventeen new spiritual sites around the world joined in the frequency boost. We're now vibrating at the eighth level. In the next few days to a week we will reach the tenth level with a total of one hundred sites in the matrix. Just this week, five more mosques joined us. They will also support the White Soul extrication."

He turned from the computer screen and looked directly into her eyes. "We are about to enter our live phase, and we need to reach the tenth frequency as projected. Are you confident we will get there?"

She nodded vigorously. "Absolutely." She paused before adding, "Success is in my every vibration."

"Good. How is the security for our network? Can it be hacked?"

"Oh, no, sorry, I should have explained," she replied, her cheeks flushing. "The worldwide chanting is the energy of this dimension, and our web frequency that tracks the energy vibration for the earth in this dimension is going through the seventeenth dimension." She walked over to the center screen in front of them and pointed. "When we see the earth frequencies we are in the Universal web, measuring from the entry level of the Divine dimension. Our presence is undetectable by humans in this dimension. In the Universal web, it is in a much different frequency than the worldwide web."

She walked back to a computer station where another technician was hard at work. "Ram, can you pull up the world web and universal web side by side for Angyo to see?"

One of the small screens turned on, and a map of North America appeared. Ram opened a control panel on the side of the map and quickly turned things on. Waves started to form around the continent, and numbers popped up on the screen across the continent.

"Now I am in the world wide web," Tammy said, pointing at the screen. "Look at Canada, their vibrations have already reached the tenth dimension, the mainland U.S. is a scattering of 7, 8, and a few 9s.

Alaska is a 6, Hawaii is a 10. So when these are tabulated, the United States is considered close to the 8 range." She turned towards Angyo. "So, when we measure the earth frequency, we need to be in the seventeenth dimension. Think of it as the matrix of the Divine Energy that is all and flows through all in its purist form."

He looked up at the screens to see the web of light circling the earth. A feeling of awe took his breath away. "Is the seventeenth the highest dimension?"

"No, as you move into the center of the Source Energy that creates all or is the Heart of God, we would be as high as 24. That is where our Souls are re-absorbed into the divine. It is the oneness muck!" Her cheeks blushed a bright pink and she clapped her hands in joy.

Angyo smiled and broke into a full-throated laugh. "The Divine Energy chooses very well," he said. He smiled and bowed to Tammy and Ram.

Before he left the lab, he turned to look at each of the young people who had answered the Divine's calling. When he was young, the calling was to pray and serve through the monasteries, temples, churches, and mosques. Now he saw a new order, one created by young people using skills in sciences and technology to serve the Divine by creating an etheric power grid that would tip the scale back from the negative path the earth was on to a loving, harmonious path. This was just one line of service. Soon a new line of White Souls would build an etheric army, a legion of light to travel across the

many dimensions from past, present, and future to save
Souls who lived in the darkness of the egotic mind.

Chapter 18

Eleazar clutched the stone wall as he climbed the steps of the monastery. His long beard and shabby clothes had become a part of who he saw in himself. He had been raised to believe that service to God should be through selfless acts and poverty. Now, at seventy-five, he had traveled the world as directed. His new orders were to return to the Bhutan Monastery for his next mission. As he got closer to the monastery he heard the voice of the Divine. He stopped on the step and took a deep breath to let the presence come through.

A wise old Soul you are. You have great power to help others. It is time to leave the life of humble servitude for an active role as spiritual warrior.

Feeling weak, he asked, "What does this mean, *warrior*? I have prayed and meditated for peace and humility for a long time. I have been singing chants for healing as I walked around the world. Now you want a warrior, a killer, to emerge? I must think before I answer." He leaned into the wall feeling confused by the message. The energy shifted again, and the impression flowed quickly.

A warrior of peace and love, one who helps the Dark Souls expand. I have never asked a human being to kill for me. Regardless of what the ego leads them to do, I always love the divine Soul within. You will work with Souls who have fallen under the shadows of the ego's darkness. I am asking you to be a warrior who ends the fight within the human who has fallen to the ego's control.

The energy within Eleazar quieted until a stillness filled him. He struggled to lift his tired legs on the steep, narrow steps. He laughed and said, "Do I look like a warrior to you? I am barely making it up the steps." He stopped to catch his breath as he held the rocks tight. "It was a much easier climb ten years ago when I arrived. The three extra years has put a lot of strain on my body."

As you enter the next phase, it will again be easy.

It was a sun-filled day as he climbed the stone steps. Each step felt heavy, and his movements were deliberate and slow. Looking to his right, he felt a chill go through him as he contemplated the steep fall a misstep would bring. He pushed the thought out of his mind and refocused on his climb to the monastery.

At the top of the stairs he stood still, waiting for his sense of balance to return. As he held onto the wall he noticed a tiger walking along the edge of the woods. Eleazar watched the big cat until he was distracted by the door of the monastery opening. Angyo emerged and strode toward Eleazar, smiling. "You have returned, a little older and perhaps more tired."

"Yes," said Eleazar. "I am still trying to catch my breath. Should I worry about our friend over there?" He nodded toward the tiger.

"No, no concerns, we live peacefully together." Angyo stopped in front of Eleazar and frowned. "It looks like you could use some rest and food." He extended his arm for the high priest to grasp.

Together they entered the monastery. As the old wooden doors closed behind him, Eleazar heard chanting. "It seems lighter here, you brightened up the monastery since my last visit. It is different than I remember." He took a moment to look around the entrance, taking in the glowing lights along the old stone walls. "The voices are louder, and what a beautiful chant. I feel it stirring within me." He turned to look at Angyo.

Angyo smiled and nodded. "We have grown since your last visit. We now have forty-two apostles and eighteen monks. The building itself is different. We have electricity and heat for the winter. Our power comes from solar panels, wind mills on the mountain, and the flow of the river." Angyo couldn't stop smiling.

"Very nice," Eleazar said. "The modern Spiritual centers I visited were very nice as well. One Imam described his mosque as being like the Hilton. I've never been to a Hilton, so it was a treat." Both men laughed before Eleazar added, "You look younger, or are my eyes better at seeing the truth?"

"The monastery has come to life and lifted me with it," Angyo replied. "There has been a great calling to the young around the world. They have chosen to work for Spiritual Centers throughout the planet for this next phase of enlightenment. Your efforts and our initial chants were frontline work of the first phase. Their work is phase two of three. Sometime today we will meet the first White Soul who has been called to enter phase three." Angyo raised his gray eyebrows as he gave Eleazar a searching look.

Eleazar smiled weakly. "I was called to return here to be a warrior of love, peace, and harmony. I'm not sure what that means, but I accepted the call. At 75, I only know how to accept the Lord's request." He reached out to steady himself on Angyo's arm. "It's funny to think that at my age and with my stiff joints and failing body I can be a warrior, in the Legion of Light." He chuckled under his breath.

Angyo looked his old friend in the eye and put a hand on his shoulder before leading him toward the library. "Stranger things have happened. We have about thirty-six women working on the campus in the physics and IT labs and forty-five men. They are not here to be apostles but to provide the services needed for the second and third phase of the Divine plan to succeed. I almost had a stroke when the first woman showed up."

Both men laughed as they wandered into the library. The red pillows were stacked in a pile against the wall. In their place were six overstuffed armchairs and two ottomans. "You will rest here for now," Angyo said. He gestured toward the old desk, which held a pitcher of water, a bottle of wine, and glasses. On a plate in the center of the driftwood table sat a plate of nuts, breads, and cheese. "Help yourself to a snack. I will return when dinner is ready. You will have a room upstairs. When you are stronger I will help you up the stairs. I will explain all this evening." Angyo bowed to Eleazar out of respect for God's chosen Soul, soon to be a member of Archangel Michael's Legion of Light, an extricated Soul.

Eleazar spent the next ten days in prayer, eating, and resting. On the ninth day he looked at his cleanshaven face in the bathroom mirror. One of the apostles had shaved his head and given his face a clean shaving of his beard and mustache. The gauntness of his thin face was gone. He pressed in his full cheeks to feel his cheek bones. He had put on weight, and his frame, though slender, was no longer frail. His legs and feet felt strong and sturdy. "Not bad for seventy-five," he murmured.

On the morning of the tenth day, Angyo met Eleazar in the prayer garden.

"When is the time right for the next phase?" Eleazar asked his friend after Angyo sat down on the stone bench.

Angyo smiled. "It may be tomorrow. You will meet with a shamanic healer today."

Eleazar raised his eyebrows and nodded in agreement. "I am glad of it."

"You will need three ports implanted for the energy to be infused into your body," Angyo said. "One will be in your thigh, the second in your arm on the same side, and the third over your heart. These will be the ports of entry for the ethereal energy that supports your form while your spirit leaves to do the work of the Divine."

"I see," Eleazar said.

"The shaman has been making a detoxification mixture, so your body will not break down chemically, as with death of the human body. I do not know the time of your Spirit's extrication. The Angels will guide you. Once you enter the etheric incubator we do nothing other than check on you through a glass window and monitor energy frequencies. The energy fields and beds we have set up will support your form as your Soul is traveling. Your body will receive energy from your Angelic caregivers through the ports. Crystals are used to intensify the magnetic waves needed for your body's suspension in a viable energetic state. The crystals act as a conduit to ensure the energy stays focused and moves smoothly through your human form. The etheric energy will work as if your spirit was embedded into each cell. The room will become very warm from the energy work that is being done. We were told we may not enter for any reason."

Eleazar laughed. "Can you bring me back with a younger and stronger form?"

"A Soul is always healthy, strong, and agile, as you know it to be. Only the form of this dimension fails. You will return to this form, and it will be stronger, more agile, and younger. That is the gift the Divine Universe provides for your devoted service. You will pick what you want to look like for your return."

"I request blue eyes and a strong, lean body with flexible joints. Maybe a man of forty to fifty." Eleazar's expression turned serious. "Will I return to my duties as a priest?"

"What if I told you that you could retire or do anything you want when you return?"

"I want to paint, make music, and fall in love. I want to find my Soul mate." Eleazar stared past Angyo as he spoke, as if he was seeing the future in his mind.

Angyo smiled. "That request has just been approved."

"How long will I be in Spirit form?"

Angyo laughed. "In Spirit form there is no time, so it may feel like a few minutes or just seconds. But I believe that you and many of the others will return in my lifetime. Early tomorrow we will go to the physics lab where the etheric rooms are set up. If your detox and port implantation goes well today, you will be ready to enter your room and start the process of Spiritual extrication. You are the first to go through the process. We expect a total of sixty White Souls to come over the next year. Other centers will be going live soon, but you are the first White Soul to extricate."

A cold wind whipped around the mountainside as Angyo and Eleazar walked in silence to the physics lab. The once-thick wooded area was losing its fullness as winter crept in. As they passed barren trees and naked bushes, the walk felt stark and lifeless. They moved quickly to avoid the cold sting of the wind. Dawn had broken, but the early morning sun provided scant warmth.

At the entrance, Angyo placed his fingertip on the pad, and the door unlocked. The warmth of the building was a relief. There was a large command station with rows of computer stations. The scientists could monitor several energy incubators and track the energy levels in each cubicle. The incubators were two to a cubicle with separate energy zones. The glass wall of each cubicle was made of thick, triple-pane, heat-resistant glass. Each cubicle had an energy generator that would support both incubator mats until the Angelic beings took over. The Angelic beings would produce and deliver all the energy needed to maintain a human body during and after Spiritual extrication.

Sam looked up and nodded when the two men entered.

"Good morning, Sam, meet Eleazar, our first White Soul," Angyo said. "He has been eating and resting for the past ten days. The shaman completed the detox last evening, so he is ready to go." Angyo turned to Eleazar and said, "Thank you for your service, my friend. I look forward to your return and to hear about your journey."

Sam extended his hand to Eleazar. "I'm honored to serve you for this mission."

Eleazar nodded and pulled Sam into a bear hug. "We all serve the one source, our Divine Creator."

Sam went to a nearby closet and returned with a thick elastic jumpsuit, which he handed to Eleazar. "You will need to put this on," he said. "It's different from your normal clothing and will fit snugly. The material in the suit is woven with diamond and amethyst particles. It will help with the suspension of your body above the mat. When you first go in you will lie on the mat. As the Angelic beings arrive, they will generate energy that will flow through the mat. Your body will begin to rise. Once your body is in the right position within the crystalline pyramid, your ports will be opened. When the energy infusion starts, your Spirit will begin the extrication. The level of consciousness of your human form will decrease, and your egotic mind will drift into a very restful state. Your Spirit will take all cognition with it at extrication. Your body will be in a coma of some sort. The cells of your body will be fed energy through the infusion and a small portion of your Animantien particles. The true 'God particle' will remain behind." Sam looked at Eleazar to see if he was comprehending what was being said. In a slower tone Sam continued, "Your human form will be anchored to tho crystalline pyramid by the same silver cord that is anchoring it now. For our Spirits to exist in this dimension, our bodies must be suspended and anchored for Spiritual incarnation to occur and be maintained. Each one of us is suspended like this."

"Very impressive," said Eleazar.

"Yes," agreed Angyo. Both men looked at each other with a nod before turning back to Sam.

Sam smiled and nodded back. "The detoxification of your cells last evening will prevent them from breaking down on extrication."

"I am amazed and humbled to serve in this way," Eleazar said. He looked at Angyo. "I will return in a younger and stronger form?"

Angyo nodded. "Yes. We don't know how long the extrication will take, so we must begin. When you are in your suit, speak and we will turn on our monitors for visualization."

Eleazar took the suit and walked into the cubicle. The windows darkened to provide privacy. Angyo and Sam walked to the scientist at the computer station. The monitor was dark, the cameras in the cubicle still turned off.

"I am in the suit. Where should I put my clothing," asked Eleazar.

"A door on the back wall will open," Sam replied. "Drop the items down the chute. You'll get new clothing when you return. Okay, the windows will become translucent. We'll watch everything through the windows and on our screens. I'll give you directions and tell you what's happening as we go on. You may speak to us as long as you're able."

The darkened window faded as the transparency reappeared. "We have you in sight, and our monitors and cameras are on," Sam said. "When you're ready, please lie down on the mat. It's okay to take a few minutes to adjust yourself. Let us know when you're ready."

After a minute Eleazar said, "I'm comfortable."

"Good. You'll start to feel warmth and pressure on your back as the generator starts the energy flow for the incubator. As it's building, you'll start to rise off the mat."

The men watched as Eleazar's body rose.

"You're rising and will stop about a foot above the mat," Sam said. "You should be feeling warm. The room is warming up from the Angelic beings. We can't see them, but we can measure their energy. Once they're all in the room, we'll turn on a special light that will allow us to see their energetic forms as well as yours as you extricate."

Angyo walked back to the window of the cubicle and stared intently to watch what was happening.

"Just a few more minutes and the light will change," Sam continued. "You'll see the angels that are working with you. Once they start the infusions, your consciousness will start to change. Just relax into it as if you're falling asleep."

Sam watched the computer screen as the energy levels rose in the room. "The light will change now."

The room filled with a lavender and pink light that looked like sparkling dust particles. The Angelic beings in the room were at each of Eleazar's port areas. The Angelic beings' forms became more visible as the light particles settled on their energetic mass. The energy waves of each Angelic being were dense in the center of their shape, but the waves became loose and free flowing on the outer edges. It took several minutes until the beings could be seen in their wholeness. Their forms were a free flow of energy that fluctuated in shape and size.

"I guess I thought they would look like the Angels we see in books and movies," Sam said. "Can you see them, Eleazar?"

"Yes, they are a very loving presence. I have never felt so much love embracing me as I do right now."

As Eleazar spoke, Sam saw several of the energies reshape into a classic Angel form with wings. A beautiful female Angel with long flowing blond hair and a long, beautiful dress looked out through the window and waved. Sam felt her eyes on him before she receded back into her energetic shape.

Sam chuckled. "A sense of humor. I love it."

The Angelic beings started the energy infusion. Strands of sparkling light came out of the air and flowed into the ports. The movements of the waves were fluid and mesmerizing. The infusion continued, and the men watched as Eleazar's aura fluctuated in waves moving above and around his body. At first Eleazar's auric energy waves were moving in a smooth manner. Then suddenly a large energetic blob popped out of his body and through his aura, pulling the aura with it. Sam and Angyo just stared in awe as they watched the blob continue to morph.

"Can you change your energetic form to look like your human form?" Sam asked.

Eleazar's energy started to reshape into his human form. His features appeared, and he floated to the glass window and tapped it in front of Angyo. Both men smiled and waved at each other. Suddenly, his energy started to flash in and out until he was gone from the cubicle.

"Wow, it's working perfectly," Sam said. "I'm in awe."

Angyo stayed still at the cubicle's window. Sam, at his computer, felt a hand on his shoulder and looked up. He saw Angyo standing in front of him staring into the room. He turned and looked from side to side. No one was there. He let out a laugh. "Is that you?"

He heard a faint whisper from Eleazar's energy. "Yes, it is."

Chapter 19

"Jill, I am so impressed you're more than two years sober," China said to Jill over the phone. "That's quite an accomplishment."

"I just wish you hadn't retired," Jill replied. "You've always been my biggest support. Some days I still feel lost without you."

"Just keep believing in yourself, Jill. I have never stopped believing in you. How about a home cooked meal on your day off this week?"

"That sounds wonderful. Thank you, China."

"Send me a text with your schedule, and we'll make dinner plans."

"Okay. I love you, China." Jill's voice cracked as she said the words.

"I love you, too. Bye." China hung up the phone. She walked to the back door and looked out into the garden. A feeling of yearning stirred within her. She opened the door and headed to the pond.

China sat silently in her garden, staring into the pond for some time before speaking. "Spirit, I am conflicted. Bernard has become so distant and angry over the growing divisiveness he is seeing in our country. How can I help him? It's been weeks since he's taken a call from me." She paused and looked up to the sky. "He didn't even come to my retirement party or acknowledge it in any way. Did I do something to provoke this?"

She sat in silence hoping for an answer. "I choose to serve you and those you place before me. Perhaps I can serve Bernard and help him to find his way back."

As dusk fell upon the garden, China felt a stirring within and felt an acknowledgement of her question move through her.

In due time. You will soon have your next assignment.

Warmth filled her being, and she felt a calm acceptance come over her. "Thank you. I will wait for that time."

˙˙•ͺͺͺ•*˙˙*•☆•*˙˙*•ͺͺͺ•*˙˙*•☆

Eleazar's energy shifted from the monastery effortlessly, without intention. He had no cognition of how he landed where he did. Instantly a knowing feeling came over him. He was in Darfur for his first assignment. He followed a group of rebels into the small house of a minister.

"Where are they?" the rebel leader screamed at the minister. "You are hiding them."

"No, no, no one is here but me," the minister answered.

Eleazar, who stood translucently in front of the men, placed one hand on the first rebel's heart and his other hand on his neck. The infusion was quick, and Eleazar felt the energy shift within the man. He quickly infused two more rebels before he walked through an inside wall and into a tiny room the size of a closet. Inside were six girls and a young woman. They were crouched and trembling and holding each other, fear written on their faces.

Eleazar placed his arms around them and felt them calm, despite the screams coming from the other side of the wall. Eleazar continued to calm them as he watched the activity in the house, stretching his neck through the wall to watch the rebels go from room to room. They checked closets, looked for loose floor boards, and searched for openings in the ceiling. Eleazar watched them enter the last room before pulling his head back into the space. They stood in front of a large wooden armoire that covered the wall.

"Move this," a rebel commanded.

Another rebel entered the room and frowned at the armoire. "That is too heavy to move," he said.

"He is ... he is right," the minister said, wiping perspiration from his brow. "It has been here a long time. It took six men to place it there."

Eleazar poked his head through the wall and stretched his hand to the minister's heart. Eleazar felt the man calm, felt his confidence return. Eleazar released his grasp.

"You will find no one here but me," the minister said. "Now get out of my home."

A rebel raised his gun at the minister. "I should shoot you."

"No, you shouldn't," said the first rebel. "Let's get out of here."

The men left the home. The minister said in a low voice, "We must wait to ensure they do not come back."

He paced the floor for several minutes. At length, he said, "We are going to be okay. I will keep you safe." He went to the armoire and pushed it. It barely moved. "God give me the strength for this."

Eleazar reached his arm through the wall and put one hand on the armoire. It moved effortlessly, revealing a door. Eleazar smiled at the surprise on the minister's face. The man opened the door, and the girls and young woman emerged.

The minister embraced the young woman, his wife. "Once it is dark, all of us will leave here. God is protecting us."

Eleazar placed his hand on each girl's head to bless them and relieve them of the fears stirring within. In a gentle voice he said, "God has ensured your safety." He watched as the group hugged each other. As he floated over the house, he spun an energy shield to protect it from further harm. "This will keep you safe from the rebels if they return."

Eleazar served in the Sudan as the genocide spread. On some days, he touched upwards of 300 rebels and villagers. Throughout the region, he saw other White Souls working as quickly as he was. Their work was important, and they only had a moment to acknowledge each other.

Without any sense of time, Eleazar moved from situation to situation. One moment standing before the murderous rebels, the next healing victims, shifting energy to the point in time he was sent to, jumping in with a Divine knowledge of how to serve. He moved through his experiences in the Sudan with barely a thought.

Eleazar heard screaming. He spun around and saw several rebels grabbing a young girl and running to the cab of a truck. One man held his hand over her mouth and held her tight in a headlock. Though small, she fought hard, kicking and trying to bite him. He shoved her into the front of the truck where another man sat in the passenger seat. Then he jumped in the open bed and the truck took off. The dirt was flying when her parents came running from a house screaming. Eleazar shifted himself into the bed of the truck and grabbed the man's heart and neck and let the energy go quickly. The man fell to the floor of the truck and appeared in shock as the energy infused.

Eleazar entered the front of the truck and infused the driver, this time being more cautious with the speed and volume of flow. He did not want the man passing out while driving. He turned to the man who held the young girl. He infused the energy with the intent to cause confusion, so he would loosen his grip as his hand occluded the child's mouth and nose. The man's hand fell from her face and she tried her best to open the door to jump out. The driver grabbed her by the leg and started screaming for help. The truck started to weave on the road. The rebel in the back pushed open the partially broken window and reached in over the men to pull the girl back to him. He held her tight against his body as he sat down in the truck bed.

Eleazar sat next to the man and placed his hand on the child's head to comfort her. She immediately opened her eyes and looked to see the man's two hands. She then looked over to where she sensed Eleazar and looked right into his eyes. He immediately heard her words within his energy, "God sent you?"

He smiled and said, "Yes."

Tears welled in her eyes. "Please take me home. I'm scared."

"You will be home soon. The longer we drive the more time the men will have to absorb the energy and gain greater control of their free will."

"Don't leave me alone with them."

Eleazar felt the trembling of fear from her small body. He closed his eyes and comforted her, his big hand stroking her head and cheek.

They had traveled a couple of miles out of town to a heavily wooded area when the truck stopped. The man in the truck bed lowered the girl down to the other two men. They grabbed her and started to run to a cluster of big rocks. The men ran behind the rocks as if they knew the area well.

Eleazar thought, *Spirit what am I allowed to do? This is the first time I don't know what to do.* The answer resonated within his energy.

Just as I will not take away free will, you may not either.

Eleazar felt disappointment move through him. *There must be something I can do,* he thought. Feeling unsure, he searched the area around him. Then he felt a presence not far away. He focused his eyes and allowed his vision to search far into the woods. His eyes were quickly drawn into a thickly wooded area where he saw three lions feasting on a large animal a half mile away. He realized that the female lions had heard the young girl's cry. One stood up and turned her nose in the direction of the young girl. Eleazar gazed into the lion and said, "She needs you to help her now."

The large lioness took off rapidly, running toward the screaming young girl. The other female and the male followed. Eleazar stood over the girl as two of the men held her naked body down. The third opening his belt buckle. The girl kicked and screamed. Eleazar infused her heart, and she calmed as she stared deeply into his eyes. Her fear quieted. She turned, and her eyes widened as she saw the lion come up from behind the man standing over her. The large lioness jumped in the air and pushed him off his feet. Both the lion and the man flew over where Eleazar's energy was kneeling next to the young girl. The man with his pants down at his ankles was unable to get up easily and the lioness grabbed him by the leg and started to pull him away from the girl. She continued to pull him into the wooded area behind the rocks. The other two men let go of the girl as the other two lions arrived. The big male roared as he trotted toward the men. They started to walk backwards as they watched the lion move toward them. They continued their walk, moving to an opening in the rocks. They saw the second lioness sit next to the young girl and roar. Once in the opening, the two men turned toward the truck and ran.

The lion followed, moving fast. The massive animal could have easily overpowered them but slowed as they approached the truck, giving them time to get away. With one last roar he turned and trotted back to the rocks to rejoin the two females.

Eleazar helped the young girl put her torn and tattered clothing back on. He reached out to the first female lion and said, "Thank you for helping to save her." He looked at the other two lions and said, "I need you to protect her until I can bring back help."

The female that had tackled the rebel lay down next to the girl, put her front left paw around her, and pulled her to her side to cradle her. The male and second female took up positions on either side of the child.

Eleazar touched the girl's face and said, "I will return soon. You will be okay, I promise."

"You didn't stop them," she said shyly.

"I cannot stop someone from using their free will. My job is to give them energy and the opportunity to use their free will wisely. If you ever need someone to protect you, just call out for Archangel Michael and he will be there."

"Are you an Angel?" the girl asked as she nestled into the lioness. "My grandma likes Angels."

"No, I am actually more like you, just doing a special job for God."

"Please get my mom and dad." Her little voice quivered, and the lioness turned and snuggled the child into her neck.

Eleazar's energy shifted and landed in a police truck with two officers and the child's father, who was screaming frantically between his tears. The officers sped down the road that led out of town in the direction the rebels had driven. Eleazar infused the father and watched his composure return and his mind and thoughts become clear. He placed his hand on the heart of the officer in the passenger seat. As he slowly infused the energy, he spoke directly to the man's Soul. "In ten minutes you will see a large cluster of rocks off the side of the road on the edge of the forest. She is behind the rocks and protected by three lions. They are taking care of her and will let you take her home."

He shifted again, this time back to the rock cluster. He sat on the top of the smallest rock and looked down at the lions and the sweet child sleeping with her adopted protectors. He turned to watch the road until the truck came into view. It stopped at the rock cluster, and the father jumped out, calling her name. "Lila, Lila, Lila!" he yelled. The two officers were right behind him.

The little girl's eyes opened wide, and she called out, "Daddy." She sat up and turned to her lioness and kissed her big face. "Thank you," she said, and then she stood up and ran toward her father's voice, trying to hold her clothing together to keep it from falling off. Her father and the officers stopped when they rounded the edge of the rocks and saw the three lions.

Lila stopped and looked back at the lions before turning to the men. "They are my friends and saved me from the bad men." She turned and smiled at the beast and turned backed to her father. He took several steps toward her before scooping her up into his arms.

Eleazar rode back to the village in the police van with Lila, her father, and the officers to ensure they had a safe return. Back at her home he watched as her father carried her into the house, with her mother crying at her side. Lila looked over her father's shoulder and waved goodbye to Eleazar.

Eleazar was still standing outside Lila's small house when he felt a breeze. He looked up to see a large wing span overhead. The power of the wings bent branches and sent leaves flying. Eleazar stood in the shadow of the wings as he watched Archangel Michael land several feet away. Standing more than seven feet tall, the magnificent Angel was radiant with light. His skin sparkled, and his clothing, made of gold threads, reflected the sun.

Looking up at Archangel Michael, Eleazar asked, "What happened to me today?"

"You were right when you told Lila you were more like her than an angel," responded Michael. "Although you are an extricated Soul, you still have attachments to your body and human emotions. Today those emotions were triggered. You have been handling your assignments well. And today you utilized your powers to save her life. They would have killed her."

"She asked me to not let them hurt her, and I didn't know how to do that without taking their free will," responded Eleazar. "They don't deserve free will."

"Is that your place to decide?" asked Michael.

Laughing Eleazar said, "No. Thank you for that reminder."

"Trust in your Soul's wisdom and you will always find the answers," said Michael. He turned toward Eleazar and smiled as he spread his massive wings and started to lift off. "I'm always around if you need me. Just call me by name."

2012

Chapter 20

Bernard sat behind his desk in his law office staring at the phone. He picked it up and dialed. A moment later, he hung up. "Am I ready for this?" he murmured.

He pulled out the old fading photo from a box in the top drawer. He looked at his father standing in front of one of the University of Pennsylvania's old stone buildings with ivy climbing up the walls. He remembered standing in front of that same building 22 years later. He put down the picture and picked up his cell phone. This time he felt more confident and dialed again.

On the third ring Sadiki answered. "Hello, Bernard, what a nice surprise."

His accent sounded the same to Bernard as it did at their first meeting almost seven years earlier.

"Hey, I just wanted to tell you I moved to D.C. My firm had an opening in the corporate office, so I applied and got it. "

"That's my boy, you see the gold ring and go for it. Just like your old man."

Bernard felt a wave of revulsion go through him as he heard his father's boasting, but he fought back the negative feelings. "Oh, thanks," he said. After a brief pause he added, "If you're ever in town give me a call. I would like to get together."

"I will be in D.C. in a couple of weeks and will call when I know my schedule," said Sadiki. He did not acknowledge their first meeting. It was as if it had never occurred. "I will be in England for the next week or two depending on my sales. I can stop by Washington on my way back home."

Bernard's stomach twisted in a knot of betrayal as he thought of his mother, but he forced himself to respond. "Great, that's great."

"I am proud of you Bernard. Even though I haven't been in your life for long, I will always feel proud," Sadiki said.

After he hung up the phone, Bernard felt wooziness in his stomach and a pang of guilt. "Damn it, Mom, it can't always be about you," he muttered. A fit of rage rose up quickly, and he slammed his fist onto the thick mahogany desk.

Several weeks later Bernard picked up the *Washington Post*. Like all of America he was saddened by the shooting at Sandy Hook Elementary School in Connecticut the week before. Every day since, the front page of every newspaper was dominated by stories of bravery, cries for gun control, and comments by deaf politicians. He couldn't understand how children could be denied the right to be safe in school while the mentally ill had the right to buy a gun. He thought about his mother and how she would say that the universe will deliver back to you what you give to others, yet the message will be twice as strong to drive the point home.

He sat silently for several minutes wondering if what had happened to his Pops and Grams was a result of the lie about Sadiki coming back as karma on them. He shook it off and turned back to the newspaper, turning to the international section. He was stunned when he read, "England's top gay rights activist murdered in cold blood." The police reported it as a break and entry, the gunshot through his head, execution style.

A chill ran through Bernard as he thought about his own emergence in the firm as a gay lawyer. He felt accepted since several of the partners were gay. At the firm's monthly meetings, the partners were open about the public coming out of the firm. Bernard felt proud to be a gay member of a firm that was helping drive gay rights and diversity. He knew his mother would accept anyone he loved, but he was unsure what Sadiki would think. He decided he would wait to share the information until he knew him better.

Chapter 21

Bernard looked at his cell phone's screen. The ID said "Mom." He hit ignore, and let her call go to voicemail. Eventually she would figure out that he didn't want to talk to her and leave him alone. At least he hoped so. He waited several seconds before opening his contact list and typing in Sadiki.

"Hi, Sadiki," he said when his call was answered.

"Son, when will you start calling me Dad?" Sadiki asked. "It has been several years since we have been getting to know each other. It is time to acknowledge who I am."

"Well, I wanted to tell you how much fun I had last weekend when we met in New York City. I felt like your son when we went to the football game. And I am not a big sports fan, but it felt good. Thanks for inviting me out to meet you." Bernard felt a warm feeling flow through him as he acknowledged their time together. "I will get there, I promise."

"Good, I will not pressure you. I like that we have been speaking every week and meeting often. It is good. One of these days you will need to introduce me to your girlfriends. I am shopping around for one myself. Perhaps a young one would be refreshing."

The warmth left Bernard, and he felt a queasiness. One of the difficult aspects of developing a relationship with his father was the man's male chauvinistic views of women and their value. He spoke of women as if they were possessions, often referring to them as "arm candy." Bernard questioned his father's version of what happened when his mother got pregnant. Inside him was the sinking feeling that Sadiki was not the man he wanted Bernard to believe he was. Bernard pushed the doubts away and focused on his anger at his mother. The internal tug of war was strong, and he felt powerless. He just could not forgive her.

October 2014

Chapter 22

China turned on the kitchen TV and tuned to the early morning news to hear the anchor say, "There will be a march on City Hall today to show the city's support to our LGBT members. As violent crimes have been increasing against the LGBT community, there has also been an increase in political rhetoric by members of the conservative party against gays. There is speculation that if the conservative party wins there will be a dismantling of the federal rights act approved by the current administration."

The scene shifted to a shot of Philadelphia's mayor. China watched and listened intently as she spoke.

"Our city will continue to set the example for freedom for all," the mayor began. "All our LGBT members are welcome to join our community leaders and myself. We will set the stage for the strengthening of our great city through love for all our brothers and sisters regardless of sexual preference, race, nationality, or religion. Philadelphia has been a great role model to other cities with our inclusive legislation and our loving acceptance of all community members. While many are calling this march a protest against the conservative party, I would like to correct that erroneous impression and announce it is a celebration of our great community of Brotherly Love."

China closed her eyes for a moment and murmured, "I am always grateful for you and your good work. I'm proud I voted for you."

She looked at the clock. The march would start on Broad Street in three hours and head to City Hall for the speeches. "Maybe," she said, nodding.

China turned the volume down on the TV and started her coffee before walking to the refrigerator for eggs. The kitchen had been the center of joy and family events, but without Bernard it felt cold and stark. It had been six weeks since she left her last voice message for her son. She could no longer remember when she last spoke to him. It was before she retired, which was almost three years ago. He did not respond to the ICU staff who planned her retirement party. Never a call back, nor a congratulations for her. She thought being retired would give them an opportunity to heal and rebuild their relationship. In her last message she offered to visit D.C. and take him out to dinner. She never heard back.

Seventy-five minutes later China boarded a bus on Market Street several blocks from her home. She was feeling good. It would be a 25-minute ride straight down Market to City Hall. She was more interested in the mayor's speech and other speeches than the march. Sitting down on a side seat she saw the digital sign on the bus flashing in bright red, "Due to march bus route ends at 18th and Market."

"I can walk the rest of the way, it is a beautiful sunny day," she said out loud. The traffic was heavy as they moved slowly down Market Street. Buses, including school buses and church buses, lined the street, moving slowly toward City Hall. The traffic bottlenecked at the I-76 ramps at 30th and Market streets. China started to feel concerned as she saw tour buses with outside digital displays with church names, most from other areas of Pennsylvania as well as other states. In some bus windows, she saw signs reading "Stop the Sinners" and "Fight Against Evil LGBT Sinners." There were so many hate signs she felt a sick feeling within her.

China prayed silently, her lips moving. "Spirit, I trust and know you have brought me here for your good. I am grateful to serve and thank you for your right thoughts, right words, and actions that flow through me to serve you. I trust all you ask me is a service of love and will result in only good for myself, others, and all who are here today. I pray for a blessing for all who protest, the LGBT community who march. Bless them to recognize it is your pure energy that flows through them. With your infinite intelligence bless them with the knowledge that hate is of free will and turns them from you and your love. I thank you, Spirit, as your presence is within me. It is my strength and power for good in whatever way you ask me to serve today. I trust your message will be clear and quickly understood without doubt and fear. I thank you, Spirit, for your eternal love of my Spirit and me. I thank you for this opportunity to serve."

The traffic congestion was so heavy that the bus had stopped moving. China went to the front and turned to the driver. "Can you let me off soon?"

The man smiled. "Sure, we aren't going anywhere fast." He grabbed his microphone and made an announcement. "It looks like we may be here for some time. If you are interested in getting off I can let you off here safely." He opened the door for China, and several others followed her.

When China reached the sidewalk, she turned and waved to the driver. "Thanks," she said.

The sidewalks were filled with others getting off buses, many holding signs and chanting anti-gay slogans. China picked up her pace to get out of the crowd of haters. She moved quickly, not wanting to be seen with the hate-chanting people. The traffic jam and early bus unloading led to the start of an informal anti-gay march down Market Street. Arriving at 18th Street she could see a large police presence along the street. Some were on bikes or horses, and there were many on foot. Traffic was at a stop, and people were walking everywhere. The shouting from one group to another was loud. The religious groups of anti-gay haters were screaming their slurs to groups that were in favor of LGBT rights. The pro-LGBT groups were slinging it back with their own hateful messages. Signs for both were everywhere. Rainbow flags hung off buildings and were displayed in the windows of some businesses.

"Spirit why did these people come here when many are not even from the City?"

The answer came quickly and in the spiritual voice she knew well.

They choose to use my name to feed their ego of fear. Fear breeds hate. It is how they have chosen to use my gift of free will.

"Can't you just remove their free will for today, so they're friendlier?" she asked from her own place of fear. Her stomach twisted in a knot as the message emerged within her.

That is the same as they are doing, taking away others' free will. Each person chooses how they use it.

China nodded. "Of course, I trust in my safety and have no need to take anything from anyone else to feel safe. Everyone has the right to use their free will. I release any fears that gave me that thought."

She felt a peace and calm come over her again. She continued to move quickly, this time visualizing a white light around her, blocking the negative people and chants until she arrived at the corner across from City Hall. Police barricades were up, and officers lined the street, not letting anyone cross.

"Spirit, is this where you want me? Open the path that I need to travel," China said as she looked around and quickly locked eyes with a police officer.

He saw her and smiled. "China," he called out.

She remembered him instantly and smiled as he approached. His name was Sean, and they had met at the hospital five years earlier after he was shot in the head and shoulder. He was 36 at the time, big and burly, a larger than life Irish cop. The media had described him as fierce, a cop who shot first and asked questions later. His Soul was in its third incarnation without expansion when they met, but she had given him an energy infusion.

"You shouldn't be out here," he said. "It may get ugly. Is this how you're spending your day off?"

"I retired. I came to support the mayor and our city leaders in building our city of inclusion."

"Of course, you did! I find myself thinking about you so many times. In many ways, I still think you did something special in the ICU after my shooting that gave me a new lease on life. Even my wife thinks I'm a better person and a better cop. I can get you into the speech area if you would like. It's the least I can do."

"Yes, that is what I want." The words flowed easily from her, and her gaze became focused on the roped-off area around city hall. "I am fine in the back right," she said.

"I'm sure I can get you a seat right up front instead of the standing area. All I have to say to the commissioner is you were my best nurse, and it's yours."

She pointed to the area she wanted. "No, I'll be fine there. Then I can slip out quickly when it's done."

"If I can, I'll come back to get you," he said.

She nodded and gave him a smile. "Thank you. God really blessed you well with your healing." Silently she acknowledged to God that she was grateful to see such a positive outcome to the healing work they did together. Her heart swelled at the thought he used his free will to find a place of peace and harmony between his inner Soul and his ego.

"Guess I got lucky," he said. "Especially with getting you for my nurse."

"After leaving the hospital you did the rest with the blessing you received," she replied. "I can tell life feels different to you now."

He gave a laugh as they crossed the street to the roped-off area. "That's what my wife says. I ain't religious, but I find myself talking to God all the time. I ask for guidance every day, and things go smoothly. The unfortunate part is it has caused some conflict. My wife has become an evangelist against evil since my shooting. She thinks being gay is a sign of the devil. I thank God that I no longer look for evil, I'm now a true peace officer. My partner teases me all the time that I went from creating the riots to calming them." With his big Irish smile and twinkling blue eyes he looked down at her and said, "Stay out of trouble."

She watched him walk away with a great feeling of love and satisfaction in her heart. She knew that true Divine intervention had taken place.

She moved slowly through the crowd searching for the perfect spot. She found herself standing in the center of the group and had a good view of the large screen that was hung over the stage. Looking around, she saw many gay couples holding hands, hugging, and waving rainbow flags and banners. She smiled at the love, yet it was evident that it came at the price of fear. She saw the energy of fear running through the crowd.

"I call upon the Spirit of the Living God, the archangels and all my angels, and the angels of all these people to embrace them to raise their vibrations and release them of fear."

China felt energies surrounding the crowd, and many angels started to vibrate into her vision, some in energy waves and others in physical form with glorious sparkling wings. Those with a human form fluttered without a clear definition of gender in neutral beige, pink, and coral tones.

"I thank you for the safety of all, including myself," she whispered.

The marchers finished filing in behind the stage. Many sat in the rows of chairs up front. On the large screen, she watched the mayor climb the stage. The crowd cheered and clapped. The applause and cheers were so loud around her she could not hear any of the anti-gay chants. Mesmerized by the moment, she focused on the large screen. The mayor moved confidently, waving and clapping to the cheers. She smiled a beautiful bright smile. China saw her aura, a bright white expansive one. "A wise old Soul you are," she said with love.

"Wow! What a day to have this celebration of inclusion, acceptance, and love," the mayor said. "While I welcome each of our community's LGBT members, I also welcome those who come in protest. Our country was birthed by those who chose to find a place to worship without persecution. It happened right here in Philadelphia. I respect that there are many churches and religions represented here in protest of our inclusion legislation. It is our belief our LGBT citizens should have the same rights as everyone else. I ask all to respect each other's right to share in this day peacefully. We need to recognize you may not agree with everything the other says, but it is the free will that God grants us that leads to this level of diversity."

She stood quietly waiting for the loud cheering to settle down. As it quieted, China heard loud bullhorns chanting, "She's the Antichrist." China glanced to the area where the bullhorn cry was coming from and then quickly turned back to the stage. As she was turning, she caught sight of a flash from a high-rise building several blocks away. She felt frozen as she watched in slow motion the projectile fly gracefully on a declining trajectory through the air until it pierced the mayor's head. On the big screen China saw the mayor's body turn to her right. In slow motion, she saw her body collapse as muscle by muscle it gave way to gravity. Blood spattered those standing near her.

China could not move as her gaze bore into the falling mayor. She saw the mayor's Soul exit before her body hit the stage. "I honor your Spirit within. You did a good job here. You answered God's calling."

As the mayor's Soul shifted into its next dimension, it was lost to China's sight. It took a few more seconds for China to realize what was happening around her. The anti-gay protesters were charging into the LGBT members on the square at City Hall. Some ran past her as they grabbed and yelled at the people around her. "Spirit what am I to do?"

In that second, she saw him running toward the place she was standing. He was screaming hateful words, "Kill the gays." She heard others around her screaming back hate. She saw James pull a gun and point it. She looked to where it was pointed and saw a man yelling back, hate vibrating through him. A bullet went past her, and she started to move toward the yelling man, who was hit in the chest. He fell. She reached him and knelt at his side. She placed a hand over his heart and one on his neck, and said, "Spirit of God flow through me quickly to infuse the energy needed for his Soul's expansion."

As she finished her words a pair of energetic hands came down on the man's opposite side. She saw the big hands and the rapid flow of energy. She looked up into Eleazar's eyes and felt their Souls connect. Her heart skipped a beat and swelled. "Thank you!" she said. They both watched as the Soul of the man between them left his body to continue with its expansion and return to the Divine. She breathed a sigh of relief and turned toward James, who was pointing his gun at a police officer.

"Drop it!" the officer yelled. "Drop it now!"

James looked past the officer and at China as she rose from the ground. She felt a thump on her head and a slight push from people running past her. She steadied herself and looked directly at James. Defiance was written on his face, and turned his gun to point at

China. She stood frozen in that moment but felt a confidence that he would not shoot her. She let her gaze drill into his Soul. She heard several shots from the police off to her side. She watched in slow motion the bullets rip into his chest. He released his gun. It moved slowly through the air as his body fell backward. Her gaze intensity continued to bore into his Soul and then she saw it release as he hit the ground. She smiled a sad smile and whispered, "Now, Linda, you are free."

"You did good today," said Eleazar.

"It's bittersweet." Her gaze stayed on James. "I infused James years ago when he was in the ICU. The bitter is that he still used his free will for hate. The sweet is that he is back in the Divine love without continuing as a Dark Soul."

Eleazar nodded. "You are a very powerful White Soul."

She turned toward him. "Are you an angel? Maybe an Archangel?"

He laughed and said, "No, I still have a body but have been extricated so I can infuse within seconds compared to the time you need."

"Is your body in a coma? Maybe I cared for you when I was working at Penn."

"No, I am not in that kind of coma. My body is being cared for by angelic beings in Bhutan. I will return to it and continue to live my life when I am done serving God."

China was drawn back to the moment when she heard the voice of Sean. "You've been hurt." His strong hands picked her up, and he carried her in his arms. He started moving quickly toward an ambulance on the other side of the broken barriers. "Why didn't you run when the shooting started?"

"I had to help him. God put me in that exact place to help him. He died quickly." She realized her hands and clothing were covered in blood. "I'm not hurt, this is his blood."

"Well, how did you get the black eye and bump on your head?" Sean asked. He slowed his pace as he carried her through the crowd.

She thought for a moment and it came back to her. "Someone banged into me with their shoulder, and then I was hit by a sign as people started to run. It felt like a big thump, thump." She laughed as she put her hand to her head where it hurt.

He put her down as they approached the ambulance. "You're safe. I still have you," he said as he kept his arm wrapped around her. "The mayor was shot. They were working on reviving her. Not sure it was working."

"Where is she now?" she asked.

"They rushed her to Jefferson's E.R. You'll be going to Penn."

"I don't need to go to the hospital. I'm a nurse and can take care of myself."

He laughed. "Yeah, you did a good job at that. You were so focused on helping someone else you didn't even realize you were hurt."

"I trusted in God that I would not be hurt, so it can't be life threatening," she said after a pause. "But I guess I won't argue, I do feel a little nauseous."

"She has a good-size egg on her head and a black eye," Sean reported to the first responders. "The blood is not hers. She's a nurse and jumped in to help the man who was shot back there. The shooter and the guy he shot died. She is the priority."

"We'll take care of her," the ambulance emergency medical technician said.

"Can you take her to Penn? That's where she works."

"Will do," the E.M.T. said.

China started to say something, but Sean gently put his hand over her mouth.

"She needs to be checked for a concussion." Sean turned to China and smiled. "Your friends are there, they'll take good care of you." He left her with the paramedics and went back into the crowd.

As she watched Sean walk away she glanced around looking for her new spirit friend, but he was nowhere that she could see.

Chapter 23

As the paramedics rolled China into the emergency room, one called out, "Head injury victim from the march." He rushed her past the triage area into the main ER.

A nurse approaching her shouted, "Looks like she's been shot, she's covered in blood." She grabbed China's blouse and ripped it open popping many of the buttons off.

"I'm not shot," China said, feeling nauseated. "It's not my blood."

She barely heard her own words above the frantic commotion and screaming staff that surrounded her as the paramedic rushed her into the trauma room. Panic seized her. She rose halfway up from the stretcher and yelled, "Stop! I was not shot." Her head pounded as she fell back down onto the stretcher. The room took on a new calm.

"Do you know where you are?" asked the nurse.

"Penn's ER ... I think?" she answered.

"Yes, is there a family member we should call for you?" the nurse asked as she hooked China up to the monitor.

"Call Dr. Jill Buggy," she murmured, feeling weak. "She works in the Neuro ICU. She's my friend. I was a nurse here. Just retired." China felt groggy and let herself drift into a restful state.

"China, China, can you open your eyes? What is your name?"

China heard Jill through the grogginess and whispered, "Jill."

"No, that is not your name. What is your name?"

"Not Jill. I China, you Jill."

Jill let out a long sigh. "Yes, that's right. You scared me when you seemed unresponsive. I'm going to exam you, and then you will tell me what the hell you were doing at the protest. You better have a good answer."

China nodded and gave Jill a wan smile, the best she could do.

"What day is it?" Jill asked.

"The day of the march," responded China, still feeling the room spinning.

"What is the day of the week?"

"I need to sleep, then I can answer." Her voice was weak, and her body went limp.

"STAT, we need to get her to the CAT scan now!" Jill ordered.

The staff quickly got China ready for transport. At first China heard the noises and voices around her, and slowly they became inaudible. She slept through the transport and scan. Occasionally she recognized she was being jostled around. She was tired, too tired to raise her eyelids. She kept hearing Jill call her name. Jill's voice sounded loud and angry and was piercing to China. Her mind drifted, and she couldn't bring it back. She did not answer and did not care.

"Jill is angry at me, God. Either shut her up or wake me up so she will shut up." China heard herself say the words, not knowing if anyone else heard her. The fogginess of her mind took over and she drifted into a deep sleep.

"China, you are in the ICU," Jill said. "You are going to be fine. There is no bleed in your brain and no skull fracture. It's a soft tissue bruise. You have a concussion."

China mumbled and tried to speak. Her vocalizations were faint and incoherent at first. She asked, "God, flow through me, so I can wake up." She started to feel the fog shifting within her. The sounds around her were becoming clearer. It took several more moments before she could open her eyes. She saw Jill looking at her. "Hi," was the best China could force out.

"Hi, China," Jill said. "You're going to be okay. I'm not sure I will. I had about a dozen strokes today thanks to you." Jill tried to smile, but her voice betrayed her. "I got ... I got scared you were going to leave me."

As China stared at Jill her face and figure came into focus. "Sorry."

"You'll be here for twenty-four hours, and I'll make sure you get the best nurses. I'm not going home until I can take you with me."

"Bernard okay?" asked China.

"He's on his way from D.C. I expect he'll be here this evening."

"Okay." China closed her eyes and drifted back to sleep.

Chapter 24

"Bernard, I don't understand your distance," China said to her son, who was pacing back and forth in her kitchen. "Ever since you moved out you have become more and more distant. We never dine together, I have no idea what is going on in your life, and I don't know how you're feeling with all that's going on in the government."

Bernard stopped pacing and glared at her. "You want to talk about the political climate? That's a joke! You just pray the candidate who does the least damage wins." His voice was escalating into a loud burst. "Well, are you happy? Is this what you prayed for? A nationalist gay hater running for president?" Bernard resumed his pacing.

"No, no, I feel very positive about Caroline. I know she will make a wonderful president. Her day will come. We have to believe, just like we had hope in 2008."

"See, that is the problem, you live in La La Land. This may be our last election if the would-be emperor gets in. It is expected he is going to dismantle our government and the rights of protected groups. He is going to suppress voters and remove environmental protection legislation." He stopped pacing again and looked at her. "What does your God say to that?"

China could see the seething inside him. "Bernard, if all you care about now is attacking me, then why did you come out after I was injured at the march? I thought when you arrived we would get closer. But no, here we are six months later." She paused then chuckled. "At least we're arguing. It is a form of communication."

"Mom, you were lucky to recover from the concussion as easily as you did. When I told you to live a real life, I didn't mean protest and marches." Bernard shook his head and turned away from her.

"You're always angry at me," China said, looking directly at her son. "Tell me what I did or didn't do. I want our relationship to be easy again. We once spent time together and laughed together. Now it feels like there's some undercurrent that I can't see. What is it?"

He gave her a cold stare. "Have you always told me the truth?"

"I believe I have. What have I told you that you're now doubting?"

"The stories about my father."

China turned from him and walked to the kitchen island and sat down. She turned back towards him and let out a big sigh. "I didn't know what to do. I was a senior in nursing school. He was in graduate school at Wharton. When I told him I was pregnant, he said he didn't want a baby. He said he didn't want to be tied to me or you. He offered to pay for an abortion. But I wanted you. I was so excited. Your grandparents were so supportive, I knew it would work out. It never sounded right to me to say he didn't want us. So, I made up the story. Sometimes I forgot it was not the real story. I always loved how you would beam with joy when I told you he loved to hold you." She swallowed hard before continuing. "He never held you nor did he want to see you. I've told you all this, so why are you questioning it now? Can you forgive me?"

"I can forgive you that you told me he died. But you're still lying. I met him, Mom. We have been building a relationship for the past eight years. He told me Gran-mom and Pops hated him and refused to let him be a part of our life. He said you were weak and never spoke up, so he thought you didn't want him." Bernard looked away from her. "My life has been based on lies." Raising his voice, he said, "My mother, the most important person in my life, is still lying to me. I'm a man of thirty-six now. I'm up for partner, and you are still lying to me. I don't understand why."

She swallowed hard before saying, "Yes, I lied to you when you were little." Hesitantly she said, "But I am not lying now about why. Sadiki didn't even want me to tell you his name. I told you everything I knew about him when you were growing up. I gave you his name, what tribe he was from in Africa. The lies I told you were that he died, that he loved you, and he held you. They were the lies." She bit her lip before continuing. "So, don't tell me I'm still lying. It's Sadiki who is lying. Perhaps he needed to say those things, so he could build a relationship with you. If he told you the truth, told you that he didn't want you, or me, would you still want to talk to him?"

Bernard shook his head. "I don't know."

"I would never have denied you a relationship with your father and neither would your grandparents.

You knew them, you knew what kind and loving people they were. My parents liked Sadiki. He sat right there." She pointed to the dining room table. "He sat there for every Sunday dinner during the seven months we dated. Your pops really liked him. He loved to hear about his homeland and what it was like growing up in a tribe. My parents offered to pay for his parents to come and visit. My parents wanted to meet his parents."

"So, you say," Bernard murmured.

It was China's turn to glare. "Don't even consider those ideas as truths." As she calmed, she added, "I'm glad you're talking with him. You look a lot like him. Except you do have Gran-mom's eyes. Build a relationship on who you both are now. Not about anything in the past. If he has opened this opportunity, take it and don't choose one parent over the other." She got up from the island and walked to his side. She looked at him and asked, "Can I give you a hug? I missed having you around." She took several steps towards him and stretched out her arms.

Bernard pushed her away and walked out. He slammed the front door as he left. He was overwhelmed with anger when he entered his car. He drove to Washington, D.C., without stopping and was so deep in thought he had no memory of the drive home. He walked into his condo, dropped onto the sofa, and started to sob. "I can't forgive her." Raising his voice, he continued, "God, I can't forgive you. You talk to her, is it you who told her to push my father away? Why?" He pounded his fist on the glass coffee table, and the glass shattered and dropped to the carpet.

Sumi, a thin black male, stood at the living room entrance in his boxers. He watched Bernard sit with his head in his hands and elbows on his knees. Sumi dropped his head before turning back to the bedroom. He left Bernard to sit with his pain.

Bernard rubbed his head with his hands. "You talk to my mother, why don't you talk to me? Maybe you're just another one of her lies." He lay back on the sofa. "I feel so empty. Did you forget to give me a Soul? Was I not as precious as your little Miss China?" after several minutes of silence Bernard said, "How the fuck did I get her as my mother?"

Chapter 25

Sam took Tammy's hand as the path narrowed in the woods behind the mountain. He pushed the branches away and held them back while she passed. Each time he only released her hand for a brief second as she moved passed him.

"Where are you taking me?" she asked softly. She could hear her heart beating in her ears. "I've never come this way before. It's a bit eerie—these woods are dark."

He smiled at her. "I know the perfect place for our picnic. I found it not long after I arrived. I've decided it's the place where God flows into the earth, and earth rises to give homage and to exalt the Divine Creator."

They pushed past several more bushes before he stopped and turned toward her. "At first I wanted to keep this place to myself since it inspired me and helped me understand what I needed to do here. Then when we started to work together the first two years, I felt that was not enough. And this past year of our relationship I found myself wanting to bring you here." Sam leaned over and gently kissed Tammy.

"Okay, but can we keep moving? I feel things rubbing my ankles." Tammy looked down and felt relief when she saw a clump of vines with their leaves moving against her skin. She looked back up and saw rays of light breaking through the dark, damp forest. She followed the light up to the forest canopy and its lacy display of light. She smiled. "We must be close. The sun is breaking through the trees."

"Just a few more yards and we'll be by the river and waterfalls," Sam replied. He continued to lead her by the hand on the narrow path. Tammy followed behind, holding one hand and his backpack. The light flowed in as they came to the end of the tree line. Sam helped Tammy as they walked down a small hill into the clearing. They walked from the eerie silence of the dark forest to the sound of roaring water.

"Oh my God, this place is magnificent," said Tammy as she watched Sam walk ahead to a flat area near the bank of the river. "Sam, this is beautiful." She felt her face flush as she thought how sweet he was to her. Her eyes widened as she watched the falling water glisten in the sunlight. The energy of the flow moved her and left her in awe of the fierceness and majestic presence before her.

His face lighted up as he opened his backpack and pulled out a blanket and picnic supplies.

The sun was bright and the air warm, but a cool mist rising from the rushing river gave Tammy a chill.

"Are you cold?" asked Sam. He scooched over closer to Tammy and put his arm around her shoulder.

"Sam, when are we going to stop hiding our relationship from Angyo? Besides, you're not a monk or apostle. They were the only ones he told me were off limits. I think he would be happy for us."

"You're probably right. But I don't want him to think our work is taking a back seat to our relationship." Sam gently laid Tammy down onto the blanket. He lowered himself to her side and reached over her to kiss her full lips. "I can warm you up." Snuggling his body against hers, he kissed her passionately as his right hand slid up her shirt and rested on her full breast.

Chapter 26

"What? Where are you going?" Jill Buggy asked China.

"To a monastery in Bhutan," China replied. "I saw a documentary on it, and I can't stop thinking about it. I can go, meditate, and pray for Bernard to return to me. He hasn't talked to me since his visit after the gay pride march. I need to reset myself spiritually. I need the change."

"How long are you going to stay?" Jill's voice was frantic. "Can I take you to the airport, and when will I get to pick you up." Her voice escalated as she yelled, "I can't believe you would just run away from me. What are you going to do with your house, your things, the rest of your life?" Jill's fear resonated in her words and overtook her being.

"Please understand that I find great peace and joy from my prayer and meditation life," China said. "This is just an intense opportunity to find that peace again."

"It's a monastery—will they let a woman in?" Jill's voice quivered.

"According to the documentary, women are being admitted to monasteries, mosques, and churches around the world. Many of them had careers in science and IT. I think I can fit in."

"I'm feeling selfish and don't want you to go," Jill said. "I need you here. You trained me as a resident and taught me so much. You're the reason I'm sober."

"I need to do this," China said.

Jill looked away. "It was hard getting used to you retired." She turned back to China, her dissatisfaction written on her face. "If you had died when you were injured at the march, I would have wanted to die, too. Now you want to move so far away it feels devastating to me."

"You'll be fine, Jill."

Jill's face took on a look of anguish, and she turned away from China. "Why are you not thinking of me? You're so selfish." She turned back toward China and blurted, "I am so sorry, all I can think about is what I'm losing. A good friend, a mother figure, and a great nurse. You know my mother died when I was young, and I always asked why."

China moved to Jill's side and wrapped her arms around her. She held her tight.

"Why," Jill whispered. "Why, why, why?"

"Sweet girl, it isn't because of you that I'm leaving. You're a very good person. It wasn't because of you that your mother left. Her death was not to hurt you, nor was it because of you. It was because her Spirit was ready to return to God. I think that's hard for all of us to understand. When a spirit returns to God, that can leave others feeling stranded, alone, and empty. Sometimes that's our journey, to learn how to handle those feelings. They're human feelings, and we're much more than human feelings. We need to travel from those feelings back to God." China paused as she stroked Jill's hair. "Did you know before our Souls incarnate they pick the parents they want for their spiritual growth experience. It's always a Soul they trust that will do what is needed to push the Soul to learn the lesson they're here to learn. You're on the brink of that learning and expanding. I know you can do it." China continued to rock Jill in her arms. "It isn't about you. Ever since my concussion, I've felt a need to deepen my connection with God. I miss feeling the Divine Presence within me all the time. The connection with the Creator is what I live for. Now it only comes and goes. This doesn't mean I love you less. It means I love you more, as you're much more than human emotions." China held Jill in her embrace. "I promise I will come back."

Chapter 27

China's trip to Bhutan was long and tiring. She took a cab to the base of the mountain. As she looked up she felt disappointed that she needed to climb the mountain with her luggage. She opened her suitcase, removed her "must haves," and dumped unnecessary things from her large carry-on bag into the suitcase. She hid her suitcase in a bush and said, "I'll be back for you in a day or two when I'm not so tired."

As she looked up the mountain stairs she thought, *This must be the stairway to heaven.* She started her climb humming the old Led Zeppelin song. The stairs were steep and narrow. Her size 9 shoes felt too big for the steps. "Okay, Spirit, I am here, does it have to be such a rough climb? Why couldn't I go to a place with an elevator? What am I doing here?"

She felt a stirring within as a strong impulse pushed through her.

You are here for your next assignment. It is as you asked.

"Will I see Bernard again?" she asked.

The impulse was strong and affirming.

Yes, and as requested, you will help him turn back to me.

She continued climbing. It was a long time before she reached the top.

Out of breath and tired, China took the last step and paused. She looked around to see the vast scene off the side of the mountain. In the distance, she saw the sea, and much closer was a steep fall to the rocks below.

"Thank you for getting me here safely." As she finished her words, she saw a large tiger walking her way. Frozen in her tracks, she did not move. "I honor the Divine within you. I honor the Divine within you," she said, repeating it over and over. As the big cat walked by, it looked at her and smiled. Its mouth opened, showing large, sharp teeth. China heard a response.

And I honor the Divine within you.

The cat walked past her within inches of where she stood. "Thank you, Spirit, for my safety." She approached the front door. It opened, and a plump bald man in long robes greeted her.

"Welcome," said Banko. "I saw you responded well to the Bengal tiger."

"Is he trained?" she asked.

"No, we do not interfere with their way of life. We offer only love, and they do not interfere with our way of life. Do you know why you are here?"

She laughed. "God sent me here. Is there any other reason to be here?"

He bowed and said, "Please come in. You must need rest and food."

"That sounds good, but I would like to start with a hot bath and a nap. Can that be arranged?"

"Of course. We have updated our bath facility for our visitors. I will show you to your room and the bathroom." He picked up her carry bag and led her up the steep winding steps.

···•.,.•*··*•☆•*··*•.,.,.•*··*•☆

It was dark when China woke up. She looked around, unsure where she was or what time it was or even what day it was. She felt the warmth of the fire and the heaviness of the feathered comforter. Reaching over the bed she rummaged through her carry-on and pulled out her cell phone. It was half past three in the morning. Her head fell back on the pillow, and she tried to remember when she had left home. Her mind stretched through the fog and fatigue before she realized she had left on the nineteenth. She cast her mind back to her arrival in Bhutan. After a long dull moment, she realized she had landed on the twenty-first. She relaxed into the comfort of the bed, nestling into its plushness. She quickly drifted back to sleep.

China opened her eyes to see daylight streaming into the room. Still feeling sluggish, she picked up her phone to see the time and day. It was still the twenty-second, 9:30 a.m. Again, her mind struggled with the time and date of her arrival. With each thought, she was drawn back into a deep fatigue. When she looked at her phone again, it was 11:22. "Spirit, fill me with energy and vigor so I can get out of this bed." As soon as she finished saying the words, she fell back to sleep.

The sun was bright when China awoke in the mid-afternoon. The heaviness in her brain was gone, the cobwebs cleared out. Her mind darted around in clear, energized thoughts. She looked around. The room was warm, the fireplace down to embers. She sat up to stretch. *Am I really in Bhutan?* she thought. She slipped out of bed, walked to the window, and looked down at the steep steps she had climbed. They were real. *This is not a dream.*

As she sat on the side of the bed to pray, she heard a knock on the door. "Come in," she called.

Banko opened the door and entered. He was carrying wood for the fireplace. "You are awake. The journey here is often long, and people arrive tired."

She smiled and asked, "When did I arrive? My sense of time is still distorted."

"Yesterday morning. You wanted a warm bath when you arrived. I started your fireplace and brought you wine, cheese, bread, and nuts. You ate nothing, but the wine was gone when I returned a couple of hours later. You were in a deep sleep and never heard me knock and enter. Your fire is almost out. I want to add more wood to keep your room warm."

"I came here to pray and meditate. What is the schedule here?"

"Chants occur all day long. The apostles and monks have a full chant and meditation schedule. They take place in the great room and in the gardens. We recommend you stay close to the main building until you know your mission. When you are up and ready to come downstairs, we will have a good meal ready for you, and you will spend time with Angyo. He has been here at the monastery for over forty years. He looks forward to meeting with you."

Banko set the wood into the fireplace. He poked and prodded the embers to ignite the new wood. The fireplace crackled, and sparks burst into the air.

"Thank you," was all China could say. There was a stillness within her, and her mind was empty. Watching him leave she sighed and said, "Spirit, give me some thoughts, my head is empty." She laughed.

She looked around the room and saw the suitcase she had left in the bushes at the bottom of the steps. Laughing she said, "It made it here!" She noticed a long robe hanging off a hook on the door. "Okay, I got the message." China dressed in the off-white robe. *Dress the part, live the part*, she thought. "Yes, so true," she said as she slid her feet into her pink flipflops. Before leaving the room, she opened every door until she found the bathroom.

Almost everything in the old monastery was made of stone. The walls and floors were of gray stone. Large wood beams and old wood planks were overhead. Outside her room the hallway led to a winding staircase. As she walked down the steps she noticed the oil lanterns along the walls lighting the stairwell. At the bottom of the steps to her left was an old library with wood bookshelves and several overstuffed armchairs. A small desk of dark wood sat in front of the window. The fireplace was lit and wine, cheese, bread, and nuts were set out on the glass table. She could not help but notice the beauty of the driftwood that sat under the glass top.

"Most people admire the driftwood and table."

China looked up to see an old monk with a bald head looking at her. "It is beautiful and somehow speaks to me," she said.

"The wood is over two-hundred years old and was found on the rocks below when the monastery was under construction. The monks who found it thought it would bring good energy to the monastery, so they held on to it. The glass for the top was made over a hundred years ago in the village below." Angyo approached China and extended his hand. "I am Angyo and have lived in this monastery over 40 years. I am grateful you came to visit us." He paused waiting to hear some response from China.

"I came here to pray and meditate, yet something is telling me there is more here for me," China said. "Do you understand the message?"

"Many have come here over the past year, called by Source Energy, the Universe, or God," said Angyo. "They recognize there is a mission but are not clear on what it is. I recommend you take this time to pray and meditate for the understanding of your purpose. We have a beautiful campus with a prayer garden, a meditation room, and areas to walk along the mountainside. If you choose, you may meditate and pray in any area of the monastery. Please just remember others are being called and may share the same areas. Not all who come here are being called for the same service. We have all been called to serve the Divine and to serve from a place of love."

"Several years ago, Spirit asked me to serve from a coma so my Spirit could extricate from my body. I apologized and said no coma in a hospital or nursing home. I prayed for another way to serve," said China. "I guess that sounds awful to you when you have spent your life serving." China felt something stir within her, and a sudden knowledge emerged. "Is there another way for my spirit to extricate my body? Is that why I'm here?"

"You were not alone in saying no to a human coma. Many Souls who love their life felt the same way. It took us three years to build all that was needed, and we have been more than four year into the extrications. They are going well. The human forms left behind are suspended in an ethereal incubator. They are cared for by angelic beings who provide energy infusions to keep the cells of the human form healthy and viable."

"That must be it," China said, not sure how she felt about it. "But I will ask for clarity."

"In 2001 we were asked to help increase the vibrations of the world through chants. That was a good task for us. We chanted, meditated, and prayed for peace, harmony, and love to grow. Several years later young scientists and computer experts, male and female, started showing up. They built their labs and the incubators. It has been a journey I would never have imagined. It just leaves me in a more reverent state of love for our Creator." He was silent for several moments before adding, "Rest, eat, meditate, and pray. The right answer will come to you. There will be great support and love here for you, regardless of your assignment." He turned from her and left the warm library.

Chapter 28

China and Angyo walked quietly to the physics lab. She felt in awe of her new assignment. The idea her Soul would extricate was both scary and exciting. She longed to know what it would feel like to be a Soul in her most pure spiritual form without a human body.

"Oh, I almost forgot," she said. "I wrote two letters and they're sitting in my room. Can you please mail them? I left money on the dresser. I don't know the cost of postage. One is going to Philadelphia, the other to Washington, D.C., one for my friend Jill, the other for my son. It's hard not knowing how long I'll be gone."

Angyo smiled. "Yes, it is hard not knowing right now, but soon it will not matter to you, and you will have no concept of time."

"Yes, you're right. I would appreciate it if they are mailed."

"Of course. It will be taken care of."

"•̦ ̦ ̦•*"*•☆•*"*•̦ ̦ ̦•*"*•☆

China lay on the crystal mat in her bio suit. As her infusions started, she smiled at the Angelic energies and said, "Thank you for asking me to serve." Her extrication was quick and easy. She stood in the cubical and admired the beauty of the angelic beings and thanked them for their work. She turned toward the window and waved as her energy felt pulled into another dimension.

She hit the ground running. Her Spirit was moving quickly through the hot thick sand of Iraq. She saw bullets flying past her as she positioned herself to grab the terrorist before he was hit. She needed her hands on him for just a short while to stop his Soul from continuing the journey into darkness. She pushed faster, outrunning the bullets, and grabbed his heart and neck. She felt the energy surge out of her hands into his Soul as the bullets tore into him. "You are safe to go home now," she said. She looked around, hoping he would be escorted back to the Divine. In that split second his vest bomb detonated pushing her energy fast and hard. Stunned, she felt her energy burst apart. She quickly focused on pulling her energy back into her core.

"I was wondering what you were doing," said Eleazar. "You must be new here."

"I just extricated," she replied. "I landed here, so I went for it." As they exchanged glances, they recognized they had met before. "Philadelphia, you helped me in Philadelphia during the Gay Pride March," she said before extending her energetic hand to him for assistance.

He smiled as he extended his hand to pull her up. "Last I saw you, some big guy swooped you off your feet and ran." His smile grew as he chuckled at the memory. "Don't worry, it will get easier to understand the assignment and your energetic abilities. You expanded his Soul quickly, and now he is on the right track back home. You did well."

"Thank you," she said.

"Stay with me for a little while until you are fully in control of your energy. It just takes a few times to understand the extent of your power."

"All right. And thank you."

"A young girl is about to be shot on a school bus. We need to get to the men who are going to shoot her. When we get to them first, we give them a better chance of using free will for good." Eleazar took her energetic hand again, and they vanished.

Together Eleazar and China appeared in a truck with six Taliban members. The terrain was rough, and the truck lurched and shook as it sped toward the bus. The four men in the open truck bed were laughing as they clutched the flanges of the truck's side walls to stay standing. Quickly, China and Eleazar moved to infuse each of the men for their Souls to expand. After completing the four in the back, Eleazar saw the bus not far ahead of them, filled with schoolgirls. "We need to get the two in the cab now."

China followed Eleazar into the cab. As the man in the passenger seat thrust his AK-47 assault rifle out the side window, Eleazar grabbed his neck and started to infuse him, letting his energy flow forcefully. The man dropped his weapon, which clattered to the ground. His body spasmed violently in the front seat until Eleazar felt China's hand on his.

"You did it, he's done," China said.

As Eleazar released his hands, the man screamed, "Give me a gun!"

A man in the back of the truck hesitated as he looked at the pile of AK-47s. Another man yelled, "Give it to him," before he picked up a rifle and handed it through the cab's open rear window. The rocking truck was twenty feet from the school bus when the man in the front passenger seat thrust the gun out the window and started shooting. The girls on the bus screamed and jumped away from the shattered windows, falling and climbing over one another. Two girls were hit, one in the head, the other in the shoulder. China moved into the bus and placed her hand on the young girl's head.

"What are you doing?" Eleazar said. "You cannot interfere that way."

"I'm not interfering. I'm helping her heal, otherwise she'll die. The bullet injured her brain." After several seconds of silence, she added, "She has an important role to play for the future of women and humanity."

"The assignment is to expand Souls prior to their turning into Dark Souls. She is a White Soul, and her mission may be to extricate to help us. We don't save other's lives. Everything we do in this moment is to decrease the Dark Souls in the future. It is through this action the world will be able to self-correct."

China looked at the other girl squirming on the floor and then turned again to Eleazar. "That may be your assignment. I trust in the moment. I trust that the right actions will occur as the Divine is manifesting through me. Now, just put your hand over her bullet wound and her healing will start. And you will decrease her pain. I'm sure she would appreciate a little spiritual help in this moment." She smiled at him. "Besides Mr. Experience, you can't tell me you couldn't control the force of your energy infusion on the shooter. Did you overstep your bounds, or did you feel the Divine impulse to guide you?"

He looked at her with surprise before laughing. "I guess we must respond to the moment and the inspired action of the Divine." He bent down and did what China had asked him to do. "Should we pick them up and fly them to the hospital?"

"Yes, that's a good idea." China started to stand up with the young girl in her arms when the bus took off.

"Hold on, girls, we are on the way to the hospital," the driver yelled.

China lowered the young teen back to the floor of the bus and looked at Eleazar. He had one hand on the bus driver's hand on the steering wheel and his foot on the gas pedal. His other hand remained on the schoolgirl's shoulder.

"You must have been pretty good at Twister," she said before adding, "Just get us there now."

A moment later, the bus screeched to a halt in front of the hospital.

Eleazar smiled and said, "Done."

Girls were crying and screaming. The two injured girls lay on the floor with China between them. The driver ran into the building, and moments later a medical team hurried out.

China stood up and said, "Our part is done."

They left as quickly as they had arrived.

Eleazar found himself in the foothills of Afghanistan and realized he was alone. China had gone to a different dimension and time. "We will meet again," he murmured with a smile.

Chapter 29

Jill's hand shook as she opened the letter postmarked from the Upper Paro Valley in Bhutan. She recognized China's handwriting on the envelope and hoped she might be returning soon. Five months was already too long. Jill ripped open the envelope, took out the letter, and began to read.

Dear Jill,

The monastery is a wonderful place and I am grateful to be here. I will be taking another spiritual journey any day now and plan to return to the monastery in about a year or two. I will not be able to communicate to you while I am away. Please take care of yourself and know I always love you. You are a beautiful Divine Spirit. Maybe it is time you get to know it.

Love, China

Jill sat down heavily on her chair. With tears in her eyes she yelled, "God damn you, God, why do you take everyone away from me?" She sobbed uncontrollably.

Chapter 30

Eleazar saw his next assignment in front of him. A middle-aged man with a large round abdomen stood laughing over the body of the elephant calf. Several other men were taking pictures of the fallen calf and hunter. "I just proved that elephants are stupid. This guy walked right into my gun barrel." As he continued to pose, one of his companions saw a large elephant in the viewfinder of his camera. The elephant charged and broke through the heavy thick shrubs behind the posing hunter, the ground rumbling under his feet. The man with the camera dropped it and ran. Eleazar grabbed the hunter's heart and neck and let the energy flow.

The hunter turned to see the female elephant rushing toward him and screamed, "I got you first." Eleazar did not let go. He moved with the hunter, who picked up his gun to shoot. The man stood still as he put the elephant in his crosshairs, but he fumbled for a second and lost sight of the approaching beast. The big elephant grabbed the hunter's head and lifted him off the ground, snapping his neck. She threw him to the ground and raised her foot. Eleazar let go and darted away from the crushing blow.

The other men ran to their parked Jeep. The vehicle motor roared as the large beast trampled their friend, the killer of the calf. As they looked back, they knew it was hopeless. They took off to save their own lives. Momma elephant was in retaliation mode, and she set her eyes on the men who had run away, but she did not leave her baby's side. Eleazar watched the hunter's soul exit and shift to the right for his return to Source.

"I didn't feel a thing." Eleazar walked to the calf where the female was trumpeting and crying. He touched the elephant's rough skin. With his hand firmly against her leg he sent his energy of love to aid in her healing. "Now, I'm doing it too," he murmured. He watched as other elephants approached and trumpeted. "They will take care of you. You are loved by all in the oneness of God."

He gave her a few more pats before walking away. He turned backed as the other elephants joined her in mourning. She looked right where his energy stood and bowed her head as if she knew he was there. "You're welcome," he said. "He will not return here again. Your baby and the hunter are now in God's embrace."

Eleazar was not pulled to another assignment. He wandered to a tree, sat on the ground, and watched as the elephant group mourned their loss, all circling the dead calf and grieving mother. In between the trumpeting they let out mournful cries. "Elephants know love. When I return, I will know love and that feeling of devotion to another being." He remembered his experience with China in Iraq and allowed it to repeat in his thoughts, like a video on replay.

Chapter 31

Angyo looked at Tammy. "How are we doing today? Are we holding our frequency?"

She beamed a big smile. "Even better." She led him to one of the computers on the left side of the room. "Look at this screen. It's the vibrational level of the Earth. It took us one hundred Spiritual sites to get to the vibrational level of twelve." She nodded to Ram, a tech, who brought up a screen that showed a graph. "You can see in this graph we started at the third dimension and the fourth vibration level. We started extrication when we reached tenth vibration level and were in the top half of the fourth dimension. Looking at the tech she said, "Ram, let's see the present frequency levels."

The screens flipped into a chart that showed a large jump from ten to twelve.

"Does that mean what I think it means?" asked Angyo.

Tammy nodded. "Yes, if you think it means we've elevated the world's vibrational pattern and shifted into the fouth dimension. It is." She smiled at him. "I thought this was a fluke, so I messaged all the other sites. They're all registering the vibrational level at twelve, and the fourth dimension."

"What a great blessing! There is a shift in energy occurring. Perhaps it is the work that our White Souls are doing."

"I think it's a combination of several things. Like the chanting that continues to evolve as the world is shifting. We now have many of the churches in Europe on the grid. That's an additional four hundred religious and Spiritual institutions chanting. One hundred with labs like ours. I hear the Pope himself is involved in the project. My peers in Rome are working directly with him."

"Are they extricating Souls?" asked Angyo.

"They go live later this month and will be the last of the new sites." She could not help but show her excitement as she clapped her hands. "Wow, this is an incredible experience. Do you know if there's any movement towards peace in the earth's political culture?"

"Not that we are aware of. One of our apostles provides us a daily briefing of news around the world. Last evening's briefing was very disappointing. It appears the Communist countries have banded together to build nuclear weapons." He smiled at her despite the disappointing tidings he had just announced. "So, your news is refreshing. It will take time for the earth's humans to shift to the new frequency."

"My understanding is that in Rome and elsewhere in Europe they will be able to extricate up to five hundred souls at the start and then can continue to increase their incubators to about a thousand if needed. My contact thinks they could even go to three thousand if pushed."

"Have you shared this information with Sam?" asked Angyo.

"Yes, this morning over breakfast," she said. A slight rosy flush filled her cheeks as she looked at him sheepishly.

He laughed a hearty laugh. "I am glad you are finding all you desire in your life here."

"Oh, thank you." The relief in her voice was palpable.

"•.,,.•*"*•☆•*"*•.,,.•*"*•☆

Angyo entered the physics lab and saw Sam looking his way. He wondered if Tammy had given him a heads-up that he was on his way. Sam waved and walked to one of the techs before meeting Angyo in the front.

"Good morning, Angyo." Sam smiled the same sheepish smile that Tammy had.

"Good morning. So you are up to date with the good news about the world's vibrational frequency. I am glad you and Tammy coordinate information so well." He smiled and nodded his approval.

"Oh, yes, you should have probably been told first. Sorry about that. "

"No, I want you both to coordinate without hesitation. You are guided by the Divine Universe, and I should never stand in the middle of that relationship. Even here at the monastery I am not to stand between the monks and the Divine. I teach how to connect, I help others to understand how they have blocked the Divine within and how to reconnect. The Divine Universe is the only True Spiritual leader. I am a conduit for the teachings. Now, let us review how we are doing with our work."

"We're at capacity and should be finished our satellite quarters for another two hundred incubators in about a month," Sam said. He pointed to a station with three computers. "Let's look at the readings over here."

They walked to the station and sat, Sam taking the chair in front of the center screen. He moved the mouse and the screen lit up. "We received our daily update late last evening about the work going on around the world," Sam said. "As the main information hub, we're ready to send out the analyzed data reports." He flipped through several computer screens before landing on a data sheet. "Okay, as of midnight last evening there are one thousand sites now live extricating souls. Rome is just starting the extrication process, so they have no numbers reflected in the 172,763 Extricated Souls working in all dimensions. We're now entering our fourth year of extrications, so this is much further along than our initial projection of 36,000 White Souls working at full power."

"Do we know the number of people who support the Spiritual Centers and the project?" asked Angyo.

"Yes, the numbers continue to increase each day. There was a big increase with the Vatican project coming on line. Europe alone has taken in over 3,500 to support the God project. So, as of midnight last night, we had 137,507 scientists and IT experts working to support our 172,763 Extricated Souls." Sam typed a few commands into the computer and the numbers shifted.

"So, with the coverage for each shift plus time off, if we don't add anyone else anywhere in the world, then we could support another 200,000 souls. However, not all sites can expand their incubators."

"Why not?"

"Depends on the location, but in general it's either because of space limitations, war, or concerns about safety and security."

"The Divine Universe will keep them safe, even if they're on the front lines of a war," Angyo said. "They need to maintain a safety vibration without doubt. That is why our visitors, workers, and monks can walk safely through the woods of Bhutan with a growing population of Bengal tigers in the area. The meditation and prayer vibrations surrounding us soothe the beasts and make them understand they are safe. In return, they provide our safety."

Chapter 32

Bernard opened his desk drawer and saw the letter from his mother. He could not help but stare at her handwriting. The postmark from Upper Paro Valley in Bhutan had surprised Bernard when the letter arrived. He laid the sealed envelope down on his desk before going back to work. "Sorry, Mom, I can't live with my head in the sand like you. You would think after the march you would have faced reality."

Bernard's responsibilities in the law firm had grown over the years. In 2012, he accepted a transfer to Washington, D.C. He worked tirelessly on immigration cases and discrimination cases as they ramped up during the 2016 presidential campaign. As the conservative party's rhetoric increased, his firm doubled their cases and built a more robust civil liberty department. They were the first firm ever to position themselves as an openly gay firm. Three of the five top partners were gay. They had strong connections to the left and liberal parties of Washington, D.C. Bernard's activism was supported by the company and encouraged. He proudly came out as a gay lawyer.

As the rapid rise in fear sparked by the new president continued to grow, threats to the safety of minority groups spiked. Just two weeks into the new administration, Bernard had mixed feeling about his mother's travel. Since the LGBT march when his mother was injured, Bernard had lost confidence that his mother could protect herself. "She's too damn trusting." Pitching his voice to mimic hers, he said, "God will take care of me." After laughing loudly, he stated, "Yeah right, how did that idea serve you?" The anger was growing inside him, and he struggled to shut down the negative thoughts. He found himself locked into the fear and paranoid thoughts that were spreading around the country and the world. To live his life, he now had to fight.

"Damn it, Mom, can't you think of anyone but yourself?" He smashed his fist on her letter. The desk shook under the force of his fist. He picked up the phone and started to dial when he screamed, "No! You can't play this game with me." He slammed the phone down, breaking the receiver. The shattered pieces flew. "Why do you do this to me?"

In the two years since his mother left, Bernard found himself relying on his father's weekly calls. His father shared more about his life as a diamond broker and his travels. He sold diamonds all around the world and was always traveling somewhere. When Bernard asked him about growing up in an African tribe in the bush he got vague answers, and Sadiki often changed the subject.

"Hey, Dad, how ya doing?" asked Bernard. "Where in the world are you today?" He placed his cell phone on speaker and continued to work at his desk.

"I'm in L.A. today and tomorrow," Sadiki said.

"When do you come East?"

"Maybe next week. I have a D.C. client who is interested in some diamonds I have for sale."

"Dad, I have been thinking I want to take some vacation time and would like to travel to Africa to visit your family tribe and village." He paused before adding, "I want to meet my relatives."

"No, no, no. I am no longer welcome, and neither will you be welcomed. Once I left for American schools I became an outcast. We should travel together to a tropical island. It will be my treat. We can be wingmen together to pick up beautiful exotic women."

Bernard felt a sickening sensation in his gut. After an awkward pause, he said, "Dad, how would you feel if I said I don't date women because I prefer men?"

There was silence for several seconds before the connection was broken.

"Dad, Dad, are you there?" Bernard looked at his phone. The readout said "call ended."

Chapter 33

The protesters threw debris onto the bonfire. The fire surged, and the flames whipped high into the night air. The bonfire grew quickly as the protesters continued to dump items into it. Within minutes the flaming pile filled the center of the street. Hundreds of protesters were running everywhere, some screaming, others looking for more items to burn. China heard windows shattering at a nearby store front. The sounds of sirens blared from all over the city, some in the distance, others close and loud and abrasive. The police rapidly approached where China stood. Without even looking around she knew she was in Germany. All she could see was turmoil. Angry energy vibrated through the people and the air. A lit sign in a diner window caught her attention. *Welcome G20 summit.* As she looked, rocks flew, and the window shattered. The protesters cheered.

China sighed and asked, "Spirit, what exactly is my assignment?" She waited and heard no response, did not feel her energy pulled in any direction. She intensified her eye gaze as she searched the streets hoping to get an idea of her next assignment. As she looked down the road, she saw endless crowds of people with a frenetic energy aura around them. The stream of protesters stretched as far as she could see each way. "Okay, I'll take a walk." She walked away from her point of entry and moved down the road.

She looked at a group of men and women who were lighting a store on fire. "Nope, I felt no need to help them." As she said it, another Soul landed and ran into the group. "Someone else's assignment. Spirit what should I be doing?" She continued to scan the crowds and the activity, making her way slowly down the street. She came to a group of police officers holding fire hoses and using high pressure sprays to drive the crowd back. She stopped and watched but felt nothing. "Nope, that's not it, either."

She wandered until she stood outside a high-end hotel. Crowds were blocking the doors, and police were protecting the visitors inside. There was a flurry of activity as a group of men talked with the police. A tall, handsome black man in a tailored suit caught her attention. He showed the police something and was given entrance to the hotel. China knew why she was there. She moved slowly toward the hotel, walked through the crowd and through the heavily guarded door. She stood in the lobby, watching Sadiki at the front desk. He leaned over the desk as he cajoled the young attractive women behind it.

"I see you," a woman said in French. "I see you here. Why are you here?"

"There are many people who can see me," China said as she watched the front desk. "But not usually people involved in fights and protest."

China turned her gaze from the front desk to the woman talking to her. She was young and wore jeans and a T-shirt and had a designer handbag hanging over her shoulder. Shock and amazement were written on her face.

"Resistance, fighting, anger, these block people from seeing energies," China said. "But you see me."

"I'm a Soul Seeker, and you are the first energy I have ever seen," the young woman replied, though her voice had an edge of uncertainty.

"Whose Soul are you seeking?" China asked before turning her attention to Sadiki again.

"My Soul," the young woman responded. "I wish to connect with my Soul."

China looked her in the eyes and said, "Then stop seeking and talk to your Divine Presence within, or your Soul. It's always there! It never hides. You are the only one that blocks you from finding it. It isn't out there somewhere." China extended her arm and pointed into the air. She looked back to Sadiki, who was picking up his room key. She turned again to the woman and said, "I need to go."

"Goodbye," the woman replied.

"Turn within," China said, and then she turned and rushed to the elevator where Sadiki was standing.

The lobby décor had a glamorous feel, with crystal chandeliers, tumbled marble flooring, and elegant gold-inlaid wallpaper. Hotel guests were dressed in high-end clothing and jewelry. Some people emitted frustrated energy from being locked inside the hotel because of the violence in the streets. Others were festive and happy to stay at a five-star hotel with a full complement of bars, restaurants, pool, and spa services.

While waiting for the elevator, China heard travelers from many nations speak in their various languages. She smiled. She understood their conversations. Sadiki held tight to the handle of the rolling luggage bag sitting in front of him. She looked at the monogram on the large black bag and noted his finely tailored suit. He looked older, heavier, and more serious than she remembered. His eyes did not sparkle like they did when they met more than 37 years ago. She focused her gaze into his chest until she saw his Soul. Sadiki's Soul was pinched off from the oneness grid. She understood her assignment. "You say when, and your will will be done."

She followed Sadiki out of the elevator into his room. In her human form, she had never stayed at such a fancy hotel. She rarely took vacations. To her, a vacation was prayer and meditation. *Maybe it's time I learned to live as Bernard has suggested*, she thought. She walked with Sadiki into his room and settled into the armchair across from his TV.

He turned the TV on, pulled out his phone, and made a call. "I arrived and got a room without a problem," he said to whoever was on the other end of the call. "It only cost me a dinner date after the hotel manager goes off duty. A small price to pay for access to the world's most powerful leaders." Sadiki's accent was still heavy, but his English was much improved. He looked serious as he listened. "It will be done," he said before ending the call.

The energy aura around him was dense and slow-moving. It was mixed with a coldness, a misguided righteousness, that justified his thoughts and actions.

At that moment, she felt a knowing move through her. He was on his fifth lifetime without expansion. The darkness that overwhelmed his Soul was growing and blocking the Divine light from expanding his Soul.

"Spirit, can I intervene now, or do I let it play out?" She knew the answer to her question as she asked, and it was quickly verified.

No intervention. You are there to understand what your work will be. He is too advanced in his darkness and will require expansion in the seconds before death. Until then you will learn from him.

She was filled with understanding and nodded in agreement. Then a strong impulse emerged.

You asked to help Bernard. This is the start of your service to him.

She felt relief that she was now to focus on Bernard's healing. Her inner voice repeated the message as it was received.

I must break Sadiki's patterns in this dimension.

The information continued to flow as she thought, *He is a recruiter for the egotic darkness. He has fathered many children in this lifetime for the rapid incarnation of Dark Souls.*

A sudden realization dawned. "Oh, Spirit, I brought this upon Bernard. I set this up."

She looked at Sadiki as he unpacked his suitcase. He removed a wooden box and opened it. The box contained a handgun. He checked the chambers and loaded the gun. He set it down and returned to the suitcase. From under several layers of packed items, he pulled out a long narrow case. He sat on the bed as he pulled parts out of the box and assembled a high-powered automatic rifle.

"You have fallen far from your noble tree," she murmured, words heard by no one. "Spirit, I am grateful to serve the Divine Presence within Sadiki." She stood up and walked through his door and left the room. "I understand enough and need not watch his every move."

Chapter 34

Sitting on her apartment balcony, Jill Buggy raised her wine glass to her lips. "When did my life go so wrong?" she asked. "It's pathetic. I have no boyfriend, no family, no one I feel close to. People I thought were my friends at work turned against me."

She put down her glass. Her face bore an expression of overwhelming sadness. "I just wanted one person to love me. China was everything to me. And I didn't mean anything to her. She just throws me out like trash." Her voice cracked as her eyes welled with tears. "She never loved me." The tears spilled, and she broke into a loud sob.

After a few minutes her tears slowed, and her sobs quieted. She stood quickly and grabbed her glass. As she turned, she was overwhelmed by a feeling of wooziness. She steadied herself with her empty hand against the wall, waiting for her balance to return. Unaware of time, she stood for several minutes, feeling the swaying in her head. As she entered the living room from the balcony, she tripped over the lip of the French doors. The glass flew from her hand and shattered as it hit the leg of the coffee table. She knelt down and picked up the shards of glass, piling them on the coffee table. She didn't notice when one of the shards cut her hand.

Jill continued to crawl around the floor, leaving blood smears on the rug wherever she put her hand. The voice of a news reporter broke through her drunken stupor. "While there is a divisiveness in our government and around the world, there is an unusual spiritualism emerging. Will this become a new type of war, prayers against evil? The Vatican stated today that the pope has confirmed an unusual influx of young professionals joining churches, mosques, temples, and monasteries around the world. It is estimated to be a calling that many thousands have answered. The Vatican spokesperson quoted the Pontiff as saying, 'It is with great honor that God has sent these young people of different religions, nationalities, and sexual preference to support a spiritual healing for the entire world.' Our reporting has also confirmed that several Imams in the Middle East have had hundreds flock to their mosques to partake in this Spiritual healing. This influx was first reported more than twelve years ago as IT and science professionals left universities and tech companies for a spiritual life. Tune in tomorrow evening when we will be broadcasting from a monastery in Bhutan. This is ZNN reporting."

"I wonder if they invited China?" Jill said sarcastically. She continued to the kitchen and opened a cabinet for a wine glass. She poured more red wine into her glass before noticing her hand and the slow trickling of blood. Holding it under the faucet, she watched as a steady stream of red-tinged water rushed down the drain. She dried her hand with paper towels and wrapped it with a kitchen towel. She reached up and opened a cabinet that held a collection of vitamins and shuffled through them until she found a brown pill bottle. With blurry vision she looked at the label before taking three Valiums from the bottle.

She downed the pills with the wine, emptying the glass quickly. She filled her glass again. This time she filled it to the top, draining the bottle. "I just opened you. Oh, well, I have more."

Jill walked back to the living room and sat down on the sofa with her feet on the oversized ottoman. She finished her glass of wine before drifting off to sleep.

China sat in the corner chair watching her friend. "Oh, you are so loved. God loves you, I love you, and all in this Divine Spiritual World love you." China moved to the sofa and sat next to Jill. She stroked her hair as a loving mother would do to comfort her child. "The only one who doesn't love you is you, my sweet girl." China took the glass out of Jill's hand, placed her energetic hand on Jill's heart, and moved her other hand to her neck. China hummed a celestial sound as she gave Jill an infusion of love. She gave it slowly and gently and continued her song. When the infusion was finished, she stopped humming. "You are a very special lady, Jill."

China picked up the TV remote to turn down the volume. A "Breaking News" alert appeared on the screen, which showed a fire burning in Hamburg. She turned the volume back up and sat quietly, listening to the events of the day.

"The shots were fired from a sniper's nest believed to be in a high-rise tower three blocks away from the meetings," a reporter said. "It is not known if the shooting victims were targets or just walked in front of the intended targets. The first victim was the assistant to the prime minister of England, the second was an aide to the new German chancellor, and the last was the assistant to the new French prime minister. All three were pronounced dead at the scene. The prime ministers and chancellor are reported safe under protection in an undisclosed location. The shootings took place just two hours ago, so not much is known, but many believe these killings were warnings to leaders not to resist the rising of the new world order of nationalism."

China turned the volume down and said, "Your work is done in Hamburg, Sadiki."

Chapter 35

China's energy shifted from Jill's apartment back to the streets of Hamburg. As she walked the streets she watched the riots unfold. Tear gas was shot into the crowds, and she watched as many Extricated Souls ran from person to person to give infusions. The days and nights were long for the Hamburg Police. For the first time since extricating she felt it was more than a moment. Her second night in Hamburg was many moments strung together by violence. Somehow, she sensed the time and felt an emptiness. Over and over she said, "My heart and mind are open for the Divine to manifest." The words flowed, and China felt a stillness in her connection with the Divine. "Spirit, what is happening here? What am I experiencing?"

As she walked she felt the stillness within vibrate with a confirming response.

Human vibrations of a mother watching something she does not like to see. You are processing feelings about Sadiki and his parental role to Bernard. You are communicating these vibrations to your body, and your ego is communicating back.

"I thought I had no human emotions left in this form. How can that be?"

She felt a knowing emerging and murmured, "On extrication I still have some connection." A moment later she thought, *I am a strong White Soul and can handle this.* She took a few steps and said out loud, "I am as able as you are, and there is no weakness in your energy. So, there can't be weakness in my energy."

She continued to wander the streets until she heard someone scream, "No, no, leave me alone."

China rounded the corner to see a group of police clubbing protesters, including the woman whose screams China had heard. She was kneeling on the ground with her arms over her head. China stood still as she watched, with no impulse to intervene. Then she saw Eleazar flash into the crowd. He moved through the thick of the conflict and started to infuse the officers and protesters at a rapid rate. She watched him work quickly and confidently. She saw his physical energy in a male shape, strong, tall and broad in the shoulders. She felt a connection as she watched him move from person to person.

Gunshots were fired. She turned in the direction they had come from. It was the first time she felt called to action since arriving. She was at the side of a protester bleeding from a gunshot wound, her hands on his heart and neck. The infusion was quick and intense as he struggled to hold on to life. As she removed her hands she watched him take his last breath. His energy exited and quickly shifted into the eternal dimension. She turned to an officer who was throwing a gun down at the man's side. Reaching up, she grabbed his heart and neck, and with a great intensity her energy flowed. He fell to the ground. She stood over him, infusing him rapidly and aggressively.

A hand touched her shoulder, and she turned to see Eleazar. Their eyes met, and she felt his energy move through her. She calmed and released the officer.

A dark cloud of energy surrounded the body of the protester, and before they could respond the cloud darted into the body.

She screamed, "No, a Dark Soul just jumped into that body." She moved to the man's side and turned him onto his back. She checked his pulse, which was beating faintly. "His body is being taken over." She bored her eyes into his eyes to search for any signs of light. "Help me infuse him," she said to Eleazar. They worked quickly, providing the energy a Soul needs for expansion.

"We did all we could do," said Eleazar as he moved away from the body.

China checked the pulse again. "It's getting stronger." As she spoke, other officers arrived.

"The first Dark Soul 'jump in' I saw was in Iraq when the Dark Soul of a terrorist jumped into the form of a soldier who just extricated," Eleazar said. "A good Soul replaced with a Dark Soul. It was a reminder to me of the importance of our job. We need to keep our sights on stopping the number of Dark Souls from growing." He gave China his hand to pull her up. "We only have a small window of time to infuse a Dark Soul prior to the body's death. If we miss the window, the Dark Soul will incarnate into a newborn or jump into a freshly vacated body."

"Why are you helping me?" she asked.

"I trust in the Divine to act through me. The action was God's action." He smiled at her as they walked away. "I lived my life in seclusion as a high priest in Tibet. I never loved anyone or felt connected to another person and their success. It is a human desire that has drawn many good people into the egotic rhetoric. Saving a child or loved one is always worth sacrificing others." He hesitated before saying, "I have devoutly loved God and never had a human loved one since leaving home at seventeen." He smiled and said, "I was seventy-five when I extricated." He laughed. "I have no idea how much time has passed."

She laughed with him. "I thought I was the only Soul still feeling connected to the earth dimension. You're a good Soul, Eleazar." She smiled as they walked together through the street.

"So are you, China." He took her hand in his and they smiled at each other.

Eleazar and China walked through the town and jumped into events to help others when it felt right. Neither felt pulled from one event to another.

"It is different working this way," said Eleazar.

"Spirit told me I'm still connected to my human form," China said. "That's why it feels different. My mission is to infuse Bernard's father. Bernard is my human son. So, my connection with him is making it feel different." She looked at Eleazar. "I'm not afraid of the assignment, so I'm not sure why it's different."

"As humans we often put conditions on love," Eleazar said. "As divine beings there is no condition."

She laughed and said, "What a wise old Soul you are. That feels true to me."

She turned to look at him. Their eyes met in a Soul to Soul gaze, and she felt his loving presence penetrate her energetic being. She returned the gaze and their energies felt locked as they started to blend into each other. Their energies thinned into a long twisting of particles that grew into a perfect helix. Wrapping around each other, their energies became more and more intertwined. Colors sparkled and lin the area where they stood. It became a magical show of light in an ascending crescendo of combustion. Lights of white, purple, and blue hues blended into a festival of color, a loving energy of radiant light. The beauty of their union in a combustion of color and light was in contrast to the smoke and darkness of conflict all around them, a city under siege beneath a smoke-filled sky. Flames, smoke, and heat became the backdrop to their joyous union, blaring sirens and screaming protesters their accompaniment as night faded into day. Yet neither had any connection to the events in that moment. Their energies were manifested as pure divine love.

"Oh my, that was so good," China said.

Eleazar laughed and said, "I have never had an experience like that."

China smiled. "I hope not. You've been a priest since you were seventeen years of age. Besides, I'm not sure what we call it—Soul sex?" She glanced up at him with a sheepish look of endearment. "It was my first time, too."

They both laughed as they resumed their journey down the road of protest in Hamburg.

Early in the morning they arrived at the hotel where Sadiki was staying. They entered his room and found him lying next to the hotel manager. Her blond hair and pale skin appeared ghostly against the white satin sheets. Her lips were full and had a natural plum sheen within a darker lip line of brown and plum. China wondered if her lips were tattooed for the effect. She could not help but think, *If she had a good hemoglobin, she would have a pinker or redder color. It must be a tattoo.* She snapped back to the moment and felt the lack of affection between the two lying in bed. Both were sleeping and neither gave off a vibration of satisfaction. China looked at Sadiki and then back at Eleazar. He gently embraced her and held her while they stood there.

China heaved a sigh. "I know I serve the Spirit of Bernard when I serve the Spirit of Sadiki. He's a paid assassin and the flesh and blood of my son." She looked away and said, "That was the human mother in me."

She walked to the balcony and Eleazar followed her. "We met as students at Penn. I was so attracted to his tribal history. The scar on his face is a tribal marking to show his status as son of the tribal leader. He was the first from his tribe to go to college. He was an activist standing for human rights against apartheid, against war and poverty. His heritage was a draw for me. I had no connection to my own heritage. I always felt like a mutt, an African-American father who was a janitor at Penn and my Pilipino mother, a nurse's aide on the geriatric unit. They loved me to death, but somehow I still felt unconnected to either culture. I felt confused, and I didn't know what color I was. For some reason, I thought others cared that I was mixed." She paused and reflected on her words before continuing. "Growing up in West Philly in the shadow of the growing University of Pennsylvania and its expanding community was my only connection. As a kid, I loved going to all the events that honored other countries, customs, and religions. Every nation sent their children to Penn, and I wanted to find a nation that fit."

"Did you find that connection?" asked Eleazar.

"No, I found my best fit at Penn itself. Born there, raised on campus, went to school there, and worked as a nurse there for thirty-eight years. Bernard went to undergrad there and insisted on attending Temple for law school."

"You are a powerful White Soul. You know your greatest power comes from God, not from being a human being, not from a nationality, nor from your job as nurse or your role as mother." Eleazar hesitated a moment and then looked at her to see her reaction.

She stepped away from him and raised her arms. "I am born of Spirit, I live in Spirit, I am Spirit in manifest. I raise my arms in gratitude knowing the Divine outpouring fills me to the brim (Earnest Holmes) and overflows my cup with unconditional love, eternal Joy, and abundance. I am filled to the brim with the Spirit of the Living God manifesting through me as a powerful White Soul." She stood still, her arms stretched out, her head held high. She felt the power of the Divine fill her energetic being. Eleazar could see the energy flow gracefully into her form. She lit up with pure white light and sparkling elegance.

It was eight o'clock when Sadiki awoke. He looked at his one-night conquest and poked her, first gently then more aggressively. "You need to go. I have a lot on my schedule today."

She stirred under the covers and moaned, "Soon, I will get up soon."

"No, now, you need to leave now," he snapped, his face intense, his voice sharp and harsh. He did not sound like the man China once knew.

China turned from him and walked back to the balcony. Eleazar followed her outside and placed his hand on her shoulder. "Are you feeling something?"

"Sadiki wanted nothing to do with my child when I got pregnant. Yet every day I told Bernard what a great man Sadiki was and how excited he was when we found out I was pregnant. I told Bernard his father died the happiest man in the world because he had an infant son named Bernard. I told him Sadiki loved to hold him and talk about his future. Sometimes I think I started to believe the stories I told him when he was growing up." She hesitated before saying, "Bernard has met Sadiki. He is confused by the lies Sadiki has told him. That's why he's been so angry at me." After a pause she added, "Bernard told me I lived the life of a lie. All I wanted to do was serve God and live the truth of who I am, and he is right, I lied."

China turned and looked into the room to see the woman dressing. She left without a goodbye. Sadiki went into the shower. When he came out wrapped in his towel, his dark black skin glistened. He walked to the room safe and opened it. He pulled out a handgun and ammunition. He laid them on the bedside table. He opened the chamber and checked for bullets. They were there. He left the box of bullets next to the gun.

When he finished dressing he opened his briefcase and placed the weapon and ammunition inside. Each had a designated place in the custom case. Before leaving his room, Sadiki stood for a long time in front of the mirror admiring his looks and expensive clothing.

China and Eleazar followed Sadiki out the back door of the hotel into a cab. Eleazar sat in the front seat next to the driver. China and Sadiki sat in the back. She reached out to touch Sadiki's hand and he pulled it back as if it felt offensive.

Eleazar felt the resistance and turned toward her and said, "Are you okay?"

She gave him a shy smile and said, "It's not about me."

Eleazar nodded.

The cab pulled into a back alley. Sadiki, China, and Eleazar got out of the cab. Sadiki paid by cash and threw extra money in the cab window before it pulled away.

They followed Sadiki as he walked several more blocks to a park area. He purchased a newspaper from a corner stand and entered the park. He looked around the park and proceeded to a park bench in front of an old wrought-iron fountain. China and Eleazar moved to the fountain and stood in front of Sadiki.

China placed her hand in the water for the energy of both to blend. "I love this," she said to Eleazar. "Try it."

Eleazar laughed and placed his large hand into the flowing fountain. He watched as the water molecules flowed through his hand and his energy reacted in an outward spiral. "I actually feel that."

"Of course, you do, it's an energy reaction. As energetic beings, we feel energy. The things I'm calling feelings about Sadiki and Bernard are actually my energetic response to their energies." She smiled at him and said, "Watch this." She took his hand in hers and held him steady under the water as it cascaded from the fountain. "I love each water molecule. You are the Divine in expression as water. Each beautiful, clear, and loving droplet is one in the one, and Eleazar and I are one with you."

"I felt the love from the water," Eleazar said. "I felt the oneness in our existence through the energy of the falling water."

She led his hand into the pool that collected the falling water. "I am one with the pool of water made of many individual droplets and a continuous flow of the Divine."

The expression on Eleazar's face was rapturous. "I have never touched water as an energetic being. Obviously, I have been blocking this gift of oneness." They watched with an intense gaze as the particles of water created beautiful patterns around their hands.

She released his hand as they both laughed. He quickly stood up, taking her with him. He twisted his energy around hers, and they climaxed into a combustion of energy, color, and light.

Sadiki's phone rang as he was reading the paper. He said in French, "I am in the park waiting for you. If you stop for coffee, please get me one. Black is fine. Yes, I am sitting in front of the beautiful fountain you described. I will see you soon."

"Who is he meeting?" asked Eleazar.

"His daughter, one of over three hundred children," China answered. "He fathered children to incarnate his growing troops of Dark Souls." She felt a sadness go through her and quickly pushed it away.

It was not long before a thin, beautiful black woman walked toward Sadiki with two coffees. Sadiki looked up and smiled a bright, beautiful smile. He stood excitedly as he said in French, "I could never imagine how beautiful you are!"

She laughed and looked so excited she might burst. She put the coffees down on the bench before jumping into his arms. "Papa, I have dreamed of this day since I can remember."

Sadiki laughed and threw his arms around her. He lifted her off the ground and swung her in a circle before putting her down. He looked at her and said, "Oh my God, you are not only intelligent, you are beautiful. I have thought of you every day since your birth. I was overwhelmed with joy when you were born and loved holding you."

She stepped back and frowned. "My mother said you wanted nothing to do with us. She said it was a short relationship and you left as soon as she got pregnant."

He took his daughter's hand in his and said, "We met in Hong Kong after the conflict in Tiananmen Square. Many young people from around the world wanted to protest the brutality of the Chinese government. I was young, and after growing up in the bush of Africa, in a country under apartheid, I had to go. It felt right. I was a young lawyer who wanted to fix the ills of the world. Your mother was there. She spoke at one of the gatherings. She spoke of a loving world. One in which we all recognize the Divine within each of us. It spoke to me. I was raised to believe in the oneness of the universe. Humans, animals, plant life all within the oneness of the Divine Energy of the Universe. I knew I loved her instantly." He paused before asking, "How is your mother?"

Her eyes filled. "She died last year from cancer." She swallowed hard to hold back the emotions.

"Oh, my daughter, I am so sorry you bore this pain without the love of your father." He embraced her tightly as they sat on the bench.

"Why did you contact me now? Mom said you did not want to be locked into a life with a family."

"No, that is a misunderstanding. I wanted to stay with you and your mother. Your grandparents did not like that I was from a bush tribe. They said I was a nomad. All I wanted was to marry her and to hold you in my arms and protect you."

"So why did you leave?" she asked.

"The conflict between your mother and her family was very stressful for her. I offered to leave for a year or two to see if she could work through it. I wanted you both to be happy. I did not want to be the stress in your lives." He took a deep breath and his face showed a solemn look. Looking at her he continued, "Your mother wrote to me and said it was best to not have me involved."

"You are not listed on my birth certificate," she said. "Why?"

"Your grandparents insisted on that. I was young and did not recognize it was a way to lock me out." He rubbed his eyes as if he might be about to weep. "Forgive me, Brigitte, for not being a good father. Can you accept me now?"

"The blood test says you are my father. I still need time to adjust. But it feels very good you want to be in my life," she responded. "It has been hard since my mom died."

"What do you need? Do you need money? How can I show you love?"

"Let me learn about you, and I am sure I will feel great love for you."

"I want to meet my grandchildren. Can that happen?"

"I have not shared with my husband that we are meeting. He knows of you and our blood test." She looked at him and said, "I still need time."

"You have my number. Call me any time. I will be in Hamburg until tomorrow. I leave after my business meetings. Can I call you tomorrow?"

"Yes, you can. I just need time to sort through my feelings." She swallowed hard and gave him a faint smile.

China turned away from the scene and gazed at the park. "He said the same things to Bernard. And to many of his other offspring." She gave a crooked smile and said, "I was totally snowed when I was young."

"Perhaps we are seeing the man he evolved into. On earth everything is in constant change. Nothing is stagnant."

China nodded. "You're right." She looked at the young woman and felt great love for her. China left Eleazar and moved to the bench. She sat next to the young woman and placed her hand on her heart and the other hand on her neck. She started humming as she released a slow flow of loving energy. She turned to Eleazar. "This will help her stabilize her energy, which has been frenetic since he first contacted her. She has a strong Soul and a good connection. All I'm doing is giving her more love for her Spirit's expansion. The worst is still to come from him. I trust this lifetime she has the power to complete her own expansion. Maybe this is a little insurance policy."

China turned her attention back to the young woman. After a moment, she sighed and then smiled. "It's done. This was the reason I was here. It is done."

"Are you here to give him an infusion?" asked Eleazar.

"No, he has lived more than five lives without expansion, now he can only receive the infusion at death. I will meet him again soon. I was here to learn what was happening to Bernard and to love her. She will make the right decision in the future." China gazed at Eleazar and said, "Are we staying together?"

He laughed and nodded. "Yes, I have nowhere else to go."

The violence in Hamburg ended with sixty police officers injured, two hundred protesters jailed, three protesters killed, and three political figures assassinated.

Chapter 36

Jill walked pensively toward the administrative office. Not sure why she was summoned to see the division chief, she felt a sense of impending doom. She thought back to the events of the week. In the emergency room she gotten into a loud argument with the ER staff. *They were so stupid*, she thought. *It was their fault.*

Or was it from earlier that day when she grabbed the medical student who botched the history of the new patient? But all she had done was grab his lab jacket to keep him from walking away when she was talking to him. It was hard for her to imagine that either event would require a meeting with the division chief. Perhaps they were ready to discuss her becoming a full attending. *That must be it*, she thought, and her frown turned to a smile.

Feeling better, Jill pushed open the glass door and entered the division suite. The administrative secretary looked up and pointed to a seat. "Dr. Ruane will be with you in a minute or two. He's still on a conference call."

"Thank you," Jill said.

The secretary glanced down at the phone and then looked at Jill. "Still in use. As soon as he's done, I'll let him know you're here." She went back to her computer. Jill sat quietly in her seat.

Chapter 37

"Are you ready for your trip?" asked Sam.

Angyo chuckled. "In all my life I never rode in a car nor flew on a plane. Today I do both for the first time."

"Nervous?"

"How can I be nervous when the Universe has it under control?" Angyo answered. "We need to discuss what happens when I am gone." He pointed to some empty chairs. "I would like to sit down over there."

The two men walked to the chairs and sat down.

"Good, that is better," Angyo said. "All the talk about my travels is making my legs feel weak."

"Okay, let's talk about something else," Sam replied.

"Let us start with the information about our newest extrications. How has it been going? How many incubators do we have left to fill?"

"We have room for only eight more White Souls. I'm hopeful the meeting you attend will bring to light new information about this project and the length of time we need to continue. We've started construction on an additional twenty-five beds and can add another hundred. It saves time and money if we build in blocks of twenty-five. We can have the first twenty-five ready for service in four weeks."

"Good. How are we doing with tech support? Can we stretch our staffing to match those numbers?"

"We don't need to stretch. Scientists and IT experts are still calling to join us. We have a list of another hundred and thirty-three for additional tech support." He smiled at Angyo. "All our needs are met. God is so good!"

Angyo smiled and said, "Banko will be in charge while I am gone. As you know, all this past week he has been making rounds with me each day. Trust in him to help if any problems arise. I trust all will be fine and nothing will go amiss." He started to rise from his chair and asked, "Can you walk me out? I have more to discuss and time is running short."

The two men left the physics lab and started on the path to the IT lab. "The Pope has asked if our center will be open to sharing information with him and his staff," Angyo said as they neared the IT lab. "I said we would be glad to share."

"I wish I could go with you to meet the Pope," Sam said.

Angyo turned toward Sam. "I would like to take you, but his Holiness feels there is added risk by inviting more people." He looked away before saying, "The Pope has concerns for safety. Fear has always been a part of many religions." He gave Sam a sidelong glance as they arrived at the IT lab.

"Hey, I agree," Sam said. "Safe travels. I'll miss you while you're gone." He gave Angyo a big hug.

Angyo entered the IT lab alone and saw Tammy speaking to one of the techs. She looked up and waved and then raised two fingers—two minutes—before turning back to the tech.

Angyo nodded and smiled.

Tammy finished her conversation and greeted Angyo with a big smile. "Today's the big day. Are you excited to travel?"

Angyo looked around before saying in a low voice, "Is there some place we can sit and talk?"

Her smile faded. "Oh, sure. We can go to my office."

They walked to a cubical with a glass slider door and large windows on one side. After they sat down she blurted, "Oh, is this a top-secret discussion?"

He laughed a full belly laugh. "No." He leaned over her desk and said quietly, "Every time someone talks about my travels, my legs feel weak. So, forgive me for my human weakness."

Her expression relaxed, and her smile returned. "Oh, no, don't worry, flying is fun. Just have a glass or two of wine and you'll relax."

"The pope asked if you and Sam might be available for questions from his team. Of course, I agreed."

"Sure, but they should just ask the Divine Universe. They don't need us." She seemed surprised by the idea.

"Not all religions are as spiritually based, and so that connection with the Divine is more conditional than it is here."

"Whatever, I'm game." She sighed and then added, "Have a great trip. We'll miss you."

"Banko will visit each day for the updates. He is well versed in the running of the monasteries and the labs. He will gladly assist with anything you need."

"That sounds great." She shrugged her shoulders before saying, "Don't worry, we'll be fine. Do you like to travel?"

"When I was sixteen, I traveled by foot to the monastery. The furthest I have traveled since was to the village below. I have had no need or desire to travel. All I have needed is right here." He stood up and said, "I must go now so I do not miss my flight."

Tammy stood up, and they left her office. She watched him walk out of the building.

Chapter 38

"I don't understand, you're suspending me?" said Dr. Jill Buggy with a shocked look. She was in the office of Dr. Allen Ruane, facing him across a desk. "How can this be? I should be an attending. I thought that was why I was here, for my promotion." She felt a sick feeling within her. "I was right in the ER, they were wrong. I'm tired of people punishing me because I'm right."

"Dr. Buggy, you smelled of alcohol in the ER, and that was again reported this morning," Dr. Ruane replied. "Security will escort you to employee health for a drug and alcohol test. Afterwards they will drive you home. Once we have the result, we will discuss the next steps. You're dismissed." He turned his chair to face his computer.

Jill was stunned. She couldn't move. She couldn't think.

Dr. Ruane turned from his computer to face her again. "You're dismissed," he said. "Security is outside the door and waiting for you."

Chapter 39

White supremacist groups, neo-Nazis, and KKK members from around the country met in a park in a quaint southern town in the United States. They said they were there to march against the removal of a Confederate statue, but their energy painted a story of hate and suppression of others. The group arrived intending to fight. Many wore shields and helmets and carried thick batons.

Some counter-protesters prepared to fight the KKK and white supremacist groups with baseball bats and fists. The energy of hate flowed through the crowd as they started to march toward the town center. Chants filled with hate toward Jews, blacks, and immigrants vibrated through the town and eroded the calm community atmosphere.

China stood on the cement pedestal of a civil war statue next to a large group of white supremacists. She saw the thick, dark energetic aura surrounding the marchers. The dark cloud appeared to cover the park. Searching the crowd, she looked for a sign of where to start her work. She caught a glimpse of a dim flickering light in one man's eyes. He was as good a place as any in the crowd to start.

China jumped down from the statue and landed right next to the man. Stepping in front of him she looked directly into his eyes. As she read his vibrations she knew the weak flickering light was struggling against a feeling of fear and inner conflict. She placed her right hand on his heart and her left on his neck. She let the energy flow with ease and love. Her eyes continued to gaze directly into his eyes to watch the flicker grow. She felt his Soul absorbing the energy. He was thirsty, and his Soul was eager to receive the infusion. His eyes ignited into a steady flame of hope and promise. They both stood perfectly still until she felt the Divine Soul within him gaze back at her with strength and love. She smiled and watched the man smile back. She felt his Soul's gratitude move through her.

"Welcome back," she said. "Use your free will well."

"Hey, buddy, you got to get moving," yelled a man in riot gear with an automatic weapon.

"Oh yeah, right," the man responded as his confusion lifted. "Go around me. I just realized I left something in my car." As China released her hands, he moved from the center of the crowd to the outer edge. He broke free of the crowd and walked toward his car, which was parked several blocks away.

China looked around to see hundreds of extricated souls working the crowd. She scanned the crowd to find tho next Soul to infuse

She worked quietly until she saw a moving mass of dark energy. She looked around and scanned the area and the Extricated Souls. Intuitively, she recognized a break in a White Soul's auric field. She moved quickly toward the Soul when she saw the dark mass engulf the White Soul. China reached out to grab the Soul. She felt the strength of the dark mass tugging back and recognized the darkness was draining the Soul's energy quickly. She knew that holding on would risk her own energy, and she did not want to be caught in a fight.

"Archangel Michael, I need help," she called.

A huge shadow shaped like wings fell over the crowd, filling the landscape in front of China. Michael saw China and the darkness in a struggle, with a White Soul as the prize. He took a deep breath and blew the winds in the direction of the dark mass. There was a hollowing in the winds as the darkness was torn from the Soul. China heard a painful cry from the dark energy as it was ripped into pieces. She worked fast, knowing the dark energy would eventually pull itself together and return. The injured White Soul collapsed into a small heap of energy. China went down with it, keeping her hands on it.

"Spirit of the living God, fill me with your Divine energy and let it flow through me to infuse this beloved Soul." She felt an intense energy move through her. The energy flowed for several seconds, and as she released her hands from the Soul she felt the presence of Archangel Michael. Light and love radiated from him. He bent over and scooped up the Soul. He turned to China and said, "Thank you for saving this Soul." In the next moment his energy shifted out of the earth dimension.

The man reached his car, opened the door, and got in. He started to cry. "I can't do this anymore, God, it's hard to continue with this hate and violence," he blurted through his sobs. "Can you forgive me?" A still, quiet voice arose within him.

Can you forgive yourself?

The man suddenly felt a calm within. He turned and looked at the back seat of his car. He was alone. "I'm a sinner," he said. "I've hurt people. How can I forgive that?"

I am always with you. When you hate, you stop me from sending you my love. Forgive yourself, love yourself, and my love will flow through you.

"You still want to love me? There are many better people than me that deserve your love." The man heaved a final shuddering sob. He felt a strong stirring within him. He sat quietly and waited for the feelings to pass. Then a flow of thoughts filled his mind.

No matter what beliefs the egotic mind spins, I never stopped loving you. Your ego is the one who denied my love. It is time to let my love in.

"I thought I was strong before," the man whispered.

Hatred is a character of the weak. There is a powerlessness that occurs when love is rejected. The egotic mind is imprisoning the Soul into darkness. Today your light was reignited. Follow the light.

The man heaved a deep sigh and started to sob again. "Thank you. Thank you." He pulled a napkin from his glove compartment and blew his nose. "I surrender to my Soul." He leaned back in his seat and said, "I am tired, God, so tired." He felt a peaceful stillness within and closed his eyes. A moment later he drifted off to sleep.

China and Eleazar worked the crowd of marchers separately. The hate energy consumed both sides, making the work of the Extricated Souls more intense. China worked alongside hundreds of Souls who moved from one marcher and protester to the next without judgement or feeling. Occasionally, she glanced around to look for Eleazar, but she didn't find him.

Chapter 40

Angyo pressed his body into the seat as the airplane descended into Ciampino Airport in Rome. As the plane taxied down the runway he felt queasy and unsettled. The landing felt rough, and he took a deep breath as the plane stopped. "Thank you for a safe trip," he murmured.

Not sure he was ready to stand, Angyo stayed in his seat by the window as others jumped up and grabbed their luggage. It took several minutes before the door opened at the front of the plane and the line of passengers started to move. Angyo felt no rush as he waited for his equilibrium to return.

"Do you need assistance, sir?" asked the flight attendant.

"No, I just wanted to wait until the rush was over. I am in no hurry to get anywhere."

He tried to stand, but his legs still felt weak, and he lowered himself back into the seat. "Sometimes at my age not everything works the way they used to."

"It's okay, take your time. Do you have a bag overhead?" The flight attendant checked the overhead cabinet and found a small bag. "Is this yours?"

"Yes, that is it."

"Okay, you can sit here another ten minutes before the cleaning crew arrives. At that time, I will need you to leave. There will be no one with you in the plane since the crew and I need to leave. I will ask Security to join you and they can help with your connection needs." She smiled at the elderly man.

229

The flight attendant left Angyo and joined the flight crew at the front of the plane. "Boy, I'm not looking forward to getting old. That guy has very weak legs." They all laughed as they left the plane.

A security guard arrived and greeted Angyo. "What's the problem, old man?" he asked.

"No problem, my legs just feel weak. This is my first flight and I am still feeling a little unsettled."

The security guard frowned. "No shit! At your age you never flew?"

"I'm a monk from a monastery in Bhutan. I have had no reason to travel."

"So why now?" the man asked.

"I was invited by the pope."

"No shit. You party with the pope?"

"I guess you can say that, if reading ancient spiritual works in the papal library is partying."

Angyo stood. His legs felt stronger, though his hips and knees felt a little stiff. Holding the seat in front of him he said, "I think my legs are ready to stand."

The Italian guard grabbed Angyo by the arm as he tried to stabilize his body weight over his feet. "You really lost your land legs."

"Is that what it's called?" He started to move one foot in front of the other, and with each step he felt stronger. "Can you carry my bag until I am on solid land?"

The big burly Italian smiled a big smile. "Sure. I can throw you over my shoulder if you prefer."

Angyo let out a laugh. "No, that will not be necessary. The thought of it is good motivation for me to move more quickly." They both laughed together.

Angyo was driven through the airport on a tram car with the Italian guard at his side. His new friend walked him to the luggage claim and asked for his luggage ticket. "All my luggage is here on your shoulder."

The guard helped Angyo into a cab and told the driver, "Hotel Alimandi Vaticano." He closed the door, smiled at the monk, and said, "Godetevi la vostra vista."

The hotel was ten miles from the airport, but the cab moved quickly through Rome, and they arrived in good time.

Angyo checked in and went to his room. He was exhausted. A hot shower and a glass of wine left him relaxed and ready for bed. He quickly fell into a deep sleep.

"Angyo, are you asleep?"

Mumbling, Angyo rolled over onto his other side.

"We need to talk," Eleazar said.

Angyo fell deeper into sleep.

Eleazar settled into the armchair in the corner of the room. "He will wake soon enough."

"•.ˌˌˌ.•*"*•☆•*"*•.ˌˌˌ.•*"*•☆

Angyo awoke in the early morning feeling groggy and disoriented, his mind and body fatigued from his first experience of traveling outside the Paro Valley area. He rolled over and grabbed the extra pillow and quickly fell back to sleep.

He woke up at eight o'clock to sunlight shining into the room. He sat up, stretched, and yawned. He put his hand on the bed and smiled. His bed at the monastery was a flat mat that sat on the floor of his room. Although the guest rooms had been redone, he chose to leave his own room and bed as it had been for the last fifty years. Now he wondered if it might be time for a change.

He climbed out of bed to head to the bathroom and noticed an energy in the corner chair. "Who is there?"

Laughing, Eleazar said, "It is Eleazar, my old friend." Eleazar's energy started to transform into his human figure.

"Eleazar, what are you doing here?" asked Angyo.

"I'm here to visit the library with you and the pontiff."

Angyo nodded. "Good." He eyed Eleazar, a question hovering on his lips. After another moment, he asked, "What is it like?"

"Do you mean what is it like to be a Soul without a body?"

"Yes, that is what I mean."

"It is a state of being that I could not imagine before the extrication. I love the confidence of my energy, the knowing that flows easily, and the ability to just act without doubt. I have not had a second thought about anything."

"It sounds ... fascinating," Angyo said.

"So how have you been old friend?" asked Eleazar.

"Funny you should say old. I was feeling good, more youthful and happy, before this trip. Now I am feeling worn and tired."

"Have you considered Extrication? It allows you to avoid jet lag as you move from one point to another."

"No, I have not been called to extricate. So, I will continue in my aging body." Angyo laughed. "I felt it more today because of the tight seats in the plane and perhaps some anxiety about flying."

Eleazar laughed. "That is the beauty of being an Extricated Soul, there is no worry about flying. Even if you get on the plane and it crashes, you don't feel a thing, and nothing changes for you."

"What brings you here to Rome?" asked Angyo.

"The Divine," Eleazar replied. He moved to the window and looked out over the parking lot. "Not the best view."

Angyo sat on the edge of the bed. "Tell me more, what is it like being extricated?"

"It is wonderfully freeing, no restrictions, no fears, just ease with every move. I just know what to do. It is funny, I just left one dimension and walked right into your room. No preplanning, no worrying about travel."

"Fantastic. Tell me everything."

Eleazar smiled. "No looking shabby or wearing uncomfortable torn sandals. I haven't shaved since the morning I was extricated. Yet I'm looking pretty good. It is a good life."

Angyo had the feeling there was more. "What else?" he asked.

"I met my match. She is a very powerful White Soul."

"Oh, a woman?" Angyo raised his eyebrows.

"Well, we have no sexual orientation when we are extricated. We are energy blobs that can choose to keep our last physical form or any form we like. I tend to keep my body form, and she keeps hers. How do you see me?"

"Right now, I see you as a younger version of you. When I first awoke I felt your presence, but it took a few minutes to see you. But I knew it was you. Now, tell me about your new friend."

"She was extricated at the monastery about a year after me."

"Tell me her name."

"China. We actually met before she extricated. I was called to a gay rights march in Philadelphia, and we first met there. Then we met again on her first assignment, and she came in like a lightning bolt. We did the next assignment together, and much to my surprise she taught me a few things."

"Do you go to all assignments together?" asked Angyo with his eyebrows raised.

"No, we pop into each other's assignment from time to time. We did some work together at the G20 Summit. That was the last time I worked with her directly."

"Is there anything we need to know to improve the extrication process?" asked Angyo.

"Well, I have learned most souls leave a small percentage of their energy in the body, and if they are placed in an experience that can trigger an emotion, they feel it. China came face to face with her son's father at the G20. Learning about his present life triggered feelings she did not expect. And I had an experience where I felt conflicted, but the answer came to me in time to save a child. As Extricated Souls, we are restoring free will to those that have Souls living in the shadows of the ego. Hopefully, they can use their free will not to inflict harm or evil against others."

Eleazar looked at his friend sitting on the end of the bed. "Do you want me to make you a cup of coffee or tea?"

Angyo shook his head. "No, I am fine. I got here a day early, so I could recover from the travel. Perhaps I will take a walk to see some of Rome while I am here. Are you staying with me?"

Eleazar laughed. "I don't need a place to stay. I don't sleep, go to the bathroom, or shave." He made a shrug. "I can leave at any time. I don't want to bother you."

Angyo smiled a shy smile as he looked over the rim of his glasses at his friend. "Okay. Leave and come back later."

In the next instant, Angyo was alone. He fell back down on his bed and pulled back up his covers. He quickly fell back to sleep.

Chapter 41

Sam looked at his phone when the Twitter alert came in. He felt his heart skip a beat as he read the message from Tammy:

Tammy.Bhutangodproject@twitter.com
to Sam.Bhutangodproject@twitter.com
Mosque in Turkey reports 1 White Soul not returning. Angelic beings stopped energy flow and human body has started death sequence.

Sam immediately called Tammy. "I never thought we could lose a Soul."

"We can't lose a Soul," Tammy responded with surprise. "It returned to the heart or core of Source to have its energy restored. It's served selflessly."

"You're right, I had myself thinking the White Souls were indestructible. I guess that sounds pretty dumb."

"No, my contact at the mosque in Turkey is taking it pretty hard. They'll hold a traditional Muslim funeral and burial for the body."

"Did Angyo get the tweet?"

"Yes, Banko asked me to include him."

Sam was surprised and disappointed, but he was not sure what disappointed him more: Tammy telling Banko before him, or that a Soul would not reincarnate into its body. Silence fell between them.

"Sam, are you still there? Did I lose you?" asked Tammy. "Sam, Sam, I can't hear you. I'm going to hang up."

"No, I'm here," Sam said. "I'll see you at dinner." Sam hung up first.

Chapter 42

Angyo felt the coolness as he watched the sheer curtains move to the spring breeze. The pontiff's office, an eclectic mix of simplicity and elegance, felt warm and was filled with light. Angyo looked at Eleazar before saying, "We are in the pope's office."

Eleazar smiled and said, "We are in his receiving office, where he receives the public. This is where he met me when I traveled here twice before my extrication." Eleazar looked around. "It is a nice office. His personal office is next to his bedroom suite. He is living in a small wing of the building and not the traditional papal wing. It felt too ornate to him."

"That is true," said the pope as he entered the small office. "The Vatican is a big place, and I still prefer the simplicity and humility of my calling." He moved into the room and sat down in an overstuffed armchair across from Angyo. "Welcome. I appreciate your traveling to see me. It is hard for me to travel to see you without a lot of press and pressure. I miss my anonymity when I travel. Besides, I heard the steps of the monastery were difficult for a man my age."

Angyo smiled. "They are difficult for me as well. Since our monastery has transitioned we now have an all-terrain vehicle that can travel the back side of the mountain. We needed a back road to bring in the supplies and building equipment when we started to prepare to be an extrication site. So, rest assured that if you visit we will give you a lift up the mountain."

They laughed together before the pontiff looked at Eleazar and said, "Good to see you looking so young and healthy. Extrication has been good for you?"

Eleazar nodded. "Yes, it is a confident and harmonious state of being. I feel I live in a state of inspired action. It is the epitome of living in the moment. Good to see you as well."

"I am not sure if you heard yet, but a mosque in Turkey lost a White Soul," the pontiff said. "It will not return, and the angels released the body from the energy field."

With a feeling of surprise, Angyo responded, "No, I left my phone in the hotel room. Do you know what happened?" He turned to Eleazar with a questioning look.

Eleazar looked to be in a state of deep concentration when he said, "The Soul was serving in Charlottesville in the U.S. when a dark energy engulfed it and drained its energy." He appeared to be reaching deep into the collective consciousness when he said, "China was there, and called for help. China and Archangel Michael were able to save the Soul and return it to the Divine for healing and love."

Eleazar came out of his near-trancelike state and refocused on the pope and Angyo. "It was the first White Soul to be returned to the Divine. The Dark Souls are fighting back. In Iraq I saw my first 'jump in' when a Dark Soul jumped into a freshly vacated body. It happened again at the G20. It is hard to stop the Dark Soul if it does not receive a White Soul intervention immediately before the body they occupied died. They are quickly reincarnating anywhere they can."

The pope and Angyo both appeared troubled by the news.

"I will reach out to Bhutan to ensure they know," Angyo said.

"It went out on the Twitter account to all centers from Turkey earlier this afternoon," added the pope. After a few moments of silence, he added, "I invited you here for a reason. I have spent many hours in the Vatican library. We have the largest collection of original Spiritual writings going back to the ancient Greeks, the Incas, Muslim mystics, Buddhist writings, and so on. I have found great power and clarity in these documents and cannot help but feel others will feel the same." He paused before getting up and walking to the desk to pour a glass of water. "Can I get you anything?" he asked Angyo.

Angyo shook his head. "Please go on."

"I invited you here to share these documents with you. And each week I will host Spiritual leaders from many of the religious centers involved in the God Project. It is time they also have access to these original teachings."

"I look forward to reading these documents," Angyo said. "Many of the Buddhist writings I studied were written by the students of Buddha. In early days, the teachings were passed down by word of mouth in all traditions."

"What I most appreciate is we all started with the same belief," the pontiff said. "The belief that we are one with God. As I look at present-day religion, I feel that has been lost. It is my calling to give the message back to the masses."

"Why not just release copies of these writings on your website?" asked Angyo.

"I feel it will do more good for each of the Spiritual leaders to lead their flocks," the pope replied. He turned toward the door. "Should we proceed, gentlemen?"

Chapter 43

Jill sat with her feet dangling over the edge of the roof. The night view of Philadelphia from the roof of her condo building once excited her. Now it was a painful reminder of the emptiness she felt in her life. As she looked down at the robust city, she felt jealous of those enjoying the evening, its night life, and loved ones. Her self-pity and loneliness was bubbling over. "God, why don't you ever talk to me the way you talk to China." She paused, then raised her voice and said, "Am I not good enough for you? Not perfect? Is that why you take everyone away from me? You told China to leave me and go to Bhutan. You took my mother. I was only seven, and you stole her from me." Jill's voice cracked under the strain, and she took a moment to try to compose herself.

"What kind of God are you?" she asked in a whisper. "How can you be a loving God when you have deserted me?"

She dropped her head in her hands and cried uncontrollably. Fatigue finally crept over her, and she sobbed quietly. Feeling exhausted, she swung her legs back onto the roof. She pulled herself up while hanging onto the rail that surrounded the rooftop. She stood at the rail and leaned over it.

"Is today the day I will fly?" She stretched her arms out to the side as if they were wings. "What will you do, God? Will you catch me? Or will you let me fall splat." She swayed from side to side as if she was flying. "Will you let me into heaven or send me to hell?" She

243

stumbled as she momentarily lost her balance. "All I want is for you to love me the way you love China."

China stepped up to Jill and put an arm around her. "Today is not the day." She gently guided her back from the edge. She helped Jill sit down on the roof. Jill reached for the sweater she had left there and rolled it into a ball. She lay down to rest, placing the balled-up sweater under her head.

Jill snorted a drunken laugh. "Ouch, I drank too much." Her head was spinning and her eyes heavy. Sleepiness came fast. Sitting next to her was an empty wine glass, wine bottle, and a brown pill bottle with Valium.

China lay down next to her. She pulled herself tight against Jill with her arms wrapped around her. Caressing Jill's hair, China said, "I love you, sweet little girl. God has never deserted you." China put her hand on Jill's heart and her other hand on her neck and the energy infusion started. "You can use your free will at any time to feel God's presence within you. Your life does not have to be as painful as you think it is—your life is what you think." The infusion continued but not at the normal rapid pace. It was slow and loving as it filled Jill's heart space and entered her Soul.

Jill stirred as the darkness of night turned to the charcoal gray of early morning. She rolled onto her back and grabbed her head. "Ouch, what was I thinking to drink the whole bottle? Or was it two?"

China was still sitting next to her. "You weren't thinking clearly. You were living your emotional pain." She reached over and touched Jill's cheek.

Jill's eyes popped open and she reached to her face. "I felt someone touch me." She slowly turned her head side to side but saw no one. "Is that you, God? Are you here with me? I really want you to love me like you love China."

China smiled and said, "God does love you."

Jill tried to sit up quickly but the dizziness made it difficult. "China, I just heard your voice. Are you here?"

"Yes, Jill, I'm here. My Spirit is here with you."

"Oh no, did you die, China, are you dead?" Fear and terror ran through Jill, and she started to cry.

"No, I am very much alive. God wanted my Spirit to be with you last evening. So I came."

"Is that because God doesn't want to be with me?" Jill sobbed as she asked the question.

"No, God is always with you. God is the Soul that lives within you."

"Then why doesn't God speak to me like he does you?" Her voice was cracking as her tears flowed more slowly.

"Life is as you think. You think God has deserted you, so you block the Divine from communicating to you. You think you are unlovable, so that is the energy that you send to everyone around you, and then you become unlovable."

"I think you told me this before. I thought it was some spiritual hogwash." Jill paused before adding, "For some reason, this time, I hear a truth in what you're saying." She looked around, shaking her head slowly. "Why can I hear you but not see you?"

"You have many layers of beliefs to shed for your heart and mind to open to all that is God and all that is good. Today is the start. If you do the spiritual work, you will connect with the incredible Divine Universe." China reached out and started to play with Jill's hair.

"Are you touching my hair?" Jill leaned into the presence she was feeling next to her.

China let out a giggle. "Yes, and you are now leaning against me. I am going to hug you and hold you." China's energetic arms wrapped around Jill in a warm embrace.

"Oh my God, I feel you. I haven't felt anyone hold me with this much love since I was a little girl." Jill felt a wave move through her as a new flow of tears started to fall.

"Sometimes we can use our own feelings and beliefs to block the love that others want to give. I have been here since last evening. I sat next to you as you drank. I sat on the wall with you. I was touching you and loving you. I cuddled you as you slept. You were too locked into your emotions to let the love in."

"Why can I feel it now?" Jill asked.

"Because you are more open to the Divine Presence within you. I touched your heart last night while you slept and gave you lots of love to help you start on the road back to God. You asked for this help when you said you wanted God to love you like God loves me. "

"I don't remember what I said," Jill replied.

"It doesn't matter what you said yesterday. All that matters is what you say and think now." China hesitated before asking, "Can you think God loves you since ... I was sent here?"

"Yes." Jill paused and with a stronger voice she said, "Yes, yes I can. Yes, I know that to be true." Jill sat straight up. "Wow, that felt good to say but not good to move so fast." She let out a chuckle.

"You have just opened the door for God to enter your thoughts and feelings from a place of love." China took Jill's hand in her hand.

Laughing, Jill said, "Thank you so much, China. I feel so different inside. How do I keep this feeling? I'm not sure I can be as good as you at meditating and praying." She let out a laugh. "Sorry."

"No reason to be sorry. It is not expected. It's what you do with your thoughts that will keep you growing in this feeling. You have it in you to develop the attitude of gratitude. Gratitude is everything to God. You don't even have to believe in God to have the Divine Energy expressing through you. Live in gratitude and come from a place of love in your thoughts, words, and deeds, for yourself and others. It's pretty easy once you get the hang of it."

"I guess I've been very petty and selfish. Always feeling deprived of love. I like this feeling much more."

Jill sighed and put her head in her hands. "I think I need something for this headache."

"You have done well, Jill, and it will get easier every day," China said. "I'm feeling my energy getting pulled, so I will say I love you and I am always close by."

"Can my mom do this?"

"Yes, she has been with us all night. Are you ready to forgive her and forgive yourself for being so angry?"

"Yes. Yes I can." Jill looked around but still saw no one. "Can I feel her like I feel you holding my hand?"

"Yes, you can. I gave your hand to your mom several minutes ago. She is holding it now."

China stood up on the roof and looked over the city. She admired the beauty of the rising sun and left in a flittering second without turning back.

Chapter 44

Bernard turned on the TV to get the early morning news on ZNN. It was five o'clock. He picked up his coffee and walked to the living room to see the early reports. The reporter was doing a standup in Rome at Vatican City. Bernard sat down and increased the volume.

"The pope has been meeting behind closed doors with world Spiritual leaders," the reporter intoned. "Over the past few weeks he has met with several Buddhist monks and a number of imams from the Middle East and Africa. He is expected to meet next week with leaders from the Jewish faith and Greek Orthodox Church. The church has confirmed the pontiff has been holding closed meetings, but the Vatican has not made a statement on the content of these meetings. It is unclear if the Dali Lama has been invited as well."

The reporter signed off and Bernard sat back. He wondered if the pope was preaching against gay people. Feeling annoyed, he switched channels to a local news station.

"It has been determined that the murder of the LGBT chapter president in Los Angeles was a professional assassination," the reporter announced. "Now, two months since Fran Johnson was shot with a high-powered rifle while giving a speech at a nonviolent rally, Los Angeles police and the FBI have issued a joint statement confirming that the killing was an assassination. The police and FBI have worked on this case together since the day of the shooting and will continue to work together until the assassin is apprehended. The joint statement released this morning notes that a sniper's nest was discovered in a building under construction one mile from the rally. They also said they feel confident they are closing in on the individual responsible. Earlier this week, the *New York Times* reported that there were several similarities to the shootings at the G20 summit in Hamburg and to the murder of the mayor of Philadelphia two and a half years ago."

Bernard turned the volume down. He felt lifeless. His only thoughts were that his father was in Philadelphia when his mother was at the march. He was in Germany to meet with a high political official during the G20 and in L.A. at the time of the Johnson shooting. Bernard's brain seemed to freeze. "It's only a coincidence," he murmured. He drank his coffee down and jumped up from the sofa. A great feeling of anxiety moved through him. He needed to get to work.

After Bernard arrived at work he arranged a meeting with the firm's investigator, a former police detective named John Smith, for 1:15. All morning he felt distracted and anxious, and he couldn't stop checking the clock.

A few minutes before one o'clock he left his office and took the elevator down to the ground floor coffee shop for a latte. On his return, he waited at the elevator until he felt a strong impulse to head up the steps. The stairwell, rarely used except for fire drills, was a good way to avoid being seen. The first two flights he took two steps at a time. On the third floor he stopped for a minute before continuing one step at a time. It took longer than he expected to arrive on the sixth floor. A little out of breath, he leaned against the wall before pulling the door open. He reminded himself to get back to his running program.

The hallway was set up the same as every other floor in the law firm. Bernard arrived with two minutes to spare. The office door sat open, and Bernard moved quickly into the reception area. Smith's assistant, a young woman with dark hair, was sitting behind a desk. She smiled and said, "You must be Bernard."

He nodded. "That's me."

"I'm Sue." She gestured toward a door behind her. "John is in his office. You can go on back."

"Thanks," Bernard said, and he proceeded to the door of the inner office and stepped inside.

Smith stood up from behind a large, glass-topped desk and greeted Bernard with a firm handshake. After gesturing to a chair at a round glass table, Smith closed the door to the office. Bernard sat down and noticed a model Harley Davison Low Rider motorcycle sitting in the middle of the table. He moved it closer to him to check it out. "Nice, is this your ride?"

"Yeah, I'm thinking of buying a designer bike," Smith said. He chuckled before adding, "If my wife agrees. So, what's this all about?"

Bernard handed him the old black-and-white photograph of Sadiki. "I need you to investigate this man."

Smith looked at the photo and then at Bernard. "Who is he?"

"My biological father. I want to know who he is, where he comes from, and what he does. I want financial information, personal information, and anything else you can find." Bernard handed a file folder to Smith. "Here's everything I know or have been told about him, including where he supposedly came from and the business travels he's been doing."

"Supposedly?"

Bernard nodded. "I question the legitimacy of that piece of information."

Smith nodded. "I see."

"The folder also has his cell phone number and information on his African roots—the tribe he came from."

"What kind of time line are you looking for?"

"As quickly as you can get it. Keep me up to date with any new information you find. You will bill me personally, not the firm."

"In that case, I'll have to do it on my own time."

"Can you do it?" Bernard asked.

Smith nodded. "I can do it."

"I appreciate it, John," Bernard said. "Please keep this between you and me. No one else."

"Do you know where he is right now?" Smith asked.

"No, the last I knew he was in L.A. about two months ago. He told me he lives in Johannesburg. I don't have an address. He sells diamonds to the wealthy and to politicians. He told me he'll be coming to D.C. in October to meet with a client. Perhaps the client is a politician. I thought I knew a lot about him, but I really know very little."

"What brought all this on?" Smith asked.

Bernard's head dropped, and he clenched his jaw before speaking, "My mother told me some things about him that she finally admitted aren't true. Now I question everything she told me about him—and everything he told me about himself. Help me figure this out."

"All right, Bernard," Smith said. "I'll help you."

Chapter 45

Sam and Tammy worked side by side at the small table in the garden room of the IT lab.

"Do you want to take a break?" Sam asked. "You've been working all day."

Tammy smiled at him. "I like that you're always thinking about me." She looked around before leaning toward him and kissing him gently on the lips. "Angyo isn't here, so I'm feeling a little frisky."

Sam let out a laugh. "You vixen! Get me in trouble at the monastery."

"Working on it," she said.

"I need to finish the stats for the report," Sam said. "This project has grown astronomically."

Tammy nodded. "We had no idea it would become a worldwide initiative with this amount of collaboration between religions, countries, and generations."

"If we could do this kind of collaboration, then why can't our government or any other country work together like this?" Sam asked. "Instead of doing this in secret, we need to come out of the closet and show the world our good work."

"I'm not sure others are ready to hear this. Too many people deny that we're all connected by the energy that's the very Soul within. It's sad. They follow beliefs that separate them from the energy."

Sam shrugged. "Then why not tell them?"

"Maybe you're right, maybe some people who hear what's happening would start to embrace the truth of who they are. I just don't think it's the right time. We still have work to do."

Chapter 46

A few days after speaking with John Smith, Bernard received a text from him asking for a meeting. Bernard texted back that he was available immediately, and Smith told him to come up. Bernard left his office and took the stairs to the sixth floor. He entered the outer office, rushed past Sue with barely a smile, and went into Smith's private office.

"What do you have for me?" he asked Smith.

The investigator stood and offered his hand. Bernard took it, gazing at Smith's face and reading the look of concern written on it. Smith took his seat. Bernard sat down and leaned forward, ready to hear whatever Smith had for him.

"This man you're calling your father does a lot to hide his tracks," Smith said. "But I've uncovered a few things." He opened a portfolio and glanced at his notes before looking up again. "Your father, the man who went to Penn, is not the son of a tribal leader. The son named Sadiki died in a hunting accident at age nineteen several years before your father arrived in the U.S. So far, I haven't been able to find the real name of your biological father. As I said, he's been covering his tracks for a long time."

"How do you know he wasn't the tribal chief's son? Where did you get the information about the death?"

"The tribe whose name you gave me was moving slowly into the mainstream of the national government at the time of his death. In the late fifties and early sixties, they were recording births and deaths within the tribe. I contacted the local government in that area and they provided the information on the son of the tribal leader at that time, who was named Sadiki." He pulled two sheets of paper from his folder and pushed them across the desk. "These are copies of the birth and death certificates." He watched Bernard as he looked at the documents. "You don't look surprised."

A sick feeling moved through Bernard's stomach. "Yes, I'm surprised and numb. Did you find any information about who he is now?"

"As I said, he's been hiding his tracks as he goes along. He does have a home in Johannesburg. It's worth over a million dollars. And he is listed as a diamond dealer. I did some digging and contacted several big diamond companies, even some diamond mines, and no one knew who he was or ever met him. As for his travels, I can't track the trips you mentioned by the name he's using."

Bernard clenched his fists and swore under his breath. He wanted to punch a wall. "Anything else?" he muttered.

"If you can get me a more current photo, I can use a connection I have in Airline Security with Homeland Security to run his photo through facial recognition. The name you know him by wasn't on any flights to L.A. in the past five years. We checked every airport within a day's drive of L.A., and he wasn't listed as a passenger. I couldn't find his name on any flight list that month. Also, he wasn't listed on any private charter or as a pilot. I tried everything to find him in L.A. on the dates when he told you he was there, but he might be using another name. Or he could be outright lying to you."

"Whoever he is, he is my biological father. He went to the extreme of having the tribal markings cut into his face." Bernard put his hands on his head in disbelief. "We did the DNA testing before we met. I no longer know what I should believe about him. I guess he was lying to my mother when they met." He heaved a great shuddering sigh and then smashed his fist into the desk. "Damn! What do we do now?"

"Call him, see when he'll be in town, and set up a meeting. I'll get the pictures."

Bernard shook his head. "It may not be that easy. He hung up on me the last time we talked four months ago—when I told him I'm gay." Bernard smiled and chuckled. "When I was a teenager, my mom told me she'd always love me regardless who I loved as long as they were a good person."

"Your mom sounds like a nice woman."

Bernard nodded. "As soon as she said that she told me should would always love me even if I loved a person who wasn't good and who hurt me." He laughed. "I've been a jerk toward her and haven't seen her for almost three years. I didn't even open the last letter she sent me." He dropped his head and shook it in disbelief. "I'm a chip off the old block, as bad as my father."

Smith frowned. "You can worry about that later. Call Sadiki, see if you can connect and set it up."

Bernard got out his cell phone and dialed. "He hasn't answered my previous calls, so we'll see." A moment later, he said into the phone, "Hi, Sadiki, this is Bernard. I'm hoping we can put the last call aside and start talking again. Call me back. If you're going to be traveling to the States, I'd like us to get together. Mom always says it's not good for the Soul to stay angry at someone. Take care."

"My gut feeling is that you'll hear from him," Smith said. "Call me when you do."

Chapter 47

China sat on the stone bench in her little garden. "Thank you for sending me here. I always felt I was in the most beautiful place, the garden of Eden, sitting here. Is my service done?"

She waited for an impression to emerge from within. She spoke the words as they moved through her.

No, just rest before your next assignment. Pray and meditate.

She smiled and nodded in acknowledgement of the directions. "Yes, that's always a good idea. Thank you, Spirit." She felt a tightening in her energy field where her throat would be. "Why did that happen?"

The words flowed easily into her mind.

You have a strong connection to your human heart. You need to purge any human feelings that may have surfaced through your travels. You know the thoughts and feelings of which I speak.

"Yes, I do." China sat quietly watching the waterfall at the pond. The sun was setting when she entered the house from the garden, passing through the locked door. She smelled the freshly cleaned kitchen and decided to do something special for Ruth, who was taking such good care of the house, when she returned. She walked past the island into the dining room, then meandered through the rest of the house, looking at all the things that had a special place in her heart. She went up the steps and stood at the bedroom door, feeling her heart expand as she looked at her wall of family pictures. She walked to the wall and reached gently to touch Bernard's face. She moved from picture to picture and kissed her fingers before touching her parents' faces. She lingered for some time, and when she turned, she was surprised to see Eleazar standing at the door.

"I was wondering why I was here, until I saw you." He walked over to her and pointed at Bernard's graduation picture. "Is this Bernard?"

China nodded. "Yeah, that was when he graduated from law school." She pointed to another photo. "This one was when he graduated from Penn." She laughed and said, "And over here is when he graduated from kindergarten. I have boxes of pictures that go back to his birth. I could bore you with them if you want."

"Nothing about you can bore me." He pulled her energy into his own energy form. He leaned into her and kissed her on the lips. "I saw that in a movie once and always wanted to kiss a woman like that."

China laughed. "A kiss is better in human form."

"Then we will do that again after we incarnate." He pulled her closer and their energy form flexed as it twisted into a helix of combusting colors.

After their combustions she said, "And that's better in Spirit form."

"•͵͵͵•*"*•☆•*"*•͵͵͵•*"*•☆

Jill sat nervously in the HR office. Looking around, she felt the drab paint and old furniture was a statement the hospital was making to medical addicts.

The walk to the office was a "walk of shame," through a maze of old underground tunnels. The office was far away from the newly renovated HR offices where new staff, residents, and physicians were greeted and recruited. Realizing her thoughts were triggering new fears, she repeated over and over in her head, *I love sobriety, I love sobriety.* Her legs were shaking when the inner office door opened. Dr. Ruane, the chief of Neurology, and Jill's HR representative called her into the small conference room. Jill noticed a pile of papers and a pen on the table as she entered.

"Dr. Buggy, you will sit here, on this side of the table, and Beth and I will be here," Dr. Ruane said. He pulled out a chair for Jill and sighed as if he was not looking forward to the meeting.

Dr. Ruane pulled the chair out for Beth, the HR representative who worked with all medical staff who had addiction problems. He sat down and looked at Jill. "Dr. Buggy, today is the last time you and I discuss your addiction issues. Beth has informed me you have completed your outpatient counseling, and your testing demonstrates you have been drug free since you entered rehab. Unlike the last time you returned to work, this time you will have a more structured and closely monitored return. I'm putting you in the resident schedule for coverage of the geriatric neurology ward. You'll work three twelve-hour shifts a week and will work like a resident, with attending oversight."

Jill made the slightest nod but said nothing.

Dr. Ruane looked at her over glasses that sat low on his nose. "For the next three months you will report to employee health forty minutes prior to your shift for drug testing. Once the testing is verified as clean, you will report to your job. Once a week your blood will go to the lab for the full panel of drug and alcohol testing." He pushed his glasses back up to the ridge of his nose. "Once you successfully complete the three months of monitoring, another meeting will be set up."

"Thank you," Jill murmured.

Dr. Ruane stood up. "I wish you success. I'll leave you with Beth to review the contract required for your reinstatement." With that, he left the small conference room.

Chapter 48

"Sadiki, thanks for calling me back. I'm glad to hear from you."

Bernard was excited and anxious at hearing his father's voice and was silent as he listened.

"No, I do not expect you to apologize," he said after listening to his father. "Mom taught me not to expect others to change for me. I need to accept people where they are." He made a face as he realized he sounded dumb reciting her words.

He listened some more and said, "Will you be in D.C. anytime soon? Great, that would be great. I want to meet up and get things back on track. When do you arrive?" He sat down on the sofa in his living room. "I can make that work on Thursday evening that week. I have a firm event that Saturday, so I need to be at work on Friday. Do you want me to pick you up at the airport?"

"No, I will take a cab," responded Sadiki. "I want to go to the hotel first and unpack so I am ready for my meetings. The diamonds need to be locked in a safe. I have some big sales that weekend in D.C. and Arlington. It will be one of my biggest sales ever."

"Where do you want to meet?" asked Bernard.

"I will send you a text message when I arrive. I will find a place close to the hotel."

"That will be great. I can meet you anytime that evening."

"Bernard, I only want to see you, not your friend."

"That's fine. It will only be me. I'll see you then."

They ended the call, and Bernard hung up the phone. He took a deep breath and leaned back into the sofa. He felt relieved he had set up the meeting but worried that his father might figure out his plan. He picked up his phone and sent a text message to Smith.

Mtg nxt thurs after 5pm DuPont Circle area. Place 2 come later.

A quick response came back: *OK*

Chapter 49

Angyo rolled over onto his side and opened his eyes. He took a deep breath and yawned before noticing Eleazar sitting in the corner chair. "Why are you here when I am sleeping?"

"I would prefer not to be here," Eleazar replied. "I was with China all night and would prefer to be there. Unfortunately, I got called back here and this is where I landed." He smiled at Angyo. "China makes my heart sing. Nothing personal but you do not. Besides, you snore."

Angyo pulled himself up into a sitting position. "So, Cupid has shot you with the arrow?" He smiled at his friend. "I expect to be invited to the wedding."

"Not so fast. I told her I want to see her after we are reincarnated into our bodies, and she did not reciprocate. I told her to take her time, that there was no pressure from me."

Angyo shook his head. "A man of the cloth wearing his heart on his sleeve."

They both laughed.

"This relationship is sanctioned by God," Eleazar said.

Angyo nodded. "All relationships are sanctioned by God."

Chapter 50

Bernard sat at the table in the Italian restaurant on Dupont Circle. He was moving his leg rapidly up and down. Once his father sent him the location he reserved the table closest to the window. He looked out the window and saw John Smith sitting in his car. Another investigator was sitting several tables away. Bernard was surprised when two of them showed up. It was obvious to him they were serious about getting the picture. It was another reminder to Bernard that he did not know the truth about Sadiki. As he looked around he realized the restaurant lights were dim. He felt concerned that the quickly approaching dusk might make it difficult to take a good picture.

Bernard did not see his father coming. Deep in thought, he was startled by his father's heavily accented voice. "How are you doing?" Sadiki pulled out the chair opposite Bernard and plopped down.

"Good, thanks for agreeing to meet with me," said Bernard. He tried to keep his voice even, but his leg continued to shake. "I know I just dropped it on you when we last talked. I really didn't know you and what your views were. I apologize for being insensitive to your feelings."

"I don't want your apology. You are a man in my eyes. You live your life as you like, and I will live my life as I like." His accent was not as smooth as Bernard remembered. He looked closely at his face, studying every line and wrinkle. The scar his mother told him about had faded over the years but was still there on his right cheek.

"Thanks for saying that," responded Bernard.

"I am not saying I accept it or like it. I will still see you as a man because you are my flesh and blood, and I refuse to have a fag for a son." He nodded to the waitress to get her attention. "A Glenlivet Scotch, a double, and I will need a second one in five minutes." He paused and then blurted out, "Bring them both at the same time."

The waitress looked at Bernard. "What can I get you?"

"I'll have a beer, what's on tap?"

After she recited her list, he ordered a Yuengling.

"Is this something you can get over?" asked Bernard

"I'm here aren't I? If I did not want to see you I would not come. Yes, it bothers me. It bothers me a lot. I never expected a son of mine to be a fag. That is unacceptable where I come from." His voice rose as he spoke.

"Where do you come from?"

"What do you mean? Your mother told you all about me. You told me you researched my tribe." His voice was gruff, and his dark eyes gave Bernard a piercing look.

"Yes, I did research your tribe. Perhaps I researched you. The son of the tribal chief died in 1972 at age nineteen. So where did you come from?" Bernard felt a nauseating feeling going through his stomach but could not hold back. He looked at Sadiki with contempt. "You lied to my mother, you lied to me. You may be my biological sperm donor, but you are not a man I can admire." Bernard's words were sharp and strained as he spoke.

Just as Bernard finished speaking the drinks arrived. Sadiki picked up his first drink and drank it down in one gulp. He picked up the second drink and swallowed hard and fast. "I'm done. Don't call me again." Sadiki jumped up from his chair and glared at Bernard. "I cannot have you in my life." He spun around, strode to the door, and left the restaurant. Bernard watched Sadiki walk in front of the window, his eyes straight ahead.

China moved to the table and sat down across from Bernard. He looked away and murmured, "I'm sorry, Mom, for doubting you. I was a jerk. Maybe a bigger one than Sadiki was to you."

She tilted her head to the right as she watched him drink his beer. "I don't need an apology. I love you regardless."

"I am so stupid."

China stood up and moved behind him and leaned over to kiss his head. "You are never stupid in my eyes." She knew he thought he was alone and could not feel, see, or hear her.

The investigator from across the room walked over. "We got it. It's already been sent to Homeland Security for facial recognition. Sorry it was so hard on you."

269

"Thanks, man, I'm the one who made it so hard. I wasn't intending to say anything like that, it just spilled out. Now I wish I could see my mother, but she's traveling and may be gone another year or so."

"Try calling her, you may reach her."

Bernard looked up at the man and nodded. "Yeah, you're right. I can leave a message at least."

"If she's like my mom, she loves getting the kissing emoji from me in text messages." Both men laughed. "Glad to see you smile. I gotta run."

"Thanks," Bernard said. "Have a great evening."

Just as the investigator was walking away the waitress appeared. "Are you ready to order?"

"No, just the bill. Thanks."

He sighed, and a feeling of relief washed over him. He knew he needed to fix things with his mother. Part of him knew she was always truthful, but he had wanted to get to know his father. He wanted to know who he was and what they had in common.

China leaned over him and embraced him as he sat at the table.

"Damn, that felt like you, Mom," Bernard whispered. "Squeeze me if that's you." He felt her arms tighten around him. And suddenly he knew it would be okay, that he and his mother would be okay. He felt the presence again and received another squeeze. He bowed his head and said a silent thanks to his mother for always being there for him.

"You're welcome," China whispered. "I love you with every drop of energy in my Soul." Her heart space expanded as she kissed his head. "I'm grateful I can still feel my connection with Bernard."

And then China was gone as quickly as she arrived.

When Bernard arrived home, he turned on the TV and grabbed a beer from the refrigerator. Settling into the couch, he turned up the volume on ZNN.

"This weekend the gay pride march will take over the National Mall. Crowds are expected to be the biggest of any gay pride march ever, and marches will occur across the country. Two hundred cities have approved licensed marches. In every city with a registered march, groups opposed to gay rights have been licensed to march on the same day."

Bernard swigged some beer from the bottle. He hoped the D.C. march would not be another Philadelphia, and he was glad his mother wouldn't be here for this one. After many years of witnessing and participating in marches, Bernard felt an uneasy feeling that he had never experienced before. He told himself to shake it off, to avoid negative thoughts. But he couldn't stop the thoughts from forming. In his mind's eye he saw a flash and saw people fall. He squeezed his eyes shut, trying to erase the thought. He refused to embrace thoughts of violence.

Bernard picked up his phone and sent a text to his partner, Sumi.

Will U B home soon?

He set down the phone and started to fidget. He picked up his phone again and dialed his mother. "Mom, this is Bernard, I am so sorry for ever doubting you. I love you and never stopped loving you. Sadiki lied to me and he lied to you so many years ago." His voice cracked and tears threatened to come. He took a breath and continued. "I was a jerk to you. I can't take it back, but I can say how sorry I am. And yes, I forgive myself." He chuckled. "I wish I could give you back the time I squandered from us. I wish I could hug you right now." His voice was shaky, and he quickly hung up.

Friday morning came quickly. He kissed Sumi before leaving the apartment. It was a beautiful fall day in D.C. He had a quick and pleasant walk to work.

"Good morning, Mr. Hope," his assistant said when he arrived at his office. "Mr. Smith called down to say he would like to see you. He said he just went for coffee and will be back in his office in a couple of minutes."

"Great," Bernard replied. He was stunned that Smith wanted to meet with him so soon and wondered what he'd learned so quickly. He dropped his brief bag on the floor next to his desk and sent Smith a text.

B in UR office in 5 mins.

He checked his voice messages, hoping for a message from his mother. There were none. Disappointed, he hoped she would respond when she heard his message.

Bernard left his office and turned into the stairwell. He took the steps two at a time to the sixth floor. He pushed the glass door open quickly with his full strength. "Sorry, Sue, I didn't mean to hit the door so hard." He shrugged his shoulders as he strode past.

"He's waiting for you," Sue replied, her voice trailing away as he closed the door behind him.

"Bernard, we hit pay dirt," said Smith as Bernard entered the office.

Bernard plopped down on a leather chair in front of Smith's desk. "Your old man's real name is "John Hunter or Stephan Briggate, Sean McDonald, or Charles Hope, and the list goes on.

"Charles Hope? That was my grandfather's name. He used my pops' name?" Bernard was surprised and disappointed.

"Facial recognition identified he has passports for at least seventeen identities from seventeen different countries. Even more interesting is that his traveling takes him around the world when there are major marches, protests, and political unrest. He was at the G20 in July and in Philadelphia in 2014 when the mayor was shot. He was in California when a congresswoman who supported equal rights for the LGBT population was shot. He was in Amsterdam when the world's most renowned surgeon for sex-change operations was murdered. He does all his traveling under different names."

Bernard felt an icy chill down his spine, as if a violent revolt was sweeping through his body "Are you saying Sadiki is a murderer?"

"Possibly a paid assassin," said Smith. "Homeland Security is digging through his bank records. He appears to have accounts around the world. He has one small account in the U.S., and you're the beneficiary. Germany has already notified us that he has multiple investment accounts there with deposits of over a million in several accounts. He has named a female as his beneficiary on one account, and there are other accounts in the millions with other beneficiaries. He has accounts in Amsterdam and many offshore accounts in various names."

Bernard felt his chest tighten. "Why is he here now? What's he planning to do while he's here?"

"Homeland Security is working on that. They plan to have him in a tight net while he's here. He's already under surveillance. They're concerned that his interest is the march this weekend."

Chapter 51

It was a few minutes after midnight, early Saturday morning, when Sadiki entered the stairway down the hall from his room at the Capitol Hill Hotel. He wore dark jeans, a leather bomber jacket, and a full backpack over his left shoulder. He was carrying a long leather case that resembled a musician's instrument case. As he entered the lobby he glanced around at a small scattering of people. Moving toward the front door, he stopped and turned to his left. There was a man in a cheap suit and black boots sitting in the lounge area. He seemed out of place to Sadiki. Sadiki turned back to scan the street and saw several vehicles parked and idling outside the hotel. The dark SUVs reminded him of undercover operations. He thought they might be out to minimize riots or problems as protesters and counter-protesters arrived, but his uneasy feeling remained.

Sadiki turned around and headed back to the stairway. Instead of going up he went down another flight. He came to a locked door at the basement entrance. He climbed the stairs back up to the lobby, turned left, and made his way through the hallway, looking for another exit. As he turned into a side hallway he saw an emergency exit. He pushed open the door and saw two men talking in the far corner of the lot. There were no vehicles idling. Feeling better, he moved quietly out the back of the parking lot.

One of the men from the parking lot said, "He just left the back of the parking lot."

As Sadiki turned toward the street he wanted, he spotted a young couple, a man and woman, meandering down the street. They appeared to be drunk and often stopped to kiss and grope each other. Sadiki crossed the street to the side that was darker and more isolated. The woman grabbed her friend, and as they embraced she said, "Jim, he is on a direct path to you."

A homeless man sitting in the dark entryway of a storefront startled Sadiki as he walked by. "Damn it, you piece of shit," Sadiki muttered under his breath. He picked up his pace.

After a moment, the homeless man got up and followed Sadiki from a distance. "He's still moving straight. Anyone else have a visual? It'll be suspicious if I try to keep up."

"We have him on the street cameras, but he's about to enter a blind spot." He heard the voice through his earpiece. "If he doesn't reappear on the cameras, then we have a perimeter where he's setting up his nest."

"Fuck, we'll be losing time, why was no one in the blind spot?" asked Jim.

"We had a tight net out front. Several agents are on their way to the area where he is."

Jim, feeling agitated, barked, "Anyone see him? I have no visual." Just as he finished speaking, Jim felt someone coming up behind him. He started to turn when he saw the flash of a silver gun pointed at his head. A silencer muffled the sound. Jim gurgled and moaned as he fell to the street.

"Jim, Tom is now in the blind spot. Where are you?" asked the voice on the other end of the line. "Jim, Jim, Tom is looking for him, do you have any visual?"

Chapter 52

Marchers and protesters arrived in Washington, D.C., several days early and set up camps along the march route the night prior. The D.C. LGBT march was expected to attract the biggest number of supporters ever. Two years into the new government, the frustration of the LGBT community was boiling over as the president dismantled LGBT rights. Early in the summer, the president wrote an executive order that banned transgender individuals from serving in the military. Pentagon and military leaders were surprised, as over 6,000 transgender services personnel were already serving throughout all military branches. While some political supporters cheered, others were bubbling over with frustration.

Bernard's condo sat in the Capitol neighborhood. He was just a walk away from Capitol Hill and Chinatown. He walked out to his balcony with a cup of strong coffee to see crowds gathering along the route. He often sat on the balcony to watch the day dawn; it was the one pleasure he still shared with his mother. Capitol Hill awoke to the activity of the steady stream of marchers and counter-protesters as they filled the streets around the Capitol.

China sat at Bernard's kitchen peninsula as she watched him on the balcony.

The door of the bedroom opened, and a young man in his early thirties emerged. He poured a cup of coffee before joining Bernard on the balcony. He stood next to Bernard and said, "Good morning, honey," before leaning down to kiss him.

Bernard smiled at his lover. "Good morning, Sumi." They clinked coffee mugs, and Sumi sat down in the chair next to Bernard.

"Does it look like a good turnout?" asked Sumi as he looked out over the balcony.

"It's already passed the numbers of the inaugural crowd."

They both broke into a laugh. Sumi settled into his chair and reached out to take Bernard's hand. "Do you want to leave soon to join the marchers, or do you want to watch from here?"

"My firm rented a place on the Capitol balcony. We should head out around nine. I want a good spot on the balcony." Bernard bent over his chair and kissed Sumi on the lips. "The speeches start around one. My firm is catering the event, so it will be a private firm party."

Sumi's build was much smaller than Bernard's. His height barely reached 5'10" and compared to Bernard's 6'3" Sumi seemed small. His thin lankiness was in contrast to Bernard's broad and well-nourished physique. Their coloring was different, Bernard with a darker completion and Sumi with a soft charcoal grey. They had met at an LGBT march in Boston five years earlier.

"I hate that we're celebrating our anniversary on the day of the march," Sumi said. "You're too distracted to make this day feel special. Let's make a plan to go away next weekend to celebrate."

Bernard looked at Sumi and nodded in agreement. "I know my work has been hard on you."

"No, it's not your job that's hard on me. It's your overzealousness that bothers me. It's all you think, say, and do. We haven't had any other conversation in the past year. You don't even ask me how my day was. It's felt like the day I moved in you forgot who I was." He paused and turned away before turning back with an angry look. "I left my life in Boston, my family, friends, and I sold my business for us." He turned away from Bernard. "Some days I feel like if I go back to Boston you wouldn't even notice." Sumi's eyes filled.

"Oh my, you're right," Bernard said. "I'll plan a long weekend for us to go away." Bernard stood up and felt a stiffness go through his back as he walked into the living room from the balcony. All he could think of was his mother and the betrayal of his father.

˙˙•.,,,.•*˙˙*•☆•*˙˙*•.,,,.•*˙˙*•☆

The streets of Washington, D.C., overflowed with marchers and anti-LGBT protesters. People were packed like sardines, shoulder to shoulder with little room to break away from the crowds. Bernard and Sumi went out the back door of their building, hoping to avoid the mobs. The side streets were crowded, yet there was room to navigate through the mass of people. Bernard and Sumi wove through the crowds and around groups until they approached the Mall area. Police, civil liberty police, and the Capitol Police were everywhere. Service dogs were on site with their handlers, looking for bombs.

When they entered the National Mall, they were greeted with angry chants from the anti-gay groups. Bernard grabbed Sumi's hand to keep him close to his side. The crowds were so dense the men had to move forward with the crowd. Bernard strained to see over the sea of people. He searched to catch a glimpse of the Capitol building. It was much closer than he had realized. The two men pushed their way to their right, away from the center of the crowd. As they entered the fringe of marchers, they quickly moved to the Capitol steps.

Security was heavy in the Capitol building. Visitors dumped out their backpacks, handed over their phones, and walked through X-ray machines after taking off their shoes. Bernard and Sumi finally arrived at the balcony with a sigh of relief.

"That was a drag," said Sumi as he felt the weight of the political climate and a nagging feeling of dread.

The law firm was the first openly gay practice with a prominent position in Washington, D.C. They had offices in three other cities, New York, Philadelphia, and Boston. At the D.C. headquarters, three out of the five partners were gay and continued to push the gay agenda to Congress and the White House. The challenge with the new president and the alt-right administration was a catalyst that pushed the firm to declare itself an openly gay firm. They embraced the role of the unifying voice and legal counsel for the LGBT movement. The founding partner was slated to give the opening speech at the rally.

"I just don't get this thing you have for putting us in risky situations," said Sumi.

"What are you talking about? This is the safest place at the march," Bernard replied. "You have the Capitol Police monitoring everyone who comes in. There are security details all over, and the firm hired a security company and has twenty-eight guards to protect this balcony and make sure we're safe walking around the event. We met at a march! And now you're afraid to be seen at the largest march of our lifetime?"

"I'm sorry, Bernard, I just feel so vulnerable and hated. When we met, the political climate was moving our rights forward, but now this administration is doing everything to strip us of our rights. It feels very different to me."

Bernard turned from Sumi, shaking his head in disbelief. "Everything I'm doing isn't good enough for you. Who I am is not what you want. The things important to me are not important to you. How did we get this far in our relationship if we're such as mismatch?"

"You I want," Sumi replied. "I just feel unsafe at all these marches. You remember your mother's injury in Philadelphia and the mayor's assassination, and they never found the shooter. The pro-LGBT congresswoman was shot. That doesn't feel safe to me. Some nut could be in a high-rise in the area and you or I might be in the crosshairs."

Bernard felt a sickening feeling run through him. He looked around, wondering if his father was in one of the many building that had a clear view of the National Mall. "You and I are not the kind of activists the assassin has been targeting. We're not high profile. Right now, I have a lot on my mind. We can talk more later." Bernard turned from Sumi and went to grab a beer.

China watched her son and Sumi as they spoke about the event and their relationship. She looked out over the city to see the high rises that had a full view of the Capitol and the balcony where the boys stood. She caught a glimpse of a flicker and said, "Spirit, reveal to me the truth of what you want me to see."

As she honed her focus on the spot that flickered, she saw through the walls a man with a gun. She recognized Sadiki instantly as he moved through the room. Her energy shifted to the room where he was setting up his high-powered rifle. She looked around the room and saw it was a vacant apartment. Again, she shifted her energy and stood next to him. China stood motionless watching him until she felt inspired to act. She placed one hand on his heart and the other over his neck. She squeezed hard and let the energy flow fast and furious as she watched Sadiki fall onto his side. She moved with him and continued the energy infusion, feeling no concern for his safety.

"This will help you and possibly save my son," China said. "With this infusion, I call upon your Angels and the Divine to flow through you to open your heart to make a free will decision that supports life and limits destruction." She watched his body twist and turn under the force of the energy infusion. As the energy slowed, she watched him settle into a restful state.

She heard Eleazar's voice before she saw him.

"Your mother's love is coming through as the love of a fierce lioness. He will still require another infusion within the last few moments of life here on earth for his Soul's expansion."

China let go of Sadiki's heart and neck and looked up at Eleazar. "So, what brings you here today?"

He laughed. "Spirit sent me. We need to get back to the balcony, we have some work to do. Homeland Security and the FBI have entered this building. They will find Sadiki after he enters the stairwell. We must go now and come back within those last few moments."

China offered her hand for Eleazar to help her stand up. She looked back at Sadiki and saw him squirming on the floor. "He'll recover soon," she said. "We better move."

Eleazar and China's energy shifted back to the balcony. China moved to Bernard and placed her hand on his heart and one on his neck, and this time the energy moved in a more loving and controlled manner.

"Spirit, I surrender to you my service in helping Bernard for his Soul's expansion. I am grateful to give an ultimate gift of love and devotion a human mother and Divine Soul could give." For the first time since she extricated she felt a welling of tears in her spiritual eyes. As she looked at Bernard her heart swelled with pride and love as the energy flowed. Her heart within her energy mass swelled and pulsated loudly within her.

China looked over to see Eleazar infusing Sumi, and then quickly moved to the law partners who were present. Eleazar moved from one person to another on the balcony.

"Bernard's infusion is done, are you going to let go?" asked Eleazar.

"No, I want to feel him as long as I can. His energy will soon leave, and I'll return to human form without him." She looked up at Eleazar with her eyes focused and enlarged.

It felt like just a second to China from her moment with Sadiki to her time with Bernard when she heard the shot. She watched the bullet fly past her to one of the firm's partners. Before it landed a second shot was fired and it traveled through her energy into Bernard. With her hand on his heart she refused to let go. "It's okay, Bernard, you are free to go back to God." She did not let go as she felt the energy from within vacate his human form.

Sumi reacted instantly, screaming at the first shot and rushing toward Bernard when the second shot was fired. A pair of security guards grabbed him and dragged him inside the Capitol building. He was screaming and kicking as they dragged him backwards by the armpits. He watched as Bernard fell. He felt frozen in time as Bernard's body moved slowly through space.

China dropped to her knees as Bernard fell. Kneeling at his side, with his head in her arms, she watched his spirit leave his form. Looking up at his energy she said, "You are free to go. Nothing can hold you from your place with God." His spirit completed its extrication and hovered over her and in a monotone voice, it said, "I picked you as my mother to help me recover my Soul."

He moved to the right and then flashed from the physical dimension to another plane, out of her sight and her field of knowing.

China continued to kneel by her son when she felt a hand gently wiping her tears from her eyes. Looking up, she saw the radiant light and love of the Blessed Mother. The Queen of Heaven leaned down and kissed China on the head. China felt the love flow into her energy form. She looked at the Blessed Mother and received a strong acknowledgement that Bernard was back with God. China looked back at Bernard's empty body and gently laid his head down. She bent over and kissed his forehead and then stood up and embraced the Divine Mother.

Mary spoke gently, "The loss of one parent's child is a loss for all parents."

The embrace was comforting to China, and Mary's energy was the brightest white light China had ever seen. China released her embrace and watched as the Blessed Mother dissipated. It took several more seconds before China felt a hand on her shoulder.

"He is gone now, you have safely delivered him to the Divine," said Eleazar. "We have other work to do."

She looked up at him, and he took her hand and pulled her tight to him. Within seconds their energy started to fuse. A snapping and crackling of energy ignited into a colorful hue of combustion as their helixes formed into a bright rainbow of light.

Sumi's last vision of Bernard was his body sprawled on the ground. Inside the room off the balcony, the participants were weeping and screaming. Gunshots punctuated their cries of anguish.

The crowd below was in turmoil as marchers tried to run. More shots rang out. Men and women fell to the ground as people pushed and shoved and collided, seeking safety.

On the stage, a man shouted into a microphone, "Please don't push, the police are—." A gunshot cracked, and the speaker clutched his chest and fell backward. The microphone stand spun and teetered and clattered to the stage.

The shots continued. The fleeing crowd became a stampede. More people fell, some wounded. Shrieks and cries rent the air. Sirens sounded in the near distance.

Eleazar held China's helix to his with no intention of letting go. As they looked out over the balcony a large black mass rolled in over the crowd, Dark Souls looking for a carcass to take over.

"No," said China as she stared ahead. "Archangel Michael and all Archangels, protect these human vessels from the wrath of darkness as they lay empty on the earth's floor."

The Divine presence of Archangel Michael, Archangel Faith, and all the Archangels appeared. Each ten feet tall, they loomed over the desperate scene.

Chapter 53

Angyo felt relief as he got off the plane in Bhutan. He was grateful the airport was so much smaller than Rome's international airport. The narrow airplane seat had left him stiff and uneasy, just as he felt on the flight out. As he exited the baggage claim he saw Banko standing by a cab. Angyo raised his hand and yelled, "Banko, right here." Banko was looking at his phone when Angyo called to him.

Banko looked up from his phone and saw Angyo. "Hurry, we need to get to the monastery right away," he said.

"What is going on?" Angyo asked.

Banko opened the door of the cab, and Angyo got in. He slid over, and Banko joined him.

"An alert just came across our God Project Twitter account," Banko said, as the cab pulled away and headed to the monastery. Banko's phone chirped and he pulled up the message:

Godproject@twitter-United States needs prayers as LGBT march is under siege in D.C. by sniper. Many killed from gunshots and others trampled. White Souls and Archangels working the area.

Angyo turned on his phone after he returned to the monastery. He looked at the same messages that Banko had read in the car. Saddened by the news, he prepared to pray in the prayer garden.

Chapter 54

Eleazar and China shifted into the stairwell. They hurried down the steps on Sadiki's heels. Several flights down they heard a door open. Sadiki stopped to listen. They heard footsteps coming up. The sound of many feet moving in unison echoed in the stairwell. Sadiki moved along the wall to the next doorway. He opened it quietly, peeked out, and slipped into a hallway. Eleazar and China followed him.

Gunshots rang out, fired from a doorway across from the stairs. Sadiki was hit several times. China grabbed him by the neck and heart before his body hit the ground. "No, you can't be gone already," she screamed as she felt his vacant heart and empty carcass. Spinning around she saw his energy floating on the left. "No, you can't be."

Eleazar moved quickly and reached up to grab Sadiki's Soul. They heard Sadiki laugh.

"Not today, tell your God not today." They watched Sadiki's energy cloud move to their left. "You may have saved Bernard's soul from my army, but you can't have me." As his dark energy shifted from their sight, they heard his final words: "I will be back for you, China."

˙˙•˳˵˵˙•*˙˙*•☆•*˙˙*•˳˵˵˙•*˙˙*•☆

Sadiki's energy shifted to a street corner in Paris. He scanned the area and saw a young woman jogging over a bridge. As the jogger approached the street, a car came speeding over the bridge from behind her. The driver hit the brakes hard, and the car swung out of control before hitting the jogger. The young woman's body was in mid-air when Sadiki saw her Soul extricate and shift to the right and into a new dimension. Sadiki moved quickly and jumped into the body as it lay lifeless in the street.

Chapter 55

Dr. Buggy walked into a patient's room after being called. "What's going on?" she asked the nurse, Julie Sykes, standing by the bed.

"Mr. Ashford came in from a nursing home yesterday with a UTI (urinary tract infection)," Julie reported. "He's been unresponsive to voice and painful stimuli for the last seven years. Several minutes ago, I took his blood pressure, and when the cuff tightened he grimaced like it hurt."

Dr. Jill walked to Mr. Ashford's bedside. "Mr. Ashford, Glenn, can you hear me?" She picked up his hand and put two fingers in his palm. "If you can hear me, try to squeeze my fingers in your left hand. Can you feel my fingers in your hand?" She watched his hand. Nothing happened. She looked at his face and said, "Mr. Ashford, can you hear me?" His face seemed lifeless, but she noticed his eyes appeared to be moving under his eyelids. "It seems he has some eye movements behind his lids."

Julie leaned over the bed to look. "Oh my gosh, you're right!"

Jill used the instant hand wash before putting on rubber gloves. She looked down at the patient. "Mr. Ashford, I'm going to examine your eyes. You'll feel the pressure from my fingers as I open your eyelids." She gently placed her thumb and index finger over and under his eye and used her middle finger to lift his eyelid. With her left hand she shined her flashlight into his eye. His pupil reacted quickly. When she removed the light, the pupil expanded to a very large size. When she shined the light into his pupil again, it quickly constricted. She shut off the light and watched the pupil expand. Suddenly, she was startled—an inner eye was looking back. "Mr. Ashford, I see you're looking at me." She released his eye and repeated the exam on the opposite eye. "Mr. Ashford, rest now. I'll be back to examine you again later today."

Jill looked at Julie. "Good pickup, something positive is happening. Let's review his records, and if we have old scans it may give us some idea what's occurring." Jill smiled at Julie as they left the room.

They went to the medical station, and Jill reviewed the records. The nursing home transfer note identified Mr. Ashford as a transfer from a medical center in Virginia seven years prior after a stroke that required intubation. He was 68 at the time of his stroke, and his brain waves were so diminished that he was taken off life support. But after three days his body continued to function. His daughter requested the transfer to a Philadelphia nursing facility, so she could be close to her father. This was his second UTI since his stroke.

Jill called the Virginia medical center that did the original workup and asked for the radiology records department. The office manager came on the line, and Jill identified herself. She explained that the condition of a former patient of theirs had changed, and she was trying to discover why. She requested that the center send her the results of any brain scans, CT scans, MRIs, or PETSCANS done during his workup and prior to his transfer. The office manager told Jill to fax the required signed permission forms and promised to send digital versions of Mr. Ashford's scan results. When Jill asked if they could send the information that day, the manager said she would.

Jill hung up and turned to Julie. "We should have the scans within an hour of faxing the request and permission documents. Can you pull everything together and ask the unit secretary to get these faxed as soon as possible?"

Julie smiled. "Yeah, glad to do it."

"Thanks," Jill said as she smiled back at Julie. She stood up. "I'm going to re-examine Mr. Ashford."

Jill entered Mr. Ashford's room and felt a welcoming warmth. "Mr. Ashford, can you hear me?" She saw his eyes moving behind his eyelids in response to her voice. She approached the bed and put two fingers on his palm. "Can you feel my fingers in your hand? Try to squeeze my fingers if you can." She applied pressure to his palm and noticed his fingers start to move in a claw-like motion. "Good, Mr. Ashford, I saw you move your fingers. This time I won't touch your palm, but I want you to try to squeeze my fingers resting in your hand."

A minute later Jill saw movement in his fingers, as if he was trying to close them around her fingers. "Very good, Mr. Ashford. Can you open your eyes?" He continued to move his eyes under his closed lids. "I see your eyes moving. Try to open your eyelids." The muscles around his eyes twitched, and then his eyebrows slowly rose as the twitching continued. "I can see you're trying to open your eyelids. If I open them for you, let's see if you can keep them open."

Jill leaned over the bed and placed her thumb and index finger from each hand on each of his eyes. "I'm going to count one, two, three, open." With her middle finger she opened his eyelids. His pupils responded to the light in the room. She felt his eyes looking back at her. "Great, I know you see me, so I'm going to let go of your eyelids. Do your best to keep them open."

She released his eyelids and started a silent count. As she reached twenty seconds, the lids slowly closed. "That was excellent, Mr. Ashford. Some of your cognition is returning, so I'm going to order a scan to check what's occurring within your brain. Perhaps these past few years your brain has been healing. I'll call your daughter to tell her about the changes in your condition. Oh, the infection is improving as well. You'll need a few more days of I.V. antibiotics."

Jill returned to the unit work desk where the Julie continued to pull together the needed documents. Jill sat down and said, "He's showing more responsiveness and was able to hold his eyes open for twenty seconds. Something good is occurring here. I'm going to call his daughter."

Sumi sat stunned on the sofa of the apartment. Several members of the firm were with him while they waited for his parents to arrive from Boston. One handed him a glass of wine. "Sumi, here, drink some more wine. You'll feel better." He looked at the firm's partner with eyes that showed the shock and horror of the day. As he was about to sip the wine, he saw a TV reporter flash to the D.C. march. Turning up the volume he heard the reporter say, "This morning's march was interrupted by gunshots that killed seven people and created a stampede that killed eleven more. FBI and Homeland Security have reported they shot and killed the shooter in a Capitol Hill apartment building. An unknown source said the man killed was under surveillance for the past two days as a possible threat to the march. It is believed he lost his surveillance team early this morning. Homeland Security is leading the investigation and will have a news briefing at eight o'clock this evening."

Sumi started to cry. "How could he have done that if they were watching him?"

"•.,,,.•*"*•☆•*"*•.,,,.•*"*•☆

Within a few hours Jill had Mr. Ashford's initial scans and medical records. He'd had a grade III bleed in his right temporal area. At admission, he was unconscious and unresponsive, and his cerebral spinal fluid level was elevated. He had been quickly intubated in the ER. Several days later his EEGs showed very slow brain waves. The decision was made to take him off the ventilator. Much to everyone's surprise, Mr. Ashford continued to breath on his own.

During her afternoon rounds, Dr. Buggy stopped in see Mr. Ashford. As she entered his room she saw his eyes were open. She moved to the side of his bed and smiled as he stared directly at her. She picked up his hand and placed her fingers in his palm. "Good afternoon. Can you squeeze your hand for me?"

Mr. Ashford sighed a heavy breath, and his eyes moved to look at his hand.

"Just move it for me, make a finger wiggle or any movement," Jill said.

He stared intently at his hand. It jerked slightly, and he slowly curled his fingers.

"I am speaking to you," Jill said. "Can you say anything to me?"

Mr. Ashford's eyes moved as if to see his face. He released his stare and his eyebrows moved slightly. His jaw started to move in a sideways motion without a sound coming out.

Jill smiled. "You're doing better. It should get easier for you as your brain wakes up more. You'll get some brain scans today to see how well you've been healing. I'll be back later today."

Jill turned to the sink and started the water to wash her hands. She felt great gratitude move through her. She nodded and thought, *Yes, God, there is a miracle happening here. I feel it inside me, you have blessed this man.*

Jill dried her hands and left the room. After a few steps she felt a flood of emotions come over her. "Thank you, God," she whispered. She leaned into the wall for support. "Thank you for my third chance to be a better person, a better doctor. You have blessed me." She felt a tear slide down her cheek. She took a deep breath and dabbed the tear away.

On her way to the charting station, Jill noticed staff members standing in an unoccupied room. She stopped at the doorway and saw two nurses hugging each other and others standing still with their heads up staring at the TV. "What's going on?" she asked.

She entered the room and looked at the TV. The crawl at the bottom of the newscast said, "Shooting on Capitol Hill, many dead, more information to come." The soundless video was a wide-angle view from a distance, which showed people running, some falling, the crowd in chaos.

With a paralyzing fear she said, "Bernard, please be safe. God keep him safe. China, where are you?"

˙˙•.,,,.•*˙˙*•☆•*˙˙*•.,,,.•*˙˙*•☆

As soon as Jill got home she turned on a news station. She watched a news conference about the shootings in the capital, but the names of those killed or injured still had not been released. She closed her eyes and prayed, *Please keep Bernard safe.*

Early the next morning Jill stopped in to see Mr. Ashford. During the night he started speaking. Simple words and short sentences. Jill entered his room and went first to the sink to wash her hands. As she turned toward him she saw him smiling at her. In a raspy voice he said, "Good to see you, doc."

"Wow, you're recovering faster than I thought you would," she responded. "Do you know where you are?"

"In this time, space, and dimension called earth," he replied in a matter-of-fact way.

Jill felt a quiver of surprise at the unusual response. "You're in the hospital. How are you feeling?"

"Still getting used to being back in my body."

"Where were you before you were back in your body?" she asked, recognizing that his orientation had not fully returned.

"I was working for God. I have been very busy these past eight years." He smiled and added, "I still need more time to settle into my old self. I'm feeling very tired."

"I'll give you time to rest. When you're stronger we can talk more." She left his room and thought, *God, somehow, I believe he has been working with you for these past eight years. Is China working for you right now?*

Jill felt an instant confirmation move through her. *Okay, got it. You are talking to me, aren't you?* Again, she felt the confirmation emerge from within her heart. "Thank you!" she said out loud.

The day after the march, the media published the names and pictures of the victims. Jill felt paralyzed as she watched the TV in her living room. She stared at Bernard's picture and felt her mind freeze, without any thoughts. It was as if she were under a spell. And then it ended.

"God, why, why?" Jill murmured. "Does China know?" Jill started to cry, a soft weeping for Bernard and China.

Chapter 55

> Angyo@Godproject.twitter
>
> Extricated Souls are returning home.

It was a cold and snowy day in the mountains. The snow was heavy on his feet as Angyo walked to the extrication labs. It was one week since the last Twitter message arrived as labs reported a small number of Souls returning. Entering the lab, he felt drawn into the activity of the staff. Some staff members ran from computer stations to the viewing windows, and others stood watching the Soul on return.

Angyo walked to a window where several scientists stood, and he saw the angelic beings working with a returned Soul. Two energies were infusing and preparing the human body for the Soul's incarnation. Two other energies were attending to the Soul. He watched in awe as the Angels cleansed the etheric aura with a beautiful, glistening liquid. The bright sparkling liquid showered down in a white flowing light over the Soul's energy. He saw the aura's transformation from a yellow-grey hue to a beautiful effervescent sparkling white light. Angyo was mesmerized by the beauty of the cleansed aura. The pure white light held his attention. Watching the transformation, he felt his heart swelling with Divine Love. He walked from window to window and watched the cleansing process. The first to return were ready to incarnate.

Angyo turned to Sam. "Is everything ready for the incarnation?"

"Yes, we have one already in his body," Sam replied. "Over the next twenty-four hours the body will be weaned off the etheric energy. It's a slower process to incarnate than it was to extricate. The body will continue with good support until the human consciousness and mind's activity are increased enough to awake. I'm told it may take from twenty-four to forty-eight hours, as it did in Rome."

"How many have returned so far?"

"We have seven Souls back so far."

Chapter 56

China and Eleazar sat on a cluster of large rocks overlooking the ocean as they watched the waves breaking over the rocks below. The sandy white beach was warm from the sun.

"I always wanted to vacation here," China said.

"I never imagined a vacation, so this is a gift," Eleazar replied.

"Do you feel you missed out on anything, living such an isolated, celebate life?" She smiled at the thought of their unifying combustion.

"No, it is all happening as it was meant to. I trust all will occur in its right time." He looked at her and smiled. "This moment is the right time."

"Do you wonder if we will be together after we incarnate? Will we remember this time? Will we feel the same?" she asked. "I wonder if our bodies in a coma can comprehend what we've been doing? Will we remember?" She closed her eyes and took a deep breath. "I don't want to forget this time of service and my time with you."

There was silence between them for a while, and then she asked him, "Do you remember everything you've done? I don't. It feels like I'm only in the moment of now. Was there anything before this? I believe so, because I still feel a connection to a young girl shot by the Taliban, I feel a connection to Bernard, and to many others I served." She raised her hands and turned her palms up in question. "I know there's something to these memories, but will they come back, or will they be lost? Today I still remember Bernard's transition, but it feels like it's fading. Will I remember when I return? I don't want to lose the memory that I was with him."

"It is as you say," Eleazar replied. "Choose to remember and it is yours to keep. What you remember and what you do with that memory is of free will."

As she looked out to sea, off the coast of Costa Rica, she saw the fierceness of the waves forming as clouds moved in. "Do you swim?" she asked him.

"No, I have never swum in my life." He smiled a nervous smile.

"I love the feeling of the water beating on my molecules. It's a reminder of who I am." She stood on the rock and slowly walked to the edge. She raised her arms and looked to the sky as she said loudly, "I am born of Spirit, I live in Spirit, I am Spirit in manifest, and with this knowing I unify my Divine essence with the Spirit of the living water."

She dropped her arms, sprinted forward, and leaped through the air. She arched her body into a forward dive and plunged toward the water that surrounded the rocks.

Eleazar jumped up and rushed to the cliff's edge. Looking out over the rocks he saw a beautiful pattern of sparkling colors dispersed in the water. The colors slowly reunited into a thickness and then into a form. She popped up from beneath and laughed as she looked up at him. "Will you join me?" she called.

"I don't know how to swim," he called back.

"Go down to the beach and walk in. You need to learn how to hold your energy together in the water. It's more than seeing yourself in form since the waves have a pressure to them. It's best to learn gradually."

Eleazar jumped off the rocks and landed on the sand. He stood in the water, imagined his feet in human form, and watched the water roll in and out over his feet.

"Now move into the water until it's up to your knees," said China, who was floating on her back.

Eleazar took a tentative step into the water, and then another and another, until he was submerged to his knees and waves were breaking around him. "I can feel the force of the waves against my energy."

"That's good, let yourself get use to the feeling. Keep the image of your feet as you knew them in human form, and they'll stay intact. When you feel ready, walk farther into the water, then stop and imagine your human body in the water. As long as you can see yourself standing in the water, your energy particles will stay together." She arched her body and dove deep into the water. When she resurfaced she called to him, "Now come out until you're in up to your chest."

Feeling more confident, he moved further in and watched as a large wave rolled toward him. "I got this one coming in."

China turned around to see the wave and then turned back to Eleazar. "You need to see yourself standing as it breaks around you."

The wave hit Eleazar and took him into the beach.

"Just pull yourself together," China said before diving below the surface.

"Hey, don't leave me now." Eleazar laughed as he scanned the surface, waiting for her to reemerge. Suddenly she broke the water and flew into the air. She bent at the waist, straightened her legs, and dived again, disappearing below the surface.

Eleazar watched her long, thin body sprout scales, fins, and a long flowing tail as she moved through the water. "How did you do that?" he asked.

She resurfaced. "I can be anything I imagine myself to be. As a little girl, I always dreamed of being a mermaid. Now I can be one. You can be anything you want."

Eleazar broke into a hearty laugh. "I never dreamed of being anything other than a priest. Now I am a Soul who looks forward to being an artist and musician when we return. And perhaps the man in your life you love to be with. Those are all new for me."

Looking up at him from the water she smiled. "I would like that, Eleazar. Perhaps we can come back here when we return to our bodies. I always wanted to live somewhere tropical. Winters in Philadelphia can be trying."

"You would give up your home and life in Philadelphia for me?"

She paused and looked at him with longing. "Yes and no. I'm not giving up any life, I want to expand my life. Philadelphia will always be a part of my life. It will take a different place in my existence and my heart. I want my life to focus on my relationship with Spirit and then my relationship with you. I have no desire to be your total focus or you mine. I am honored to stand and support you with your relationship with God."

"And I will do the same for you." Eleazar walked further into the water and then jumped and dived beneath the surface to where she was swimming. The afternoon was sunny, and the light flickered off their energy as a fluctuating rainbow of colors beneath the water surface. He grabbed her mermaid tail and they swam together through the crystal blue water. A school of dolphins swam up to them and surrounded them. Some of the dolphins broke the surface of the water in high jumps. Eleazar imagined himself as a dolphin. As the image appeared in his consciousness, his body morphed into the shape and substance of the majestic creatures.

The pod changed direction and swam toward the surface. China looked around and didn't see Eleazar, only the dolphins around her. One large dolphin approached and swam close to her side. She swam at the same pace as the dolphin, her tail powerful and her energy fast. The first line of dolphins breached the surface and flew effortlessly into the air. China was in the fourth line and breached the surface as a mermaid. The large dolphin on her side breached next to her. As they reentered the water she caught sight of the large dolphin morphing, particles of energy dispersing as it splashed down on the surface.

Eleazar's form returned as he flapped his arms and legs wildly, attempting to gain control. China swam out of the pod and moved toward him. The dolphins reentered the water all around them. As Eleazar was regaining control of his energy form, a dolphin swam into him, and his energy molecules burst apart into a million little sparkling lights. China laughed. As Eleazar pulled his energy together, another dolphin entered the water where he was struggling, and his energy exploded again into millions of particles of sparkling colors.

China stayed close to Eleazar, waiting for the dolphins to finish their jumping. They swam fast and Eleazar was left in the turbulent waters. As the water calmed, Eleazar gained control of his energy particles and pulled them back in to his energy form. Once he was back together, they laughed and held hands. They left the water and reappeared back on the rocks.

"Are you all right?" asked China.

Eleazar laughed. "I felt a little disorganized for a bit."

They lay back on the rocks and held each other.

Chapter 57

Every day Angyo checked into the lab to find more and more Souls returning. He welcomed each one back as they awoke, celebrated their return with a feast and wine before they left the monastery. Some took up residence in the village below, and others chose to return to their country of origin and religious faith.

On every visit to the lab, Angyo walked to Eleazar's cubicle to find no change in Angelic activity. One day he found himself staring at the cubicle, musing. *First to go, maybe last to return*, he thought to himself.

Angyo left Eleazar's cubicle and walked down the hall to check on China Hope's cubicle, but there was no sign of her return. *Hmmm, maybe they ran off together in the Spiritual realm of bliss*, he thought. At that moment an angelic being formed on the other side of the glass of China's cubicle. The being's vibrations solidified as a neutral voice intoned, "They will be back."

Angyo broke into laughter. "Could I have been talking to you all this time?"

"It depends on how well you are aligned with the Divine Energy. Not everybody can hear and see energies at the same time. There are some that feel, hear, and see. They are the ones that extricated, wise old Souls, White Souls."

As the winter progressed and signs of spring appeared in the Paro Valley Monastery, Angyo continued to look for the return of Eleazar and China. The monastery had three White Souls who chose to return to Source instead of incarnating back into their bodies. He often wondered if China and Eleazar would choose to stay with Source.

One day in late winter, Angyo walked through the physics lab and noted the many empty cubicles with lifeless incubators. Only half of the lab's incubators were supporting the physical forms of the extricated Souls. The angelic beings continued to infuse the bodies of Eleazar and China.

"Hi, Angyo."

Angyo turned to see Sam looking up at him from his computer screen. "Hello, Sam."

"No, they haven't returned," Sam said. "I know you're disappointed. It's been about a week since the last Soul arrived. We're at half capacity."

"I must trust this is all a part of the Divine Universe's plan," Angyo said. "The statistics show that many extrication sites are at half capacity."

Sam nodded. "This morning one of the news channels said that hospitals and nursing homes are reporting that patients who have been in comas for as long as ten years are waking up. Many are recovering quickly without complications. They interviewed a doctor at a military hospital in France who had a soldier injured by an IED and left in a coma with little brain function twelve years ago. They took him off life support less than a month after his injury, and he didn't die. He woke up last week. He's progressing well and regaining his cognitive and physical capacities."

"Remarkable," Angyo said.

"A jogger in Paris, a woman, was hit by a car and in a coma for the past year. Now she's awake, and her physical and cognitive skills are returning. They're calling it a miracle. There are also other reports of these miraculous recoveries after years of support on a ventilator. Some people are breathing on their own but not conscious. They're awakening and recovering in a way that mystifies the medical community."

"What a blessing," Angyo said. "If they are reincarnating, there must be a shift in the Divine plan, or we are entering the phase where earth and humanity can realign with the Divine without the burdensome overshadowing of the egotic mind." Angyo raised his eyebrows and gave a slight smile. "This is all good." As Angyo turned to walk away he noticed a concerned look on Sam's face. "Why so worried?"

"My human condition is getting in the way. I've been here nine years and the thought of this project ending is bittersweet. Tammy and I have been wondering what's next. Do we go back to the U.S. for traditional jobs?"

"How did you get here?" asked Angyo.

"I was called by God to join you."

"Ask for direction and it shall be given. It is Buddha's teaching. We must let go of the things we feel attached to. It is in the space created by letting go that we find a greater goodness or a greater purpose coming into our life. So, ask the Universe, What now?" He turned from Sam and headed out of the lab.

Angyo opened the front door of the monastery with a heavy feeling in his heart. He entered the library and sat down on an overstuffed chair. "Oh, Divine Universe, I too am caught in my human condition. I have been a leader here of a Divine project, the God Project, and it has made my heart soar with love for all humanity. Now, each day as I have watched the return of your beloved Souls, I am grateful for their safe return. I am grateful this project has gone into a maintenance level. Yet, I feel a loss. What will happen with the monastery? Do I let go of my concerns and offer them to you so I may be the conduit of your plan from this moment moving forward?"

He sat silently with his eyes closed. Slowly he felt the answer percolate up into his thoughts.

I have allowed thoughts of lack and limitation to enter my vibrations. I am concerned that I am returning to what I have called a lifeless monastery.

There was a pause in the words, and then a new burst of thoughts emerged.

A lifeless monastery is a state of mind. Find a new purpose that comes from a place of love.

"Thank you, I am grateful for your guidance," Angyo said. He took several deep breaths and continued with his meditation.

Chapter 58

The months passed and Eleazar and China did not return. After meditation and chanting, the monastery and Angyo had a new energy and a new purpose.

One early spring day, Angyo went to the lab to speak with Sam about the new spiritual center they had planned.

"The construction will start next week," Sam said. "The supplies have started to arrive, and the construction crew will be here over the weekend. I've arranged for them to stay in the IT lab, and we've moved the IT staff to the physics lab. With half the Souls returned, we have the space. We have empty work stations in the physics lab, so that will work for the IT staff. The human forms we're supporting will remain in their incubators and the angelic energy will continue to support them."

"Good, how long before the Spiritual Center is finished?" asked Angyo.

"If we have no more snow we can be up and running by the end of September."

"When can we expect our first spiritual retreat?"

"We're planning for the first of December," responded Sam. "We wanted to make sure we wouldn't have to cancel any groups in case of delays."

Angyo nodded. "Good. We are planning to set up the meditation suites and yoga studios on the grounds and in the Spiritual Center. We just signed a contract for a juice bar and vegan restaurant. It will open in the building on the first floor next to the massage centers, Reiki, chiropractic, and nutritional counseling, and we will have two restaurants. One will be a juice bar with vegetarian meals, the other will have a wide variety of organic foods including meat. I am most excited about the five meditation gardens. They will be built moving higher on the mountain. We will spruce up our present prayer and meditation gardens lower on the mountain. I hope we can connect with the village below and those that travel this way and stay in the village."

"The Spiritual Center will have sleeping capacity of sixty people in double rooms on the third floor, and we'll have two ten-bed rooms on the fourth floor," Sam reported. "The classrooms will fill the second floor. We'll be able to hold as many as two hundred participants in the classrooms. Visitors who stay in the village will be able to join us each day."

"Will the village be able to handle the overflow of participants?"

"Yes and no," Sam replied. "There are about fifty-six beds available at the inn and B&Bs. Right now, owners of forty-two homes with empty rooms are interested. The village is planning to build a boutique hotel at the base of the mountain. They're discussing another hundred rooms that would sleep two to four visitors in a room. They expect that to be done in three years. They'll start construction in the summer."

Angyo nodded. "This is all good. Are you feeling this is a good purpose and use of our resources?"

"Yes, I'm very excited about the plan," Sam replied.

"The Divine answered your question of what next?"

"Yes, most definitely."

"Good. We are both wisely led by the Universe."

Angyo left Sam and went outside to roam the wooded area along the mountain. He found a downed tree trunk and sat on it. "Thank you, old tree for a place to sit," he said as he touched the trunk with his hand. "I honor the spirit that lived within. Like you, my form will someday fall, and my spirit will soar free. Until then I am here to serve in this time and dimension." He fell silent and then added, "Actually, like me you were here to serve. Your role in the forest is important to the birds, the animals, insects, and to the dirt that needs your roots to absorb the rain. It is interesting that we all have so many things we do for the Universe. We are all a part of this oneness, the Divine loving plan."

As he continued his monologue with the tree, Angyo felt as if he was being watched. He turned to look behind him and saw two Bengal tigers lying on the ground watching and listening to him. "I honor your spirit within and thank you for your presence. If you want, you can move in front of me, so you do not have to stare at my back while I talk."

A thought popped into his head that he should turn around to face the tigers. "I have been instructed to turn around. The tree does not mind which way I sit, and I like looking at both of you. It is good to see you."

Angyo walked around the tree and sat facing the tigers. "Your spirit is here in this time and dimension as well. Like myself and the tree, you serve the Universe. We all have a place within the Universe, and sometimes our purpose changes. It can feel hard to let go of what felt good, but we must trust it will always be filled with more good, even better than before."

Angyo looked around and saw a small tree growing out of the mossy ground. "Like you, a young tree now, someday to be the biggest tree in this area. A seedling from the tree that now provides me a seat. In a hundred years, you too may fall and leave seedlings along your path."

Angyo turned again to the tigers. He saw contentment in their faces as they lay resting before him.

"What a divine scene this is. A gift of the Universe, of how we can live peacefully together. If beasts can feel peace around humans, then humans can feel peace around other humans and the great beasts. Perhaps once they recognize the divine within themselves and the divine within others they will awaken to the love and peace they can feel and live."

He sat quietly, listening to one tiger snore in a raspy throat murmur. The other tiger cocked her head as she stared at Angyo. "I hope I can keep my students awake when I start teaching classes." He smiled at the tigress. She turned toward her partner and swatted his head. He growled and pushed her paw away. "It is time for me to go back. You may walk with me if you like."

Angyo got up and the tigers jumped up in unison. The large male stretched and took the first steps towards Angyo, the female at his side.

Chapter 59

Eleazar's energy stood in stillness as he looked around using his powerful 360-degree vision. He sensed a familiarity about where he was. His surroundings started to move like a misty cloud, touching and embracing him, first with a sensation of effervescent delight, and then with penetrating love and peace. He allowed himself to move with the energy as he felt his consciousness pull him into a deep, comfortable space. Going deeper within himself, he traveled with love. Sparkling lights moved with him. He felt free of form and matter. He knew existence of the All-Creative Power. Quickly he became encapsulated in a cocoon of colors, soft colors, with an etheric radiance. Loving celestial sounds filled the space, and his energy continued to expand into the space of no time, no boundaries, no thoughts. A space of consciousness filled with Divine Love pulsated into him, through him, with him.

The euphoria of being home within the Spirit of the Living God was a gift that Eleazar had longed for throughout his time in human form. He had lived in the earth dimension with deep devotion to God. He had served with gratitude, yet he always longed for a feeling of completeness. He rationalized over the years that the completeness he desired could only come from his Soul's reabsorption into the Creative Energy of the Spirit of the Living God.

Unfolding in front of him was the image of his 75-year-old physical form traveling on his journey for

God. He heard the words within himself, "Oh, God, each step I take I feel ready to return to you, and to leave this life behind. Bring me home when my service is done. This form has served me well, and my Soul longs for completeness with you."

Ask and you will receive. Your request is being answered. You are here for a point of decision, another opportunity to use your free will. Are you ready to leave the earth plain and return for total absorption, eternal love, peace, and joy? Are you ready to reap the rewards of a life well lived? A life of devoted service?

"Yes, I did make that request, not once, but many times as I walked the world. I was tired, my joints stiff. Before extrication I never allowed myself to feel a loving union with another human form. I could not imagine the depth of feeling it could stir. I didn't think I could be good at it. Many times, as I traveled the world, I saw couples, young, old, racially mixed, culturally different and same sex couples that radiated with a beautiful energy that vibrated brightly. Sometimes they sat for an artist to paint their picture, other times they stood in the streets embracing each other while listening to street musicians. I found great comfort in watching them radiate love. It was beautiful. Then Angyo said you would grant me any wish I may have. I asked to paint, make music, and fall in love."

Your union with China would not feel as it has in Energy form if you return to the earth's dimension. What you have experienced is true love without judgement, without conditions, without expectations. In the earth dimension the restraints of the egotic mind return, and for you this will be a new experience. You will still have your devotion and calling to serve and will need to find a new way to serve in a new human life, with new opportunities much different from a life of isolation and prayer. Your Soul has expanded and expanded over your eternity. Your rewards here will never disappoint you. You will even have other Soulmates who will love unconditionally. Now you have a decision to make. Do you want to continue your journey within the creative energy that you exist of and always have? Or will you return to your human form, this time undergoing a great alchemy of that human form. In this life you will need to learn to balance your divinity with your humanness.

"Perhaps this will feel easier if I continue to work as a Soul alongside China."

Your decision is yours alone. It cannot be dependent on China.

"Can I fail?"

That is always your choice. In the human dimension, every thought, word, and action is of free will. Your thoughts, words, actions, and beliefs will send vibrations into the earth's magnetic field, and they will return to you in the manifestations of your life. You will create a wonderful life if you procreate positive thoughts and beliefs and serve all in human form as if you are serving the Spirit of the Living God. If you live with negative thoughts and fears, you will live a life that attracts negative events and things to fear. Whatever life you live is your choice.

"Yes, that is true."

You have been serving in your Soul form for more than eight earth-bound years. If you choose to stay within the Spirit, your energy in your human form will quickly leave, and your body will be taken off the etheric incubator. It is now your choice.

Eleazar felt a stillness within. He knew his answer deep within himself. It felt right.

Chapter 60

The summer sun was fading, and the colors of fall were filling the mountains in Paro Valley. The monastery, now fully functional as a Spiritual and education center, was full of new arrivals. Each arrival called by God came to take classes, learn meditation, and quiet the egotic mind. A new mission and a new passion for the scientists and monks at the monastery created a great energy and joy.

Angyo had stopped visiting the lab weeks before. It weighed heavy upon his mind that Eleazar and China had not returned. Once each incubator was full; now half were, supporting half of the extricated Souls. Not one had returned in the past year.

Angyo had just finished his class on Buddhist teachings when his phone beeped. He looked at the text message.

please come to lab asap

Angyo put his phone back into his cloak and dismissed the class with a few words about their preparation for the next class.

Angyo moved quickly to the lab. As he walked through the woods, the tiger couple came through the bushes. The male tiger turned his head toward Angyo with a wide-mouth moan. Laughing at the beast's response, Angyo said, "What are you telling me?"

The tiger let out another loud moan, which ended in a smile.

"Okay, I think you are happy. Perhaps it is a good day."

The female tiger walked ahead of the male and turned toward Angyo. She rubbed her head on his cloak close to his hip. He reached down and gave her a pat on her head. "Thank you for your affection."

Angyo entered the lab and moved to the etheric incubators, where Sam stood. "What is happening?" he asked.

"Eleazar returned," Sam replied. "By the time I got to his incubator he had already incarnated. I rushed to see if China had returned. So far, she hasn't, but her Angels looked busy, as if they were preparing for her return. I wanted you to know he was back and that she might be back soon."

"Good," Angyo said. "It will be good to have him and China back."

Angyo left Sam and walked to Eleazar's cubicle. He asked the Angelic energies, "Did he need to be cleaned as other Souls have needed to be on return?"

"No, he just returned from the Source itself," the Angelic energy replied. "He was cleaned before entering the center of oneness and has had great expansion. With this mission ending, he has become a very powerful white Soul who is honored by the Divine."

"Will China return soon?"

The Angelic energy moved to the window and gazed at Angyo. "Yes."

"Is she a powerful Soul, as powerful as Eleazar?"

"Will you love him more if I say no? Will you love her less if I say yes? Is this the question you need to ask? How does it change your love for them?"

Angyo shook his head. "It doesn't."

"Then why ask? It is a problem with humans that they want to judge one against the other. Look to see the power they both offer as unique and a gift of God. See both as equal within your eyes." The energy broke its gaze with Angyo to look at Eleazar. A moment later, it turned back to Angyo and said, "All are made equally within the Universe."

"Yes, yes, you are so right." Angyo stood looking at the Angelic being before saying, "Some of the Souls who have reincarnated have said they went deep within the Source and were given the choice to return here or stay within the loving presence of God, our eternal home."

The Angelic energy said, "Yes, that is right. Until the death of the body the Souls still have free will. They chose to serve as Souls when asked, and some who have longed to return home to God have requested to stay. The alchemy of a Soul's life is a powerful tool that makes the earth plane a much easier journey. "

Chapter 61

On the second day of Eleazar's return, he felt a shift back into consciousness. His thoughts were clear, and he knew where he was. Looking up he saw the Angelic beings removing the etheric ports from his body.

"Welcome back," one Angelic being said.

"Thank you," he replied. "Is China back?"

"Yes, she incarnated last evening."

Eleazar felt a leap in his heart, and his mind soared with anticipation.

His Angels continued to finish their work and turn down the mat. Eleazar's body slowly lowered back down to the mat on the table. He lay flat, waiting for permission to move.

"How long do I have to lie here? Will I be dizzy when I get up?"

"You can get up whenever you are ready," the Angel said, smiling. "Are you feeling well?"

Eleazar nodded. "Yes, I feel perfect."

The Angel smiled. "We will be with you the next few days as you move back to the monastery. You may stay as long as you like."

Eleazar sat up on the mat and swung his legs off the side of the bed. He faced the large glass window and saw Angyo and Sam watching him. He lifted his hand and waved. He stood up and stretched before he turned to his Angels and sent them love and gratitude. "Thank you for taking such good care of me." He felt emotional and asked, "Is that normal?"

"You will continue to reconnect your energy with your human form and mind, and as things come back to you, it can trigger emotions." The Angel touched his face. "You will need to reconcile your human emotions with your Divine self. You will feel your energy shifting over the next day or two, and then you will be totally reconnected. During this time, you may feel sudden emotional shifts."

"Okay," Eleazar murmured. He rubbed his damp eyes and took a deep breath before walking out of the cubicle. He smiled as he walked up to Angyo and Sam. He grabbed Angyo for a big hug, and then hugged Sam.

"Welcome back," they both said in unison.

"It is good to be back. It still feels a little funny to be walking on my feet, but I am sure that will get better."

"You will need some rest," Angyo said. "Let me walk you to your room in the monastery. It has been set up with your things and some new clothing. Tammy went shopping for it."

"How long was I suspended in the incubator?"

"More than eight years," replied Sam. "Do you remember what it was like to be a Soul?"

Eleazar nodded. "Yes, I remember everything. Can you take me to China's cubicle? I want to wait for her."

"It might be best for you to return to the monastery for food and rest," Angyo said.

Eleazar laughed. "I am not hungry, and my body has been resting for eight and a half years. I will sit and wait for China to awake."

"Okay, we can visit for a few minutes, but then you must rest," responded Angyo. He led Eleazar to the back of the lab, and Sam typed some commands into the computer. The dark window of China's cubicle turned translucent. "There she is. Does she look like she did when you were with her?"

"She looks more beautiful," Eleazar said, smiling at her sleeping form.

"Walk with me to the monastery," said Angyo.

Eleazar shook his head. "I will sit here and wait. She will wake soon."

Eleazar watched the Angelic beings as they slowed down China's infusions, and within a couple of hours they were stopped.

Angyo sat by Eleazar throughout the day. It was late afternoon when he said, "Six months after Bernard's death, China's friend Jill Buggy came to the monastery to find her. I told her China was traveling. Jill stayed two weeks. Banko worked with her on chanting and meditation. She did very well and continues to improve. She shared with me that China visited her when she was at a very dark place. She understands that China helped her save herself from the painful life she was living."

A moment later, China was standing in front of them. "I love her as if she was my own," China said.

"You have a lot of love to give, China. Focus on giving love, and you will honor Bernard's memory and heal your human heart," replied Angyo as he looked up at her.

"I was there when he died. As a Soul, I felt not a twinge of emotion as I watched it unfold. Then as we moved through the scene, I felt connections to my human form and knew my body and mind were grieving. After that Eleazar and I moved from moment to moment together."

Eleazar stood up and looked deeply into China's eyes. Their Souls connected in a loving gaze. He reached out to her and pulled her to him in a strong and comforting embrace.

The lab became quiet as everyone watched the bright sparkling light radiate from them as they embraced.

The End ... for now!

About the Author

M. Suzanne, AKA Mary Barrett, has a Master's Degree in Nursing from the University of Pennsylvania. Over her 35 years in health care, she worked as a bedside nurse, a nurse practitioner, a researcher, and administrator. She also held an adjunct faculty professor in a Nursing and Allied Health program at a Philadelphia University/Medical Center.

Mary's nursing experiences have been vast. She has been blessed to learn from her patients and families and their diverse religious and spiritual beliefs. She has been with many Souls when they made their transition from their earth journey to the true self in spiritual form. She holds dear the bedside conversations, before a Souls transition, as some of her most heart-warming and memorable experiences. Mary is also an Energy Healer trained in Reiki; She has worked with a wide range of clients, including the dying, non-communicative disabled, children, adults and the divine creatures we call pets. In The Extricated Soul, she merges her deep Spiritual beliefs with her love for healing into a unique and suspenseful novel.

Mary's desire to write was a yearning for many years/decades that popped in and out of her thoughts. When she first experimented with the craft, she started writing poetry. She then delved into short stories and now her first full novel. Mary has been a member of several small local writer's groups, and she worked exclusively with an editor that coached and pushed her outside her boundaries.

www.ingramcontent.com/pod-product-compliance
Lightning Source LLC
Chambersburg PA
CBHW070913260626
47162CB00007B/2656